Adalbert Stifter

The idyll and the abyss

A startling bard of environmental disaster is almost unknown in the English-speaking world

Motley Stones. By Adalbert Stifter.
Translated by Isabel Fargo Cole. *New York*
Review Books; 288 pages; $17.95 and £14.99

her introduction, he is less a writer of idylls than of "the abyss in the idyll". The tension between what he claimed he was writing and what he actually wrote generates a singular and unsettling suspense.

Over time, German-speaking readers and writers reappraised Stifter's work. Franz Kafka, that master of the uncanny, identified him as an artistic brother. Thomas Mann called him "one of the most extraordinary, the most enigmatic, the most secretly daring and most strangely gripping narrators in world literature". Today, Stifter can be seen as one of the first authors to engage seriously with the theme of environmental catastrophe.

Characteristically, he disavowed any such intention, claiming in the preface to "Motley Stones" that he was less interested in "the surging of the sea" or "the fire-spewing mountain" than in "the force that makes the milk in the poor woman's pot swell and boil over". Yet of the six stories, four are about hailstorms, blizzards, plagues and floods. Storms are common in literature, often as projections of a hero's inner turmoil. But in Stifter's narratives, storms do not represent anyone's interior drama. They are the drama. He eschews the type of hero who comes into conflict with others and changes the world; in the story "Tourmaline", in which a character's flat is

to "Motley Stones", Stifter described the book as "an assortment of fancies for young hearts" and himself as an imaginer of "only ser...l things". In his lifetime he

The Business Mind of Clever Mpoha

The Group MD who built Savenda Group of Companies into an African Conglomerate

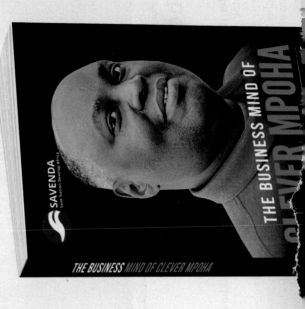

THE BUSINESS MIND OF CLEVER MPOHA

Clever Mpoha's rise to the corporate world has been described as "meteoric". It is surely one of the most inspiring stories for any young Zambian. From hunting to watching over the cows and helping his family run their small shop, he was born in a small village and in this autobiography he explains how the village setup gave him the survival skills he needed to run the business empire he runs today as managing director of the Savenda group of companies.

He started with buying and selling South Korean phones to the local market, focusing on anti-magnetic wave products. From the profits made he increased our volume and started diversifying. The book follows the rationale of every business crossroad and gives useful pointers with the personal stories involved, a valuable insight since Mpoha rarely appears in public. For example for farmers he explains how by aggregating their products and ensuring the right quality controls they can sell their products in a healthier market environment with real price discovery and transparency while also giving consumers better locally grown food.

The business intelligence of the author is practical and down to earth but also inspiring. Clearly he was always gifted in

Brigitta

The translator: Helen Watanabe-O'Kelly is a Fellow of Exeter College and Lecturer in German at the University of Oxford. Her translation of Schiller's *On the Naive and Sentimental in Literature* was published by Carcanet Press in 1981.

ADALBERT STIFTER

Brigitta

with Abdias; Limestone;
and The Forest Path

Translated with an Introduction by
Helen Watanabe-O'Kelly

ANGEL BOOKS
London

DUFOUR EDITIONS
Chester Springs

First published in the United Kingdom 1990 by
Angel Books, 3 Kelross Road, London N5 2QS

First published in the United States of America 1990 by
Dufour Editions Inc., Chester Springs, PA 19425

British Library Cataloguing in Publication Data
Stifter, Adalbert, *1805-1868*
    Brigitta; with, Abdias, Limestone, and The forest path
    1. Fiction in German. Austrian writers, 1830-1856. English
texts
    I. Title
    833.7

    ISBN 0-946162-36-0
    ISBN 0-946162-37-9 pbk

Library of Congress Cataloging-in-Publication Data
Stifter, Adalbert, 1805-1868
    [Short stories. German. Selections]
    Brigitta: with Abdias, limestone, and the forest path/Adalbert
Stifter; translated with an introduction by Helen Watanabe-O'Kelly.
        p.   cm.
    Translated from German.
    ISBN 0-8023-1288-8 – ISBN 0-8023-1289-6 (pbk.)
    1. Stifter, Adalbert, 1805-1868 – Translations, English.
    I.Title.
    PT2525.A26   1990
    833'.7 – dc20   90-39502
                                                         CIP

Front cover design based on *Portrait of Frau Josepha von Zallinger*
by Friedrich Wasmann, 1842 (oil on canvas), detail; Staatliche
Museen Preussischer Kulturbesitz, Nationalgalerie, Berlin

This book is printed on Permanent Paper conforming
to the British Library recommendations and to the
full American standard

Typeset in Great Britain by Trintype, Wellingborough, Northants.
Printed and bound by Woolnough Bookbinding,
Irthlingborough, Northants

Contents

Translator's Acknowledgement

My thanks are due to Antony Wood, publisher and translator, for many helpful and stimulating suggestions during the making of these translations and for saving me from numerous solecisms.

Stifter and I are very grateful to him.

Introduction

There is nothing glamorous or sensational about Adalbert Stifter the man. He was a country boy, born in 1805 in the village of Oberplan in Upper Bohemia. His father died when he was twelve and it was only thanks to his grandfather that he was able to continue his schooling, rather than start work in the fields to support the family. He studied law at the University of Vienna, though he never took a degree, earning his living as a tutor with various notable families in Vienna. In the late 1820s, he fell in love with a girl called Fanni Greipl, whose parents forebade the match. On the rebound, as it seems, he married the beautiful but uneducated Amalia Mohaupt in 1837. Stifter did not publish anything until 1840, when he was already thirty-five, and, as far as we know, he did not write very much before this either. During the 1840s his stories became increasingly popular, though he continued to earn his living from teaching, tutoring among others the son of Chancellor Metternich. He was in Vienna during the abortive revolution of 1848, to which he lent his support at first but from which he recoiled in horror when he saw the violence and chaos which was its inevitable concomitant. In 1850 he became the Inspector of Primary Schools for Upper Austria, a post he held for fifteen years and filled conscientiously, though he found it hard to reconcile the demands of the civil service with those of authorship. He was also very much interested in landscape painting, devoting more and more time to it in his later years. He and his wife were childless and they made at least three disastrous attempts to adopt nieces of Amalia's. One of these children ran away, aged ten, and another vanished and was found four weeks later drowned. Stifter was filled with grief and depression and in the 1860s his health and general state of mind began to decline. In December 1867 he took to his bed in great pain from cirrhosis of the liver. In January 1868 he cut his throat with a razor and died two days later.

His entire oeuvre, apart from some journalism, consists of prose fiction. He published first of all in the fashionable periodicals of the day, the so-called *Taschenbücher*, where three-quarters of his stories appeared between 1840 and 1848. These magazines were the reading-matter of the bourgeois public, particularly women. They were attractive little books containing stories, poems and engravings which were often given as presents and there was a veritable explosion of them in the 1820s and 1830s, with between thirty-three and forty-eight new titles a year.

The Revolution brought about a decline in the number of such periodicals which coincided with Stifter's development as a writer. Quite soon after the first appearance of his stories, Stifter began extensively rewriting them and publishing them in collections. Thirteen of the stories that first appeared between 1840 and 1852 reappear in the six volumes known as *Studies* (*Studien*, 1844-50), from which *Abdias*, *Brigitta* and *The Forest Path* (*Der Waldsteig*) in the present volume are taken (first published in 1843, 1844 and 1845 respectively), and five more in the single volume entitled *Coloured Stones* (*Bunte Steine*, 1852/3), which contains *Limestone* (*Kalkstein*; first published in 1848 with the title *Der arme Wohltäter* – The Poor Benefactor). Stifter was therefore moving away from individual stories in ephemeral publications towards works on a larger scale, though we have to remember that earlier stories were appearing in their second or book versions at the same time as other new stories were appearing in magazines. His first and best-known novel, *The Indian Summer* (*Der Nachsommer*), appeared in 1857 and the unfinished historical novel *Witiko* – one of the works Dietrich Bonhoeffer read and reread in his concentration camp – appeared between 1865 and 1867.

So in Stifter we have a childless civil servant, detached from the great currents of European history and art, who wrote thirty-two stories and two novels, whose work is virtually unknown outside the German-speaking world and not all that well within it. Yet he is the writer whom Thomas Mann called 'one of the most extraordinary, the most enigmatic, the most secretly daring and the most strangely gripping narrators in world literature'.[1] It is not just that Stifter is an unknown writer. His reputation has suffered even more from the fact that where his work is known it is misunderstood.

Many of Stifter's stories are set in the forests of his home region of Upper Bohemia. *The Forest Path* in the present collection is an example. Many of his stories centre round children – the *Coloured Stones* collection, from which *Limestone* is taken, is ostensibly a set of stories for and about children. This fatal combination of pine-trees and apple-cheeked country children, the quintessential expression of which is the story entitled *Rock Crystal (Bergkristall)* in *Coloured Stones*, convinced generations of readers and critics that Stifter was a charming chronicler of the countryside and nothing more, 'idyllic' being the favourite critical term used. Stifter himself elucidated the ethos behind his stories in the preface to *Coloured Stones* written in 1852. Here he explained that he chose to describe small-scale events and gradual happenings rather than large-scale violent ones because such mild and gentle happenings demonstrate the forces that govern the world more clearly than do the violent ones. The same force that causes the milk to boil over in the poor woman's saucepan leads a volcano to erupt and emit streams of lava, he says in a famous passage, and the latter event is not of greater intrinsic importance than the former. Indeed, the former, because it is typical and universal, is of more significance than the latter. Similarly, he says, greatness in human conduct does not reside in grand gestures and heroic acts. 'An entire life full of justice, simplicity, self-control, rationality, effectiveness within one's own circle, admiration of the beautiful together with a cheerful, calm death – this is what I call greatness,' he tells us firmly. He goes on to state that we must strive to gain insight into the 'gentle law' which governs the human race. According to this law, the individual should strive for the common good rather than at all costs for his own happiness and satisfaction. A whole series of unspectacular virtues is enumerated which are necessary to achieve this: marital and parental love, industry, social order, moderation, self-sacrifice. This 'gentle law' can be seen in operation in all human societies, 'in the sacrifice of the poor woman as well as in the calm contempt for death of the hero who dies for fatherland and mankind', and it is the continuous operation of this law, rather than its unusual manifestations, that preserves the human race. Stifter makes his moral stance perfectly clear when

he says: 'If in these currents [of the human race] the laws of
justice and virtue can be seen, if these currents are brought into
being and carried on by them, then the whole human race feels
itself ennobled, we feel ourselves united in a common humanity,
we become aware of the sublime as it sinks everywhere into our
souls, where by means of incalculably great forces in time or in
space everything is working towards a well-formed, rational
whole.'

Thus, for Stifter order is a key concept. Man must behave in
an ordered manner, submitting to the guidance of the 'gentle
law' (*sanftes Gesetz*), the ordering principle of the human race,
just as it is of Nature. But how do evil, pain, disaster and death
fit into this seemingly universal harmony? Here we come
up against the Stifterian concept of fate, and its related
phenomenon, chance. Stifter states the problem at the beginning of *Abdias*. 'There are people on whom such a series of
misfortunes falls out of the blue that they finally stand and let
the hailstorm roll over them, just as there are others whom
good fortune visits with such extraordinary wilfulness that it
seems as though the laws of Nature had been reversed in a given
case so that things should turn out solely for their good. In this
way the ancients arrived at the concept of fate, we at the milder
one of destiny.' But this fate only appears to be arbitrary, to be a
chance occurrence. In reality, there is 'a serene chain of
flowers', 'the chain of cause and effect' whose extremity rests
in God's hand and which can be unravelled by human reason.
As Stifter says, 'and if some day we have counted correctly and if
we can comprehend what we have counted: then chance will not
exist for us any more but consequence, not misfortune but only
guilt'. Stifter is thus again enunciating a belief in an underlying
order which man has to comply with, whether he understands it
or not.

It has often been maintained that these ideas are the very
epitome of the values of Biedermeier Vienna, where between
1815 and 1848 the middle-class virtues and the values of hearth
and home were allied with a political conservatism and with-
drawal. This is said to have produced not just a particular style
of domestic architecture and interior design, and painters who
depicted this bourgeois way of life, but also narrators such
as Stifter, dramatists such as Stifter's Austrian contemporary

Grillparzer and poets such as Droste-Hülshoff whose work is maintained by some to concentrate on the same subject-matter and embody the same virtues and limitations. Whether 'Biedermeier' is a helpful term to use in a literary context is very debatable, but it is the preface to *Coloured Stones* that has done more than anything to label Stifter the single-minded advocate of passive Biedermeier virtues, of resigned self-denial, of purity and goodness, coupled with an over-insistence on order and harmony. It may be this too that has led other critics to maintain that Stifter's characters have the simplest psychology. Thomas Mann knew better. In the same passage from *The Genesis of Dr Faustus* quoted above he talks of the contrast between 'Stifter's bloody and suicidal end and the gentle nobility of his writing. It has only rarely been noticed that behind the quiet, inward exactitude of his descriptions of Nature in particular there is at work a predilection for the excessive, the elemental and the catastrophic, the pathological.' Stifter *is* advocating passive virtues, resigned self-denial and the subordination of the self to the greater good but the signs of tension and doubt are unmistakable and the price paid by his characters, and indeed by himself in his own life, is immense. Erika and Martin Swales, in their excellent book *Adalbert Stifter. A Critical Study*,[2] talk of 'Stifter's struggle to reconcile passion and morality, to uphold, in the face of a problematic reality, Reason as inherent in both nature and history, to worship that double deity of Religion and Art despite latently persistent doubts', concluding 'it is surely difficult to insulate his life from the reverberations of its catastrophic close.'

How could this so often go unnoticed? It went unnoticed because Stifter deliberately suppressed it. Read the magazine versions of Stifter's stories and there is a wildness, a sensational quality in both the subject-matter and the style that he has gone to great pains to eliminate from the book versions, which are what is read nowadays and what is translated here. The book versions are seamless stories, where apparently unnecessary details are narrated at length, where landscape plays as large a part as the humans peopling it, where characters are distin-guished not by sudden acts of heroism or speeches of grand pathos, but by carrying on living and coping in the face of difficulties and handicaps of which they are often only half-aware or which they are unable to face.

This change from magazine to book version could, of course, be expressed in terms of literary history. It is clear that Stifter begins writing within the context of late Romanticism, strongly influenced by the prose fiction of the then popular Jean Paul Richter (1763-1825) and following in the footsteps of E. T. A. Hoffmann (1776-1822). As in the works of these writers, the first versions of Stifter's stories deal with the emotions of strange individuals and quirky outsiders. Mysterious events and people cross their paths, madness and supernatural interventions are hinted at. These elements are eliminated remarkably quickly in favour of what is often referred to as the 'poetic realism' of Stifter's later work, that is, from the revised versions of his early stories on, and at its most marked in his extraordinary novel *The Indian Summer*. 'Poetic realism' is a term peculiar to German literature of the nineteenth century and one that attempts, on the one hand, to pin down the common denominator of all 'realism' in art, that is, the depiction of things and people in so complete a manner as to mirror reality, but on the other hand, to recognise that the realism of such writers as Stifter, Keller, Gotthelf and Droste-Hülshoff is imbued with a timeless conservatism and predilection for the small-scale and the provincial. But having attached this label to Stifter's later work, we are not really any closer to grasping the nature of the narrative experiment he is conducting from *The Indian Summer* on, nor does it help us to understand what it is he is depicting in *Studies* and *Coloured Stones*.

One way to approach the latter is to remind ourselves of one of Kleist's most famous stories, *The Marchioness of O . . .* Here Kleist, another suicide, writes of a world in which a noblewoman is raped in a swoon, becomes pregnant, marries her rapist and lives 'happily' ever after, bearing him many more children. Why? To preserve 'the fragile organisation of our world', says Kleist. It is frequently overlooked that Stifter is dealing with similar individual tragedies, because he shows them taking place, just as they do in real life, behind lace curtains and closed doors, unacknowledged because unacknowledgeable by those who suffer them. The fragile organisation of the world never pretended to be so solid, nor revealed such dangerous cracks.

Take the way familial relations, the great linchpin of the Stifterian world order, are depicted. Abdias is a Jew born and raised in the North African desert and an only child. His mother ostensibly adores him but treats him like a dressing-up doll, tricking him out in jewels and different costumes, including girl's clothes. It does cross his father's mind to have him educated in some way, 'but nothing came of that because it was forgotten.' Thus reduced to little better than a pretty animal, Abdias is driven out into the harsh world by his father, forbidden to come back and threatened with disinheritance if he does not earn enough to support himself for life. It takes him fifteen years of constant suffering and hardship to fulfil his father's command. This ostensibly stern but loving family produces a maimed human being, whose fate is narrated in the rest of the story.

Families in general fare very badly in Stifter. Brigitta, the ugly woman who puts on men's clothes and makes the desert of the Hungarian steppes bloom, is shown in some of Stifter's most poignant writing to have been mutilated psychologically by her own parents. Her mother finds her so ugly that she turns away from her as a baby, fixing her attention on her two beautiful elder sisters. 'When strangers came, they neither criticised the child nor praised her, and asked after her sisters,' writes Stifter in one of those deceptively limpid sentences. 'When she cried, no one saw to her needs. If she did not cry, she was left to lie there.' She is so neglected that she is not even blamed or taken to task. Her father beats her long after she has reached puberty. The alienated, loveless child develops a strange inner world of fantasy. Tiburius Kneigt, the hero of *The Forest Path*, is an equally loveless and alienated child. His father is deranged, his mother is obsessed solely with the boy's physical well-being, his tutor eradicates all traces of imagination in him, and the child is so starved of love that he uses a boot-jack as a substitute love object, wrapping it up in cloths and cuddling it. *Limestone* tells of a repressed priest, an utter failure as a boy, not so much because he is stupid as because his education is so rigid that it cannot take account of his individuality. His twin brother thrives initially where he does not. Love, affection and fun are qualities conspicuously absent from his upbringing, as they are from that of all the other three characters mentioned. Duty, monotony and a rigid adherence to outmoded tradition characterise his education.

He, like all the other characters, turns into a sexually disturbed adult. Abdias becomes so hideously pock-marked that his wife develops a physical abhorrence for him. Yet, some time after this, she bears him a child. Stifter does not comment. Is this the married love he meant in the preface to *Coloured Stones*? It takes Tiburius Kneigt and his healthy peasant wife five or six years of marriage to produce a child – and this after he is supposedly cured of his sexual repression. The priest in *Limestone* has one erotic encounter in his life, so slight, so seemingly innocent, and yet so deeply shaming and so engulfing that it determines his strangely obsessive and repressed behaviour for the rest of his life, as John Reddick demonstrated in a seminal article published in 1976.[3] In an extraordinary speech Brigitta's husband says to her on her wedding-night: 'When I first saw you . . . I did not yet see that I should either have to love you infinitely or hate you infinitely. How happily things have worked out that it is love.' The relationship between the ugly Brigitta and her handsome husband, while outwardly constituting the first happiness and emotional warmth she has ever experienced, is at the same time a mixture of love and hatred, attraction and repulsion, insight and blindness.

This is perhaps the greatest Stifterian theme of all: seeing and seeing truly. Sight and blindness is a major plot element in *Abdias*, which we cannot discuss more fully without giving away the story. Here the theme is overt. Yet as well as this the whole story is shot through with the idea that if one sees with the eyes only, one is blind. One must see with the heart. Deborah, Abdias's wife, has never learned to see with the heart, says Stifter. Abdias never learns to see truly either and this is his failure as a father and as a man. It depends how you see things, says the narrator in *Limestone* over and over again. He is a surveyor and therefore, as he goes to some pains to explain, a professional when it comes to seeing and observing. Yet he never sees the priest truly, just as he never sees the landscape he is surveying correctly until the priest shows him its details. He lays claim to be an expert on weather phenomena, yet cannot tell there is a thunderstorm in the offing until the priest proves it to him. The

Major in *Brigitta* has to learn to see with the heart too. He is led astray by his eyes, mistaking outward beauty for inward beauty, just as the nameless narrator in that story is so often led astray by his: forever misjudging distances, misinterpreting objects in the darkness, mistaking Brigitta's identity. The Major makes a hobby out of scientific observation, but this is not real seeing. In *The Forest Path*, a humorous story, sight and seeing is again at the centre of the plot. It is no accident that Tiburius's father, in a metaphorical sense the blindest of all the characters, actually makes himself blind on purpose. His son later on cannot at first see the forest, then cannot see the path and naturally cannot see the woman he meets, just as he cannot see his own condition and so cannot cure it.

In the four stories in this volume landscape plays a prominent part, functioning variously as man's best teacher, as his moral amphitheatre but also as a symbol of his most insoluble problems and as an inimical and destructive force. Each of the four stories embodies at least one of these characteristics of the landscape, in some of them two opposing ones, in a typical Stifterian paradox. For Tiburius, the forest is a teacher, yet it almost destroys him, or so he thinks, before he finds his feet in it. The North African desert, its drought and harshness the very quintessence of inimical Nature, is a symbol of Abdias's own fierce and destructive nature. He goes to a verdant Austrian valley and, though his daughter learns from Nature in this setting, for him it is merely another desert and the house he builds in it is a desert house. The priest in *Limestone* learns to see and love the unpropitious karst which most people find hideous. Here he finds his moral purpose, yet the karst, like himself, is hiding something, for all its flora and fauna are to be found only by attentive searching in little cracks in the stones. At the same time this very landscape can erupt in a thunderstorm which both at the time and in its after-effects can bring death. Brigitta's inner life is described as a desert by the author and when her life is hit by tragedy, she sets out to find another desert, that of the uncultivated and primitive Hungarian steppes. This outwardly barren region conceals hidden treasures of fertility, which she unlocks and then manages to interest others in her project. In Stifter's words, 'on the barren blind heath a human free activity began, like the opening of a

beautiful eye.' So for her the steppe brings life and enlighten-
ment, yet it too conceals malaria and deadly danger from packs
of wolves. The Major is first described on the very edge of Mount
Vesuvius, the harshness of the landscape here being no accident.

This dangerous element inherent in man's relationship with
Nature can be limited if man tames Nature. Agriculture, the
slow process by which man harnesses the landscape, has for
Stifter a moral force which he elucidates at greatest length in his
Bildungsroman *The Indian Summer*. As the Swales have said, *The
Indian Summer* 'is essentially an intensified version' of *Brigitta*.
Again we must avoid giving away the plot of *Brigitta*, but it is clear
that the title-figure's role as agriculturalist is a prime factor in
her development, in that of the Major and in that of the
nameless narrator too.

Part of what gives Stifter's work its unmistakable flavour is its
style and narrative method. The four stories here are all told in
the first person, which should in theory make them more direct
and immediate. The opposite is the case, for Stifter goes to great
lengths to make them indirect, placing his narrator and at the
same time his reader at one remove from events. He does not
plunge straight away into the action, but usually begins with a
preamble, stating a general premise which he intends the
ensuing story to exemplify, or so he says. Fate is discussed in the
opening of *Abdias*, virtue in *Limestone*, beauty in *Brigitta* and
foolishness in *The Forest Path*. Then the actual narration begins.
Here we find that further narrative layers are interposed
between us and the action. In *Limestone* we have one narrator
telling us a story he was told by one of the characters, the
surveyor. The surveyor in his turn inserts into his own narrative
the priest's story, told in the first person by the priest. The
narrator in *Brigitta* narrates those events he took part in, with
one whole section being a flash-back dealing with events the
other characters have told him.

And what strange people these narrators are, only a whit less
odd than the characters they tell of. The surveyor in *Limestone* is
the only friend the priest has because he is almost as odd and
obsessive as himself. The surveyor purports to be an open-air
type capable of sleeping rough at a moment's notice and taking
pot luck, but note the manically fussy arrangements he makes
for his own comfort. He sends for special wine and special bread

to his inn, he lugs around the countryside a whole set of contraptions for cooling his wine by means of ether.

These oddnesses are reflected in the characters' speech. The translator becomes particularly aware of them. The surveyor in *Limestone* narrates his story in the most convoluted, awkward, jerky way possible. The description of natural phenomena, which one would have thought to be his forte, causes him to go into convulsions of subordinate clauses and qualifying phrases. The priest, in contrast, has a rock-like simplicity when it comes to his story, all simple sentences and lack of qualification. There is equally a change of tone between those parts of *Brigitta* that are told by the narrator as one of the participants and the part he narrates at second-hand.

The oddness of these narrators, like the oddness of some of the characters, shows them to be latter-day variations on the Romantic figure of the eccentric, the square peg in the round hole, the so-called *Sonderling*. E. T. A. Hoffmann's Anselmus in *The Golden Bowl* with his two left feet, Peter Schlemihl in Chamisso's story *The Wondrous Tale of Peter Schlemihl*, whose very surname means a maladroit person, are two of the predecessors of the surveyor and the priest in *Limestone* and the doctor and the hero of *The Forest Path*. On one level these are all misfits but on another they all, like Anselmus and Schlemihl, learn to see, and see better than those who fit in. Poor stunted repressed Tiburius Kneigt in *The Forest Path* is, after all, the one out of all the visitors to the spa who discovers the beauties of Nature all around and in the end carries off a prize the others never even suspected existed. The priest in *Limestone* takes on a task his parishioners did not know was necessary.

But apart from these thematic aspects, the importance of the narrators and their strange perspective on the story places an emphasis on the narrator within the narration which has to do, at least in part, with the particular genre Stifter is using. Stifter himself, like many other nineteenth-century German-language writers of short fiction, simply called his stories 'tales'. Yet they belong within that body of prose fiction, both varied and extensive and utterly characteristic of nineteenth-century writing in German, which can be subsumed under the title '*Novellen*'.[4]

Goethe inaugurated the form in 1795 with his series of stories *Conversations of German Emigrants (Unterhaltungen deutscher*

Ausgewanderten), modelled on the *Decameron,* and wrote a famous
example of the genre which he entitled simply *Novelle* (1828). It
was Goethe too who provided one of the most useful, as it is the
briefest, definitions of the Novelle, in one of his conversations
with Eckermann in 1827. 'What else is a Novelle but an unheard-
of event which has actually happened?', he says. There is thus a
tension built into the form between the everyday nature of the
central event it narrates and its strange and inexplicable quality.
Novellen are set in a recognisable world but cast a lurid light on
that world. The operation of fate and chance within the lives of
the characters is frequently one of the motive forces of the plot.
Since one of the characteristic structural features of the Novelle
is that it is narrated at one remove from the events depicted,
either by a whole series of Novellen being set in a *Decameron*-like
framework or by placing a narrator within the tale itself to tell it
at second-hand, the question of how to interpret the events in
the story becomes a theme in its own right. There are other
thematic and structural features that are from time to time
adduced as essential to the form: a turning-point in the action, a
recognisable symbol to function as a recurring motif, the
restoration of order at the end of the story, and so on. In the
course of a century and more, and within the vast corpus of work
coming under the heading of the Novelle, many variations
are possible. Kleist, Brentano and Büchner, Grillparzer and
Mörike, Storm and Meyer, Keller and Droste-Hülshoff all use
the form in a different way, but all address sooner or later
precisely those themes we see Stifter exploring: the tension
between the everyday and the extraordinary, the part chance
and fate play in man's affairs, the problem of interpretation. It is
not an accident that Thomas Mann and Kafka, the last great
writers of Novellen, should use the form to investigate some of
the same questions. Nor is it an accident that Günter Grass calls
his story *Cat and Mouse* a Novelle, labelling it as such on the title-
page, for it too has the narrator and his narration as one of its
central themes.

　　Part of Stifter's appeal for the modern age, like Kafka's, is that
in his work the narration is as much a veil as it is a window. The
reader, like the characters, must learn 'right seeing', seeing
'with the eye of the heart'. Two sentences by Oscar Wilde in *The
Portrait of Dorian Gray* seem to sum up Stifter's method

admirably: 'It is only shallow people who do not judge by appearances. The true mystery of the world is the visible, not the invisible.'

Notes

1. Thomas Mann, *Die Entstehung des Doktor Faustus. Roman eines Romans*, Amsterdam, 1949, p. 124.
2. Erika and Martin Swales, *Adalbert Stifter: A Critical Study*, Cambridge, 1984.
3. John Reddick, 'Tiger und Tugend in Stifters "Kalkstein": eine Polemik', *Zeitschrift für deutsche Philologie*, vol. 95 (1976), pp.235-55.
4. The English-speaking reader will find a thought-provoking guide to the Novelle in Martin Swales, *The German Novelle*, Princeton, 1977.

Abdias

1. Esther

There are people on whom such a series of misfortunes falls out of the blue that they finally stand and let the hail-storm roll over them, just as there are others whom good fortune visits with such extraordinary wilfulness that it seems as though the laws of Nature had been reversed in a given case so that things should turn out solely for their good.

In this way the ancients arrived at the concept of fate, we at the milder one of destiny.

But there is indeed, too, something terrifying in the indifferent innocence with which the laws of Nature operate, so that it seems to us as though an invisible arm were reaching out of the clouds and enacting the incomprehensible before our eyes. For a blessing comes with the same smiling face today and tomorrow the terrible happens. And when both are over, Nature is dispassionate as before.

Here for example the beautiful silver mirror of a river swells, a boy falls in, the water ripples sweetly around his locks, he sinks – and after a short while the silver mirror swells as before. – – There the Bedouin rides between the dark cloud of his sky and the yellow sand of his desert: then a light, glittering spark leaps onto his head, he feels an unfamiliar shiver run through his nerves, still hears drunkenly the thunder in his ears, and then nothing more for all eternity.

For the ancients this was fate, frightful, final, inflexible cause of events, farther than which one cannot see and beyond which nothing more exists, so that even the gods themselves are subject to it: for us it is destiny, therefore something sent by a higher power which we should accept. The strong submit to it humbly, the weak rebel against it complainingly, and the base are dully amazed when the monstrous occurs, or go mad and commit crimes.

But in fact perhaps there is neither fate as the final irrationality of existence nor is its individual occurrence visited upon us; rather, a serene chain of flowers hangs through the infinity of the universe and transmits its shimmer into men's hearts – the chain of cause and effect – and into man's brain was cast the most beautiful of these flowers, reason, the eye of the soul, in order to attach the chain to it and by means of it to count his way down flower by flower, link by link, until he comes finally to that hand in which the end rests. And if some day we have counted correctly and if we can comprehend what we have counted: then chance will not exist for us any more but consequence, not misfortune but only guilt; for the gaps which now exist are the cause of the unexpected, and misuse creates unhappiness. Certainly the human race is already able to count from one millennium to another, but only individual petals of the great chain of flowers have as yet been discovered, events still flow past us like a sacred mystery, suffering still enters and leaves the human heart at will – – is this suffering perhaps itself a flower in that chain? Who can fathom that? If then someone says, why is the chain so big that in thousands of years we have uncovered only a few petals which pour forth their fragrance, then the answer is: the supply is immeasurably big so that each coming generation can find something for itself – the little that has been discovered is already a great and splendid treasure, and the more people in the future who live and reveal it, the bigger and more splendid this treasure will become – and we can divine scarcely a thousandth of a thousandth of what lies behind the great wave of the future. – – Let us not ponder the nature of these things further but simply tell of a man who exemplifies much of this and of whom it is uncertain which is stranger, his destiny or his heart. In any case one is stimulated by the course of lives like his to ask: 'Why did this happen, exactly?', and tempted into a gloomy brooding about providence, destiny and the ultimate cause of all things.

It is the Jew Abdias whose story I want to tell.

Anyone who perhaps has heard of him or who has even sometime seen the bent ninety-year-old figure sitting in front of the little white house should not think of him with bitterness – should neither curse nor bless him, and he has earned both richly in his life – but should rather, as he reads, bring his image once more before his eyes. And let him who has never heard of the man follow us too, if he likes, to the end, since we have simply tried to show what Abdias was like. Then let him judge the Jew Abdias according to the promptings of his heart.

Deep in the deserts behind the Atlas Mountains stands an old Roman town lost to history. It has gradually fallen into ruins, has been nameless for centuries, and it is unknown how long it has had no inhabitants, the Europeans up until very recent times did not mark it on their maps because they did not suspect its existence and the Berber, whenever he dashed past on his swift horse and saw the crumbling walls, either did not think of it or of its purpose, or else he soothed the unease he felt with a few superstitious thoughts until the last piece of masonry had vanished from his sight and the last sound of the jackals that dwelt there had vanished from his ear. Then he would ride happily on, surrounded by nothing but the image of the desert, lonely, well-known, beautiful and dear to him. Yet, unknown to the rest of the world, other inhabitants besides the jackals lived in the ruins. They were children of the most exclusive race in the world, rigidly taking one place as their sole point of reference, yet scattered in every land known to man, and having as it were splashed a few drops from its great ocean into this deserted spot. Dark, melancholy, dirty Jews moved around in the rubble like shadows, went in and out among it and lived in it with the jackal which they sometimes fed. No one knew of them except other members of their faith who lived outside. They dealt in gold and silver and in other things brought over from the land of Egypt, also in contaminated rags and wool fabrics from which they themselves probably caught the plague and died – but then the son took up his father's staff with resignation and patience, and wandered and did as his father had done, waiting for what destiny should send him. If one of them was slain and robbed by a Kabyle, then the whole tribe scattered over the wide desert land would weep, until, perhaps a long time afterwards, the Kabyle was found slain somewhere.

Thus was the nature of this race from which Abdias was descended.

Through a Roman triumphal arch, past the trunks of two dried-out palm trees, was a heap of masonry whose purpose was no longer clear – now it was the dwelling-place of Aaron, the father of Abdias. Above, the remains of a viaduct stretched over it, below lay fragments which were no longer recognisable and which had to be climbed over in order to reach the hole in the wall which gave entrance to Aaron's dwelling. Inside the broken hole steps led downwards, made from the cornices of Doric columns that had found their way here at an unknown date by a series of unknown destructive accidents. They led down to a spacious dwelling such as, from outside, one would never have suspected under the heap of masonry and rubble. Here was a room surrounded by several of those small apartments the Romans loved, but on the floor were no flagstones or parquet or mosaic, just the naked earth, on the walls there were no paintings or decorations, just the Roman bricks, and numerous packs and bales and odds and ends lay about everywhere, showing with what inferior and diverse objects the Jew Aaron traded. Principally, however, clothes and torn rags hung, of all colours and ages, carrying in them the dust of almost all the lands of Africa. To sit and lean against there were heaps of old cloth. The table and the other furniture consisted of stones that had been collected from the old town. Behind a hanging bundle of yellow and grey caftans there was a hole in the wall which was much smaller than the one that did duty for a door and that looked out of the darkness as from a pit in the rubble. It looked impossible to pass through. However, after bending, clambering through it and traversing the winding passage beyond it, one again entered a room surrounded by several others. On the floor lay a Persian carpet and in the other rooms there were similar or comparable carpets, at the walls and in niches cushions were placed; over the niches hung curtains, and nearby, tables of fine stone and bowls and a bath were set. Here sat Esther, Aaron's wife. Her body rested on silk cloth from Damascus, her cheek and her shoulders were caressed by the softest and most glowing of all fabrics, the woven fairy-tale from Kashmir such as the Sultana in Istambul owns. About her were two maids who wore beautiful cloths around their clever beautiful foreheads and pearls at their bosoms. Here Aaron collected everything that was good and that poor mortal man thought flattering and beneficial. Jewels lay around on the tables and were scattered on the walls. Windows overgrown with myrtle sent light down from above, sometimes letting in the yellow desert sand – but when evening came and the lamps burned, then everything glittered and sparkled and was bright and radiant. Aaron's greatest jewel, apart from the woman Esther, was her son, a boy who played on the carpet, a boy with black rolling pupils, equipped with all the Eastern beauty of his race. This boy was Abdias, the Jew whose story I want to tell, now a tender flower which had blossomed from Esther's bosom.

Aaron was the richest man in the old Roman town. The others who lived there with him knew that very well, since they often partook of his good fortune, just as he too knew everything about them: but no occasion has been heard of on which the Bedouin dashing past or the lazy Bey in his harem found it out. On the contrary, over the dead town the dark secret hung silently as though no other sound was ever heard in it but the soughing of the wind which filled it with sand, or the short hot cry of the beast of prey when the flowing disc of the moon stood over it and shone down on it. The Jews traded among the different races, they were tolerated and few questions were asked as to where they lived – and when one of their fellow inhabitants, a jackal, emerged into the outside world he was slain and thrown into a ditch. On his two greatest treasures Aaron heaped everything that he thought good for them. – And having been outside, having been beaten and driven from pillar to post and having then come home to enjoy what the ancient kings of his race, above all Solomon, considered the joy of life, he felt a terrible voluptuous pleasure. And if at times he sensed that there were other pleasures which belong to the heart, then he decided this was suffering to be shunned and he shunned it too, only that he thought one day he would set the boy Abdias on a camel and bring him to Kahira to a doctor so that he might become wise as the ancient prophets and leaders of his race had been. But nothing came of that because it was forgotten.

The boy, therefore, had nothing, except that he often stood high on the rubble and thought the wide immense sky he could see was the hem of Jehovah's cloak, Jehovah who had once actually come down to earth to create it and to choose a people to eat with and associate with to his heart's content. But Esther would call him down again to dress him in brown, then in yellow and again in brown. She put jewellery on him too and let the beauty of the pearl shimmer on his fine dark skin or the fire of the diamond sparkle against it – she put a band around his forehead, stroked his hair or rubbed his little limbs and his face with soft, fine, woollen cloths – often they dressed him as a girl or his mother put ointment on his eyebrows to make them into very fine black lines above his shining eyes, and she held the silver mirror up to him so that he could see himself. –

When the years had passed, one by one, his father Aaron led him out one day into the outer room, put a torn caftan on him and said: 'Son, Abdias, go out now into the world and since man owns nothing in the world apart from what he acquires for himself and what he can acquire for himself again at any moment, and since nothing makes us secure except this ability to acquire, go out now and learn it. Here is a camel and a gold coin, and until you have gained enough for a man to live on for life, I'll give you nothing, and if you turn out to be a useless man I'll give you nothing after my death either. If you want to and if you are not too far away, you can visit your mother and me from time to time – and when you have enough for a man to live on, then come back and I'll add sufficient to it so that a second person and several others can live on it too, you can bring a wife and we will try to make another room for you in our cave for you to live in and enjoy what Jehovah sends you. Now, son Abdias, a blessing on you, go out and betray nothing of the nest in which you were reared.'

Thus Aaron spoke and he led his son out to the palm-trees where the camel lay. Then he blessed him, touching the curly crown of his head with his hands. Esther lay inside on the carpet, sobbing and beating the ground with her hands. Abdias, however, since the blessing was now over, mounted the camel which was lying before him. The camel stood up as soon as it felt his weight lifted the boy on high, and when he felt the fanning of the strange breeze that seemed to be coming from afar, he looked once more at his father and rode obediently away.

From now on Abdias bore the beating of the rain and the hail in his face – he wandered far afield, over streams and rivers, from one season to another – he knew no language and learned them all, he had no money and acquired it in order to hide it in ravines where he found it again, he had no learning and could do nothing when he sat on his skinny camel but fix his fiery eyes on the huge, frightening emptiness and meditate, he lived in such a needy fashion that he often had nothing but a handful of dried dates, and yet he was as handsome as one of those heavenly messengers who at one time appeared so often to his race. In the same way Mohammed, alone with his animal for days and for weeks amid the vast sands, pondered the thoughts that afterwards became a flame and swept the universe. Otherwise Abdias was simply a thing that the most stupid Turk thought he could kick aside, and did. Abdias was hard and implacable when it was a question of his advantage, he was spiteful towards Muslims and Christians – and when at night in the midst of the caravan he stretched himself out on the yellow sand, then he laid his head very softly on the neck of his camel and when he heard the camel's breathing in his sleep and in his dreams, this gave him a good and friendly feeling, and when the camel was chafed somewhere, he denied himself fresh water, washed the sore spot with it and smeared it with ointment.

He had passed over the place where the ancient trading queen, Carthage, had stood, he had seen the Nile, he had crossed the Euphrates and the Tigris, he had drunk from the Ganges, he had scrimped and practised usury, amassed and conserved wealth, he had not visited his parents even once because he had always been so far away – – and after fifteen years had passed he returned for the first time to the forgotten Roman town. He came in the night, on foot because his camel had been stolen; he was wrapped in very tattered clothing and carried pieces of a horse's carcase to throw to the jackals in order to keep them away. In this way he reached the Roman triumphal arch and the two old palm-trunks which were still standing, two dark lines pointing up into the night sky. He knocked at the door made of three thicknesses of plaited reeds which stood in front of the hole in the wall that formed the entrance, and called, his own name and his father's – and he had to wait for a long time until he heard someone and wakened the old Jew. Everyone in the house got up when they heard who had come and Aaron, having first spoken with him through the door, opened it and let him in. Abdias asked his father to take him into the cellar and when he had closed the reed door behind him there, he counted out to him the gold coins of every country that he had acquired, a larger sum than might have

been expected. Aaron looked silently at him until he was
finished, then he pushed the gold coins together on the stone
and put them back in handfuls into the leather bag in which
Abdias had brought them and placed the bag in a hole which
ran sideways between marble friezes. – – Then, as though an
outer crust were suddenly to burst or as though he had had to
wait with his parental joy until business was finished, he threw
himself on his son, embraced him, pressed him to himself, wept,
blessed, murmured, touched him and wetted his face with tears.

But Abdias, when this was over, went back into the outer
room, threw himself down onto a pile of mats lying there and let
the fountain of his tears flow – it flowed so mildly and sweetly,
for his body was weary unto death.

His father, however, had him stripped of his rags, his body was
placed in a soothing purifying bath, his limbs were rubbed with
exquisite and healing ointments and he was dressed in a festive
garment. Then he was brought into the inner rooms where
Esther sat on the cushions, waiting patiently for the father to
bring him in. She stood up when the new arrival entered under
the curtain at the entrance – but it was no longer the sweet
gentle beautiful boy whom she had once loved so much and
whose cheeks had been such a soft cushion for her lips; he had
become very dark, his face harder and prouder and his eyes
much more fiery. But he too looked at his mother – she, no less
than he, had become a different person and the mysterious play
of the years was visible in her face. When he had advanced to her
side she took him to her heart, drew him towards her onto the
cushions and pressed her mouth to his cheeks, his forehead, the
crown of his head, to his eyes and to his ears.

Old Aaron stood to one side with bent head, and the maids sat
in the next room, behind yellow silk curtains, whispering.

The other members of the household, however, were outside
carrying out another task they had been ordered to perform.
Although the night was already tending from midnight towards
morning and the well-known images of the stars, which in the
evening had come over from Egypt, were already standing
behind the peaks and moving down towards the desert, Abdias's
arrival still had to be celebrated according to custom. A lamb
was killed by candlelight, roasted in the kitchen and put on the
table. They all went and ate of it and the servants were given to

eat too. Whereupon they laid themselves down to rest and slept long into the next day when the desert sun was already shining down on the ruins like a great round diamond which glittered every day all alone in the empty sky.

There were celebrations throughout the next three days. The neighbours were called in, the camels, donkeys and dogs belonging to the household were not forgotten and in a distant part of the ruins a portion of food was put out for the desert animals, for the masonry stretched far out into the plain and the animals came to seek shelter in the parts uninhabited by man.

When the celebrations were over and a period of time had elapsed, Abdias again took his leave of his parents; for he was travelling to Baalbec to fetch Deborah of the beautiful eyes whom he had seen there and remembered, and who, like all her relatives, belonged to his race. He journeyed as a beggar, arriving after two months. He returned as an armed Turk in the middle of a great caravan, for the treasure which he had brought with him could not be hidden in a ravine, nor could he acquire it again if it were lost. At that time in all the caravanserais people spoke of the beauty of the Muslim traveller and of the even greater beauty of his slave; but the talk gradually died away like a shining river on the desert and after some time no one gave any thought to where the two had gone nor spoke of it any more. They, however, were in old Aaron's dwelling, rooms were being furnished in the vaults under the rubble, curtains hung and cushions and carpets spread out for Deborah.

Aaron shared his possessions with his son as he had promised and Abdias now went out into many lands to trade.

Just as he had once been obedient, so he now gathered from all corners everything he thought might please his parents' senses, he submitted to his father's wilful caprices and suffered his mother's senseless scolding. – When Aaron had become old and senile, Abdias went around in beautiful clothes, with shimmering well-made weapons, making business arrangements with his fellow merchants in the outside world just as the great European merchants do. When his parents had become immature children they died one after the other and Abdias buried them under the stones that lay near an old Roman capital.

From now on he was alone in the vaults under the piled-up rubble, near the triumphal arch and the two dried-out palm trunks.

Now he travelled farther and farther afield, Deborah sat at home with her maids waiting for him, outside he became better known among the people and drew the shimmering road of wealth further and further into the desert.

2. Deborah

When some years had elapsed since the death of Aaron and Esther, changes gradually came about in the house near the palm-trees. Good fortune and riches increased constantly. Abdias was assiduous in his business, constantly extending it and doing good to his animals, slaves and neighbours. But they hated him for it. He heaped worldly goods onto the wife of his bosom, whom he had chosen, and, although she was unfruitful, he brought the most diverse things home to her from his travels. However, because he was once taken ill in Odessa, contracting the terrible illness of the pox, which made him deformed and ugly, Deborah loathed him after he came home and turned away from him for ever; for the only thing known to her which he brought home was his voice, not his form – and even though she often looked up suddenly at the accustomed sound, yet she always turned away again and left the house; she had received only corporeal eyes with which to see the beauty of the body, not spiritual eyes, the eyes of the heart. Abdias had never known that before, for when he glimpsed her in Baalbec, he too had seen nothing but her great beauty, and when he went away he took nothing with him but the memory of that beauty. For this reason everything was now over for Deborah. – But he, when he saw what had happened, went into his solitary chamber and wrote out the bill of divorce to have it ready for when she would demand it, for she would leave him after all these years. She did not demand it but lived on by his side, was obedient to him and remained sad from sunrise to sunset. The neighbours, however, laughed at his face, saying it was Jehovah's angel of the plague who had come to him and left his mark.

He said nothing and time slipped past in this way.

He travelled abroad as before, came home and set off again. He sought wealth everywhere, at times he defiantly piled it up with burning greed, at other times he squandered it, and when he was outside among men he indulged his body with every luxury. – Then he came home and on many an afternoon sat, as he liked to do, behind the heaped-up rubble of his house, near the ragged aloe-tree, holding his already greying head in his hands. He thought he was longing for the cold damp continent of Europe and that it would be good if he knew what the wise men knew there and lived as the noblemen lived there. – Then he fixed his eyes on the dry glittering sand before him – and looked to one side when the shadow of the mournful Deborah passed around the corner of some broken masonry and she did not ask him what he was thinking. – But they were only fleeting thoughts, as when a snow-flake which cannot be caught falls in front of the face of someone wandering in the Atlas Mountains.

But Abdias only had to sit up high again on his camel in the midst of the baggage train, giving orders and taking charge, for him to become a different man and for the unspeakably ugly scars on his face to shine with joy and for his eyes next to them, the same eyes as before, to shine in beauty – indeed, at such times they became even more beautiful when everything was in chaos around him from the press of the people, animals and things, the greatness and daring of the baggage trains was manifest and he could set off with them like a king of the caravanserais; for in far-off places he was accorded that which was denied him at home: respect, prestige, sovereignty. He repeated this idea to himself and put it into practice very often so that he might see its effect – and the more he ordered and demanded, the more the others did what he wanted as though that was how it had to be and as though he had a right. Although he almost suspected it was his wealth that gave him this power, yet he held on to this power and rejoiced in it. Once when the richly dressed Melek-Ben-Amar, the emissary of the Bey, who had been sent to him in the town of Bona to extract a loan, had been made to wait a very long time and to beseech very fervently until his request was granted, then his heart was almost sated. On a journey from there, through Libya, he also tasted the joy of battle. Merchants, pilgrims, soldiers, riff-raff and people of all kinds had united into one great caravan in order to cross the desert. Abdias was among them, with his silken clothes and shining weapons, for since he had become ugly, he loved display all the more. On the seventh day of the journey when black rocks were all around them and the camels gripped the soft sandhills with the soles of their feet, a cloud of Bedouin flew up to them. Before those in the middle where the large baggage was could ask what was happening, the long rifles were already spitting at the edge of the caravan and blades were flashing in the sun. Immediately a crying and wailing arose from those in the middle, many of whom did not know what to do and dismounted to fling themselves on their knees to pray. Then the gaunt Jew, who had also been riding in the middle with the great bales of merchandise, rose up on his beast and shouted whatever battle order occurred to him. He rode forward into the fray, drawing his curved blade: there were the white figures with swathed heads and several members of the caravan fighting with them. One of them immediately turned towards him, aiming with his blade at his head over the neck of his camel, but in that moment Abdias knew what to do: he ducked down sideways on the neck of his camel, drove the beast close to the enemy and stabbed him from the saddle so that a stream of blood ran down over the white garment. He fired his pistols at the next adversaries. Then he shouted orders that those near him saw were right and followed – and when the others saw how things were going, their courage grew, more joined them all the time and as soon as the second and the third of the enemy fell, a wild exultation engulfed them, the demon of slaughter rejoiced and the whole caravan pressed forward. Abdias himself was swept to the front, his scars were flames of fire, his eyes in the dark face white stars, his mouth called out the deep Arabic sounds swiftly and resonantly and as he rode ever deeper into the fray, as though dipping his breast into the flash of the sabres, he stretched his dark gaunt arm, from which the wide silk sleeve had fallen back, out in front of him like a general in command. In the thin shadow of the smoke which dispersed quickly because no one had time to reload and in the fearful flash of the desert sun which stood overhead, the picture of events now changed quickly. Those who had earlier been the attackers were now hard-pressed and pitiable. They looked for aid. One first pressed the long weapon softly to his body, bent forward and shot from the circle as he fled, another threw his weapons away, let the reins hang forward on his horse's back, leaving his salvation to the noble steed which fled into the desert like the wind – others, oblivious of flight, were rooted to the ground, begging for mercy. But it was all in vain. Abdias who had given the orders could no longer control matters, the flood overflowed, and those who had previously prayed now went wild, stabbing their knives into the hearts of those who knelt to beseech them. – At last when everything was over and the victors were plundering the dead and wounded and the saddle-bags on their animals, Abdias stopped his camel and threw the bloody sabre away from him. A Turk crouching nearby misunderstood the movement and took it for an order: he wiped the blade on his own caftan and handed it back to the brave Emir.

When they moved on again after the fight and day after day the desolate picture of the desert was the same, Abdias thought, what if he now killed the Bey, if he became Bey himself, if he became Sultan, if he conquered the whole earth and subjugated it – what could happen then? These were unknown things and lay in the future beckoning dimly. – But he did not become Bey; on the contrary, if we can express it in this way, on that whole journey which continued for a long way after that, a mournful dark angel hovered over him. They had come again to the fruitful lands of men, he had to go in many different directions, he joined now this, now that caravan and often – as happens to people at times – when he travelled in this way in far countries, it suddenly occurred to him: if only no misfortune has happened at home – but he always quelled these thoughts himself by saying: 'But what could happen? No misfortune is possible at home.' – – Whereupon he travelled from desert to desert, transacting business and doing so successfully, seeing many regions and towns, and many months had passed before, after all these meanderings, he saw again the shimmering blue of the Atlas Mountains and could feel that his home lay behind them. He drew near to it. He left his beautiful clothes in a village where there was a synagogue in a cave and, on a beautiful clear starry night, he separated from the last caravan with which he had travelled and turned aside towards the plain across which the mountains were reached and, on the other side of them, the old Roman town. Then the angel flew away from his head; for what was to happen had happened. For when Abdias, a ragged man riding all alone on a camel over the sand, was already approaching his journey's end, he saw a thin blue haze over the ghost town like the brooding veil of cloud which often throws its shadow on the desert – but he paid no attention to it since the rest of the sky also seemed to cloud over and become milky and the hot sun stood above like a red mournful eye, which in these regions always means the approach of the rainy season. But when at last he reached the well-known ruins and rode into the inhabited parts of them he saw that the ruined town had been devastated once more; for the few miserable beams that had once been dragged here from distant lands and erected lay scattered about smouldering – dirty ashes of palm leaves, the roofs of huts, lay among stones blackened by the fire – he rode faster – and when he came to the triumphal arch and the two dried-out palm trunks he saw strange men carrying things out of his house; their mules were already heavily laden and from the poor quality of what they had in their hands he recognised that they were carrying the last of it. But at the palm-trees Melek-Ben-Amar sat high on his steed with several men around him. When Abdias, having quickly forced his animal to kneel, got down and ran up as though to the rescue and then recognised the man, Melek grinned down at him and smiled – and with the most indescribable heartfelt mockery and hate Abdias also bared his teeth at him – but he had no time now, he sprang past him into the outer room, where the old clothes lay, to see – – but here were several neighbours who had come up out of pleasure in another's misfortune to feast their eyes, and when these now became aware of the unexpected appearance of Abdias they shouted for joy and at once grabbing him they struck him, spat into his face and cried: 'There you are now – you are responsible, you, you!! – – You have sullied your own nest, you have betrayed your own nest and shown it to the vultures. Because you went around in their vain clothes they suspected it, the wrath of the Lord has found you and crushed you, and us with you. You must replace what has been taken, you must replace everything, you must replace it tenfold and more.'

Abdias, impotent against so many hands, let them be and said nothing. They dragged him to the door again, wanting to shout at him again and ill-treat him. Then the Bey's ambassador came in with several soldiers and called among the Jews: 'Let the merchant alone, otherwise every one of you will be spitted through just as he is standing here. What business is it of yours that he is a dog. For you are dogs too. Let him alone, I say.'

At this they dropped back. Melek's mercenaries now searched Abdias's clothes and took whatever they wanted from him; he suffered this very patiently; then Melek said to him: 'You have acted very ill, Abdias-Ben-Aaron, in concealing goods and revenue in this hiding-place, we could punish you but we won't. Farewell, noble merchant, if you are ever on your way through our town then visit us, we shall show you the pledges of your loan and pay you the interest. – Now let him go so that he can increase and bring forth fruit.'

And amid laughter and shouting they let him go – he suffered this also very patiently without moving, except that while they were mocking him, he turned his eyes timidly to the side like an impotent tiger who is being teased. – But when they were outside, had mounted and were about to ride away over the sand-dunes, he sprang after them with one leap, tore the pistols from the halter of his camel where they had been forgotten when the other bags had been cut from the skinny despised animal, and fired both at Melek. But he did not hit him. Then several soldiers turned back, beat him on the back and loins with their spears and left him for dead. Then the procession again went through the rubble towards the side of the plain that was overgrown with short poor grass and was the nearest way to inhabited territory. Abdias lay on the sand without moving. But when not a single sound of the riders' shouts could be heard any longer he pulled himself up from the ground and shook his limbs. Then he went back to the camel which still lay on its knees, took from the inner parts of its much-mended harness two little pistols that were hidden there and went with them to his dwelling. There, both at the palm-trees and in the room, were others of his race who had come together and were waiting to see what was now to be done. He went softly in through the door, pressed himself to the wall and shouted in a hoarse voice: 'Whoever among you remains here even long enough to draw breath, indeed whoever even twitches his foot as though he intended to be the last to go, I'll shoot him down with this weapon and his neighbour with the other – then come what may, praised be the Lord!'

As he spoke these words he had been creeping towards the
back of the room, fixing the stars of his sight on them. His ugly
countenance glittered with immeasurable determination, his
eyes shone, and some declared afterwards that at that moment
they had quite clearly seen an unnatural glow around his head
and the hairs standing up straight and separate like spears.

They still hesitated a little, before going out through the door
one by one. He looked after them, chattering with his teeth like
a mountain hyena. When the last had finally withdrawn his foot
over the threshold and vanished, he murmured: 'There they go,
they're going – wait, a time will come, Melek, when I shall settle
my account with you too.'

Outside they reasoned: 'If he's the man who has brought us to
ruin, then he can also help us up again, he must compensate us,
we'll spare him and put pressure on him in the future.' Their
words came in to him and he pricked up his ears. But they grew
fainter all the time and at last nothing more could be heard, a
sign that they had all gone.

Abdias stood still for a while, breathing long and deep. Then
he went to see what had happened to Deborah for whom he
began to feel sorry. He put the pistols into his caftan, climbed
over the pile of clothing that usually hung in front of the
entrance to the inner room but now lay on the ground, pulled
himself through the passage, where the lamp had been thrown
down, and entered the inner rooms. There the light fell through
the upper windows, which were overgrown with myrtles, onto
the paved floor: but now there were no carpets or mats and with
the earth dug up in many places in search of treasure and the
naked stones of the thousand-year-old walls, it looked to him like
a thieves' den. He did indeed find Deborah in the large room
where she was usually to be found, and, lo and behold, how
strange is the path of destiny: on this very night she had
borne him a little girl – because of the mother's shock it was
premature and from the heap of loose earth on which she lay
she now held it up to him. But at that moment he stood there
like one shaken by a frightful blow. The only words he said were:
'Shall I ride after them and hurl the child onto the spears of the
soldiers?'

After a short pause, however, he went nearer, lifted the child
up and looked at it. Then without putting it down he went into

the neighbouring room and looked long and closely towards one corner and the masonry there; then he came out and said: 'I thought so, you fools. I did leave you enough outside after all – oh, you great fools!'

Then he fell on his knees and prayed: 'Jehovah, praise, honour and glory to Thee for ever and ever!'

And then he went back to Deborah and laid the child down next to her. He put his finger into a little bowl of water which stood near her and moistened her lips, for there was no one, no midwife, servant or maid in the whole dwelling. And when he had done this he looked more closely at her and crouching near her head, stroked her sick, already ageing features – but she smiled at him again with her dark mournful countenance for the first time in five years, as though the old love had returned again; meanwhile the ugly head of a neighbour, the greediest perhaps, looked in even at this inner half-broken door, but drew back again; Abdias paid no attention to him, it was as though thick scales fell from his eyes, as though the greatest happiness on earth had come his way in the midst of the devastation – and as he sat near the mother on the bare earth, and when he touched the little mewling creature with his hands, then it was as though he felt in his heart the beginning of that salvation which had eluded him and which he had never known where to seek – now it had come, and was immeasurably sweeter and more soothing than he had ever thought. Deborah held his hand, pressing and caressing it – he looked tenderly at her – she said to him: 'Abdias, you are no longer as ugly as before, but much more handsome.'

And his heart trembled in his body.

'Deborah,' he said, 'there is no one to bring you anything, perhaps you're hungry?'

'No, I'm not hungry,' she answered, 'only weak.'

'Wait, I'll bring you something,' he said, 'to strengthen you, and food which perhaps you do need after all and I'll make you a better bed.'

Then he got up and had first to stretch a little before he could go out, for his pains had become very strong during the short rest. Then he went out and brought in an armful of some of the poor clothing that lay outside and arranged a better resting-place near her on to which he lifted her; then he laid his own outer garment, still warm from his body, over her because he thought she was cold, for she was so pale. He went to where the tinder-box was to start a fire; it lay untouched because it was valueless. He lit a candle, put it into the horn lantern and went outside down some steps underground to where the wine was kept. But it had all been poured out and thrown away. From a small puddle of it on the ground he got some into a container. Then he fetched water from the cistern, for the water in the little bowl was already very warm and rather foetid, and with the mixture of wine and fresh water he moistened Deborah's lips, telling her just to remove the moisture with her tongue and swallow it, that it would do her good for the moment. When she had done this several times he put down the containers with wine and water and said he would prepare her some food. From his travelling things which lay scattered around he searched out a tin in which he always carried the concentrated material for a good broth. Then he went out into the kitchen to look for a pan that he could use. And when he had found one he came in again, put water and the concentrate into it, lit a spirit-lamp and put it down on a stand. He remained standing near the pan to see if it would all dissolve. Deborah must now be much better and calmer; for when he looked in her direction he saw that she often let the lids fall over eyes with which she looked at him as though she were sleepy. In the whole house it was very still because all the maids and servants had run away. When his broth had dissolved in the warm water, he took the pan away in order to let everything cool down. He knelt down near her face, squatting in the Oriental manner.

'Deborah, are you sleepy?' he said.

'Yes, very sleepy,' she answered.

He held the pan for a little in his hands and when it had become suitably lukewarm he gave her the drink and told her she should sip it. She sipped. It must have done her good too, for once more she looked up at his face with her drowsy eyes as he sat near her and then did fall asleep softly and sweetly. He sat for a while and looked at her. The little child, covered with the wide sleeves of the caftan, slept well. Then he got up and laid the pan aside.

He wanted to use this period of sleep to see what was lying around in the dwelling that could be used as furnishings for the time being; and if it were possible, he also wanted to look around briefly outside to see whether he could see any of his servants or maids who would watch while he went out to gather enough food at least for the next short period. He went through the rooms, came out again to Deborah and as he was searching, constantly looking at the door-lock to see how he could manage to close it when he went out – for everything hung down half-torn and broken – his Abyssinian slave Uram crept in. He crawled along the ground, fixing his eyes immovably on Abdias because he was expecting a terrible chastising for having run away with the others when the marauders came. But Abdias intended to reward rather than punish him because he was the first to return.

'Uram,' he said, 'where are the others?'

'I don't know,' answered the slave, as he stopped creeping nearer.

'Did you all run off together, then?'

'Yes, but everyone scattered. And when I heard that you had returned I came back again because you will protect us. I thought the others would be here already.'

'No, they are not here,' said Abdias, 'not a single one. Boy, Uram,' he continued very softly, 'come nearer and hear what I have to say to you.'

The youth sprang up and stared at Abdias, who said: 'I'll give you a very beautiful red band with a crest of heron's feathers in it, I'll make you overseer over all the others if you do exactly what I tell you. As long as I am away — for I'm going out for a short while – you must guard your sick mistress and the child. Sit down on this heap of earth – like that – here you have a weapon, it is a pistol – this is how you must hold it.'

'I know that already,' said the boy.

'Good,' Abdias continued, 'if even one person comes in and tries to touch the sleeping woman and the child, then tell him to go or else you'll kill him. If he doesn't go, then point the opening at him, press the iron tongue and shoot him dead. Do you understand everything?'

Uram nodded and sat down in the desired position on the ground.

Abdias looked at him for a while, then went through the passage into the outer room holding the other pistol in his caftan. Everything lay scattered around as he had left it and the roomy cave was empty. When he had looked around everywhere he decided to go right outside. Because of the many pains in his loins he had to stretch again before climbing over the threshold out to the palm-trees. Here it was indeed completely desolate as he had supposed; the neighbours must have gone to their distant dwellings or wherever else they pleased. When he came to the heap of sand where he had been beaten with the spears, the camel was no longer there – they had taken it together with the rags as compensation. He went round the triumphal arch and the outlying masonry and when he had ascended the high pile of rubble that lay above his house, he climbed the even higher one situated behind it where there was sand and a great expanse of scattered blocks and which afforded a wide view of everything and of the overcast desert round about. There he lifted a stone and pulled a golden ring from under it. Then he stood and looked around a little. The sun which had previously been a mournful red, glowing point was now no longer visible and a veiled grey hot sky hung over the region. In our part of the world we should call such air very hot, but here it had become considerably cooler in comparison with days when the sun shone incessantly. Abdias breathed it in like a tonic, running his palms a few times down his sides. He looked through the silent rubble that lay under him, then climbed down. When he got to the ragged aloe small drops began to fall and, a rarity in this part of the world, a soft grey rain gradually began to hang over the whole peaceful plain; that too was a rarity, that the rainy season should approach so quietly without violent storms.

Abdias climbed down the opposite side from where he had gone up, walked a fairly long way through numerous well-known byways and twists and turns in the rubble until he reached his goal, the dwelling of his most important neighbour where he thought to find some of the others too. Several of them were indeed there and when the rumour spread that he had crossed Gaal's threshold, more began coming all the time.

This is what he said to them: 'If by my finer clothes and more extensive trade I have betrayed our dwelling-place, have drawn the robbers here and caused damage to be done to you, then I shall compensate you for it as well as I can. You won't have lost everything, for you are wise and have jewels hidden away. Bring paper or parchment and ink. I have many debtors out there who must pay me when the time is up. I'll write you a list of them here, authorising you to take the money for yourselves.'

'Who knows whether it is true that he has credit,' said one of those present.

'If it is not true,' answered Abdias, 'then you always have me here and can stone me or do what else you please with me.'

'That is so, let him write,' called others while the parchment and the ink that had been brought were pushed over to him.

'He is as wise as Solomon,' said those who had scolded and mocked him most that day.

And when he had written a long list on the parchment, had handed it to them and they had all said that they were satisfied for the moment until his recovery when he could give them the rest of their compensation, he drew the ring out of his caftan and said: 'You have a female donkey, Gaal, if you'll sell her to me I'll give you this very valuable ring.'

'You owe the ring as compensation, we'll take it from you,' called several people at once.

'If you take the ring from me,' he answered, 'I'll close my mouth and never again tell you where I have money, who is my debtor, where I made earnings in trade, and you'll never get anything more from me to diminish your losses.'

'That is true,' said one, 'let him have the ring and, Gaal, give him the donkey for it.'

In the meantime they had looked at the ring and when they realised that it was worth much more than the price of the donkey, Gaal said that he would give him the donkey if he could add a gold coin to the ring.

'I can't add anything else,' answered Abdias, 'for they took everything from me as you yourselves saw. Give me the ring, I'll go away without the donkey.'

'Leave the ring,' said Gaal, 'I'll send the donkey to you.'

'No,' answered Abdias. 'That won't do. Give me a bridle so that I can lead her away, or give back the ring.'

'I'll give you the bridle and the donkey,' said Gaal.

'At once,' said Abdias.

'At once,' answered Gaal. 'Go out, Ephraim, and lead her out of the pit where she is standing.'

While the servant went to fetch the donkey Abdias asked the

people if they had seen any of his servants or his wife's maids, 'for,' said he, 'they've all gone.'

'Have all your servants gone?' they asked, 'no, we haven't seen them.'

'Perhaps one of them is with you, Gad, or you, Simon, or one of the others?'

'No, no, we all ran away ourselves and have seen nothing of them.'

In the meantime Ephraim had come with the donkey, Abdias went out over the threshold of Gaal's cave, they put the bridle into his hand and he led the donkey away over the rubble. Heads stuck out of the windows to look after him.

He went along the paths through the rubble, intending to seek out a place well known to him to see if one or other of his servants was to be found there; it was very distant and often served as a place of refuge. In the meantime the rain had increased and, though fine, spread. He went through the sludge, past the climbing plants that emerged out of the cracks and grew over the tumbled masonry; he went past nodding aloe blossom and dripping myrtles. He met no one on the way and no one was visible anywhere. When he came to the place he had in mind, he went through the low, flat gateway up to its middle in sand, pulling the donkey in after him. He went through all the rooms of the hidden vault; but he found it quite empty. Then he went out again and climbed a piece of masonry in order to look around and see whether he could glimpse anyone, but there was nothing to be seen except everywhere the same ancient ruins over which the moisture, so precious here, was busily trickling on all sides so that the ruins shone as under a dark varnish; he could see no one, nor hear anything except the soft trickling of the running water. He did not want to raise his voice to call, for if anyone heard him who wanted to answer, then that person could equally well find his way to Abdias's dwelling and await his orders there. They must definitely be hidden by one of the others who did not want to give them away. He thought to himself that perhaps they now took him for a beggar and were avoiding him – and he found this behaviour natural. He climbed down again from the masonry, grasped the donkey's bridle which he had bound around a capital and took the path to the triumphal arch. Although he was wet through,

for he had taken off his outer garment to spread it over
Deborah, he paid no attention and pulled the animal along
after him. When he arrived home he went through the door
into the outer room, led the donkey in with him and tied her up
there. The room was empty. As he went along the narrow
passage he thought that, if there was no one inside either, he
would be Deborah's servant himself, tending her as well as he
could in his present state.

But she no longer needed any care; for while he was away
from home, she had not slept, she had died. The inexperienced
woman had bled to death like a helpless animal. She herself did
not know that she was dying but when Abdias had given her the
strengthening broth she seemed to fall softly asleep like one
who is very tired. She did indeed fall asleep, but she never woke
again.

When Abdias entered, the room was still empty, no one had
come back here either. Uram, like a bronze effigy, sat near
Deborah's bed, still watching, eyes and pistols fixed on the door;
but like a wax effigy, she lay behind him, pale and beautiful and
still – and the child lay at her side, slumbering sweetly and in its
dreams moving its little lips as though sucking. – Abdias cast a
fearful glance at them and crept nearer; – all at once the danger
was clear to him and he thought of what he had forgotten earlier
– he let out a weak cry of surprise – but then took away the outer
garment he had spread over her earlier and the other cloths
that lay there in order to see: it was clear, what had not occurred
to him and what she had not even known. From a garment he
pulled out a thread as fine as and lighter than down and held it
in front of her mouth – but it did not move. He laid his hand on
her heart, but could not feel the pulse. He grasped her bare
arms: they were already becoming cooler. In the caravans, in
deserts and in hospitals he had seen men die and knew its
countenance. He got up and, still wearing the wet clothes which
stuck to his body, he went around the room. The boy Uram
remained sitting in the same position on the floor, letting his
eyes follow his master's movements. Abdias finally went into the
room next door, threw his wet clothes onto a heap and put
together a costume from the things that were lying around.
Then he went into the outer room, took some milk from the
donkey, carried it back, twisted a small cloth together, put it into

the milk to soak it up and put it to the child's mouth. The child sucked at it as it would have done at its mother's breast. When it began to move its lips less strongly, stopped and fell asleep again, he took it from its mother's side and put it into a little bed of cloths that he had made in a niche in the wall. Then he sat down on a bench made of stone sticking out accidentally from the corner of the wall. As he sat tears flowed from his eyes like melted bronze. For Deborah stood before him as he had seen her for the first time in Baalbec when he chanced to pass her house and the gold of the evening flowed not only around the upper part of her house but also around all the others. From a section of white wall a bird of paradise had flown up, dipping its plumage in the yellow glow. He fetched her, her relatives accompanied her down over the terrace, she was blessed, and then he took her away from all her family and lifted her onto his camel. – Now she must be with her dead father, telling him what life was like with Abdias.

He remained sitting on the stones onto which he had sunk. No one was with him in the still room except Uram who watched him.

When the day at last drew to a close and it had gradually become so dark in the cave that scarcely anything at all could be seen, he stood up and said: 'Uram, dear boy, put away this weapon, there is no one here to guard. Light the horn lantern instead, go to the neighbouring women and the mourners, tell them that your mistress is dead and they should come to wash and change her. Tell them that I still have two gold pieces to give them.'

The boy placed the pistol on the loose earth, stood up, searched for the tinder-box in the familiar place, lit the lantern which Abdias had put down when he had come from the cellar, and went out. The rays of light from the lantern being borne away lengthened along the corridor and it was now darker inside than before for the light had created its opposite. Abdias did not strike a light but felt for the cheek of the woman, knelt down and kissed it in farewell. But it was already cold. Then he went to the place for the tinder-box where a piece of wax candle lay, lit it and held the light towards the woman. The face was the same as when she had looked at him when he gave her refreshment and had then fallen asleep. He thought if he only looked more closely, he would see it stirring and her breast moving with her breathing. But no breath came and the rigidity of the dead limbs continued. The child did not move either. As though it too had died. He went to look at it. But it lay in a deep sleep and lots of little droplets stood on its forehead. For in his anxiety he had covered it up too heavily. So he took some of the coverings away. As he was doing this the long shadow of his back fell over the corpse. Perhaps he was looking at the little face to see whether he could discover any trace of the dead woman's features. But he did not discover them, for the child was too small.

Uram the slave did not return for a long time as though he were afraid and did not want to come back, but when the piece of wax candle had almost burned down and Abdias had already lit another one, a confused murmuring and calling approached the door and Uram entered the room at the head of a crowd of people. It consisted mostly of women. Some had come to mourn and weep as was their calling, others out of interest in the misfortune; and others again to look. Among those who had come was Mirtha, Deborah's favourite maid to whom she had given all her affection after she had turned away from Abdias. She also, like the others, had run away in fright when the marauders had broken in and had not returned out of hatred for Abdias. But when she heard in the evening that her mistress had given birth to a child and then died, she joined the crowd of people who could be seen going with a lantern along the rain-softened paths through the dense rubble towards Abdias's dwelling. She wanted to see if both things were true. When she arrived in the room and saw her mistress's lord, she pushed herself crying and weeping through the crowd, threw herself down before him, embracing his feet and demanding to be punished by him. He, however, said nothing except: 'Get up and see to Deborah's child and guard it, for it is lying there with no one to tend it.'

When she got up from her mistress's corpse and was a little calmer he took her by the hand and led her to the child. Her eyes still fastened on him, she sat down near it to guard it, covering its face with a cloth so that no eyes looking at it could bewitch it.

The other arrivals were calling confusedly: 'Oh sorrow, oh misery, oh misfortune!'

But Abdias shouted at them: 'Let her rest, she's none of your business; but you whose occupation it is, mourn for her, bathe her, anoint her and give her her jewellery. – But she has no jewellery any more – take the best of what's lying about and dress her for burial.'

Those who had bent over her, wanting to feel her all over, moved aside and the others took hold of her to perform the task for which they had come. Abdias sat down in the shadow thrown by the knot of people into the furthermost corner; for two old lamps had been lit so that they could see better what was to be done.

'That's a stubborn man,' murmured some of them amongst themselves.

The women who tended the dead had meanwhile removed the corpse's outer garments, lifted it up and carried it into the next room in order to undress it fully. Then they fetched water from the cisterns, filled with that day's rain, made a fire in the kitchen to warm it, put it into a bath and bathed and washed the corpse which was not yet stiff and which, especially in the warmth of the water, hung down limply. When it was clean, they laid it on a cloth and anointed it all over with ointments which they had brought with them for this purpose. Then they tore out of the open cupboards and gathered from the floor what remained and dressed the corpse fully. Whatever garments were left after this they put together and took home.

The corpse was carried out again into the room in which it had been before and laid down on the earth. Deborah now lay there dressed like the wife of a simple man. Groups were formed to watch over her during the night, the mourning women came back again, many people came and went through the nocturnal ruins to Abdias's cave, and in the outer room that led to the outside world the women who had come for payment lamented and wept.

The next day Abdias buried his wife in the stone grave and paid the two promised gold pieces.

She had had little happiness in this marriage, and when it was about to begin she had to die.

The neighbours blessed her with their lips as she was lowered into the grave and as it was closed with the stones under which Aaron and Esther rested, and they said: It is really Abdias who took her life.

3. Ditha

When Deborah had been buried and the last stone laid over her body and fitted into the neighbouring one as though they lay there accidentally and were not concealing such precious things as the bodies of deceased relatives, and when they had been so heavily weighted, and rested so immovably on each other that no greedy hyena could dig up their limbs, Abdias went home and stood in front of the little child. Mirtha had found a better and deeper niche in another room. It had once been lined with silk and covered with silk cushions. Esther liked to lay the beautiful child Abdias on it so that his sweet smile presented a cheerful contrast to the dark green silk. But now there were none of these things in the niche; for the silken curtains and covers had been torn down and packed onto beasts of burden, only the cushions lay there, torn into rags so that their filling, a soft fine grass, the hair of the desert, poured out like the entrails of a human body. Mirtha pulled this fine filling out completely, loosened it up with her fingers and padded the sharp stony bottom of the niche with it. Then from the rags lying about she selected something to spread on it so as to be able to lay the child on this little bed. There was anyway very little linen in the desert and the best of it had been taken away by the horsemen. So she made diapers out of wool and other fabrics, even out of silk rags whose colour was no longer recognisable, and put them on a pile near the niche. When the newborn baby girl was sleeping on this little bed Abdias came home and stood in front of her.

'That is good,' he said, 'Mirtha, we'll have to take further precautions.'

He went out and led in the donkey he had bought, which was still in the room where he had tied her up. He put her for safekeeping in the vaulted room which had once been Esther's best room and into which light fell through the barred window. There he tied her up carefully and arranged the wooden bolt on the inside of the door so that it could always be closed at night when they slept. There was enough of the store of desert hay left with which he always fed his camel, and the hay had been in a dry cave in the rubble not far away and not in its shelter whose outside, in so far as it was inflammable, had been burnt down by the soldiers. The marauders had in fact found the hay, had tried to set it on fire also but through lack of a draught and because it was so tightly packed, it did not catch fire. So they tore out as much as they felt like in their high spirits, took with them what they needed for the next short while and what they could accommodate on their animals, and left the rest lying scattered around. When Abdias had made sure of the hay and its useful-ness he went back into his dwelling and spent a very long time among all the finery searching out the cleanest pieces of cloth and, wherever possible, those made out of linen so that they could be used to feed the child when it was being given the fresh milk warm from the donkey. He placed all these cloths together on a stone in the child's room. Then he went back to check the cisterns. In earlier times he had had two cisterns made behind the high heap of rubble that lay on top of his dwelling at the place where a very large frieze and the pieces of rock that lay on it gave constant shadow. Usually, however, only one of them was full and the other empty. This came about because the cisterns were connected with the artificially lined and paved water-tank in the cellar by means of a duct which could be closed. Abdias always let down large quantities of water when they had collected up above so that the water in the cellar should always be fresh and so that no large quantity of water would evaporate such as would happen out in the warm air where a larger surface was exposed than down in the cellar. Abdias found both cisterns quite full after the previous day's rain and he let one run down under the earth as usual.

He had completely forgotten the poor scrawny camel on which he had arrived the day before and which he had left on the sand in front of his house. He remembered it now and went to find it. It was no longer where it had still been kneeling when Abdias had pulled out his pistols, but it was in its stable. The boy Uram had taken it again from the man who had led it off the previous day as though in compensation for his losses, he had led it through the rubble, had brought it to a yellow puddle well known to him which he let no one know of, let it drink the whole puddle dry so that the water would not be dispersed again when the hot sun returned, then he had led it into the stable after taking off the harness and bridle that it had still been wearing. Abdias found it standing in the stable. It was the only beast where up till recently several much finer and better beasts had stood. It had a little of the hay in front of it, scattered and half burned, and was eating it greedily. Abdias had some maize added, of which there was still a stock, and had fresh hay fetched from the cave. Then he said to Uram whom he had found in the stable and who had carried out these provisions: 'Uram, go out over the sand-dune today while the sun is shining and look for the flocks, they must be around there somewhere, and when you've found them show yourself to the chief shepherd and tell him to give you a sheep from Abdias's flock marked with my name. Put a rope around it and lead it back here before evening so that we can kill it, roast some of it and cure the rest with sea salt so that we can survive until the caravan that sets off tomorrow comes back again and brings what we need to resume a partially normal life. If you don't find the flock quickly, then don't spend a long time searching but turn back and come home in the daylight so that we can think of something else. Do you hear? Have you understood all that?'

'Yes,' said the boy. 'I'll find the flock all right.'

'But have you something to eat?' asked Abdias.

'Yes, I filled my pocket full of wheat when I was in the upper part of the town,' answered the boy.

'Good,' said Abdias.

With these words Uram reached down a rope from the hook in the stable where it hung as usual, took a long, very heavy wooden staff and ran off over the rubble which stretched in great mounds from Abdias's stable towards the desert.

Abdias looked after him for a while until the leaping figure could no longer be seen. Then he turned round and went back to his dwelling. For his midday meal he took a few handfuls of maize kernels and drank some of the stale water in the upper cistern. He let Mirtha take a bowl full of milk from the donkey and gave her some of the dry bread that was there, for the better bread had partly been carried off and partly taken out and thrown around; it was never possible to bake a large amount at once because it dried out so quickly in the hot desert.

Abdias spent the whole afternoon arranging the dwelling so that it should be safe from any not too violent attack from outside. He gathered the rags and whatever better fragments lay about into the two rooms that now constituted the dwelling, and the rest he either packed tightly together or tied with string, using it to barricade the entrances to other rooms. In places he also fitted completely new bolts, fastening the hasps with good strong nails. When he had finished he sat on the stone bench and rested a little.

The pains that were due to the previous day's maltreatment by the soldiers were much worse now than they had been in the first excitement of the day before and had made his body much stiffer. He had been down to the cellar several times, taken a bowlful of the precious cold water, dipped a cloth in it and rubbed his loins and other painful places.

Towards evening a messenger arrived from the maids and menservants of Abdias's household. Uram and Mirtha were the only ones who had come back and stayed with Abdias during the day. The messenger demanded the back pay of the people whose tokens he had with him, and demanded it defiantly because they thought he was now a beggar. Abdias looked at the demands and then gave the messenger the money which he pulled out of his shabby caftan in lots of very small coins. He sent his greetings to his neighbours and told them that if they wished he had a few poor silken things to sell very cheaply, they could come next day to buy if it suited them.

The messenger took the money, left the servants' receipts with Abdias and went away.

The very short twilight of those countries had begun and when Abdias, knowing well how quickly the very dark night would follow it, had already looked several times over the rubble for Uram, fearing he would get lost in the trackless, featureless desert, just as the last weak rays shone from behind the dark masonry, made even darker by the overhanging bushes, the boy arrived dragging rather than leading the resisting sheep. Abdias soon saw him, went up to him and led him into his dwelling. There the sheep was tied up and after Uram had been praised he was asked to light the horn lantern again and find someone, perhaps Asser the butcher, who, for payment, would kill and cut up the sheep. For the pains in his body were making Abdias stiffer all the time as though the muscles he wanted to move were rubbing painfully against each other or as though they were swollen, and he could not easily help in the task, much less perform it himself, as he had often done at other times. The boy lit the lantern and hurried off. After a short time he came back again, leading Asser the butcher. Asser went in to Abdias and when they reached agreement after some haggling, declared that he would kill, flay and divide the carcase according to the law. Abdias took the lantern and shone it on the sheep in order to see its mark and be sure that it was his and that he was not killing someone else's. When he had reassured himself on this point, he said that the business could begin. The butcher tied up the animal suitably, laid it on a channel into which the blood could flow and killed it. Then he skinned it and divided up the meat according to their agreement and the custom of the inhabitants of the ruined town. The boy had to light a candle for him. After it was all accomplished and the butcher had taken the entrails as agreed and received payment, Uram again took the horn lantern to accompany him back to his dwelling. When he came back again, he and Abdias filled in the bloody hollow with earth, then put water, rice and a piece of meat with salt and herbs into a pot, lit the fire and cooked the whole on camel dung and some remaining bundles of myrtle twigs that had not been burned. When this food was ready, Abdias and the boy ate some and brought a portion in to Mirtha who had remained sitting the whole time inside with the child. They got water from the upper cistern to drink, for they were saving the water in the cellar. After all this was done, Abdias went to the outer entrance of the dwelling, closed and locked it from inside and after he had salted some of the meat with Uram's help and had buried part of the fresh meat for the next day in a hole dug deep into the earth to keep such things, he closed and fastened all the other doors in the dwelling from inside and the inhabitants laid themselves down to rest. Abdias, the boy Uram, the maid Mirtha and the baby Ditha now slept where previously there had been almost a crowd of servants. The baby had been called Judith after Esther's mother, but Mirtha had addressed her the whole day by the diminutive Ditha. Abdias had made a bed for himself on the floor of the room in which the child was, Mirtha slept near the niche in which Ditha lay, a lamp burned in the room and in the next room was the donkey they had bought. Uram lay outside in the anteroom on dry palm leaves.

At sunrise next day many of the neighbours came, wanting to buy the silk pieces Abdias had told them about. Because of the numerous pains in his body he lay half-leaning back on a heap of desert straw. Uram had gathered up all the cloths Abdias indicated, piling them one on top of the other. Some consisted of old clothes sorted out from other even older ones that were completely useless, others were the remains of various pieces of cloth with which he had formerly traded, others were the remnants of his own furnishings and mats that the marauders had torn and, because of their insignificance, had thrown around like the pieces of cloth. The neighbours bargained for everything, even for the most insignificant things, and bought everything Abdias presented to them. When, after much haggling and lowering of prices, the agreed amounts had been paid, the buyers gathered up their purchases and left. The rest of the day passed like the previous one in making arrangements to improve their situation. Abdias got up again at midday, went out to the piece of land near his dwelling where he had his vegetables and looked at them. Much still grew, much had perished for lack of attention. Whatever could bear the climate best he wanted to keep and tend. He took a little water from the upper cistern and watered the plants that needed it most. He felt able to do this because the rainy season was due and would bring water again. He himself provided the donkey with hay taken from the centre of the store where it had least absorbed the smell of the burning house. He gave her water, even mixing it with a portion of the cool water from the cellar; he had Uram lead her out for an airing in the evening and, present at this himself, let her eat the various grasses, thistles and scrub that grew in the sand, mortar and rubble. The poor camel standing alone in the stable was looked after by Uram. Outside among the flocks that were kept in common in the desert there were a few animals of his; those that had been in the ruins had been driven off by the marauders.

After a few days some of the departed caravan came back and brought everyday things that helped them gradually to begin life again as it had been before the attack. In the succeeding days Abdias gradually bought what he needed and in a short time there began again that daily buying and selling that is necessary among people in a community so that they can live in society, arranging their way of life as they want, no matter how lowly it is. The neighbours were not surprised that Abdias had

money, and more money than he could have acquired by selling
his goods, for they themselves also had some money which they
had kept buried in the sand.

So time passed slowly. Abdias lived on quietly, each day like
the next. The neighbours noticed this and believed he was only
waiting for the moment when he could be revenged for all past
iniquities. But he stood in his dwelling and looked at the child.
It had tiny fingers which it could not move yet, small unrecog-
nisable features which had scarcely begun to develop, and in
this little face it had blue eyes. These eyes, of a very beautiful
blue, stood open but did not move yet because they had not
learned to see; the world outside lay heavily on them like a
stillborn giant. These blue eyes were peculiar to Ditha since
neither Abdias nor Deborah had blue eyes but deep black, as is
usual in their race and in that part of the world in which they
lived. Abdias had never previously looked very closely at children. But he did look at this child. He did not go off on his
travels, either, in order to trade and make money as previously,
but remained at home. He often thanked Jehovah for having
directed such a stream of gentle emotion into the heart of man.
When night had fallen, he sometimes sat down as he had done
in earlier times on the piled-up rubble of his house, on the spot
where the ragged aloe stood, and gazed at the stars, the deep
sparkling eyes of the South which looked down on it daily,
innumerable and fiery. From his numerous wanderings Abdias
knew very well that in the course of a year different stars shine,
the only decoration that is renewed in the course of a year in
the seasonless desert.

At last, after a very long time, the second part of the caravan
sent out into the world after the devastation returned. The
sunburned, tattered members of it brought all the things that
were still needed; they brought goods and jewels to use for trade
and finally they brought those monies that had fallen due just
as the caravan set out and that Abdias had made over to the
others in compensation. The neighbours were satisfied now,
they respected their comrade Abdias, thinking that if he went
out again and traded, he would soon become so rich that he
could compensate them for all the injuries they had suffered
and that he alone had drawn on them by his careless and daring
way of life. They soon equipped a caravan again, giving it

everything necessary to set up trade and barter, as they had done before being plundered. Abdias took no part in the undertaking. It seemed as though he wanted to do nothing but protect the little creature which was not yet a human being, not even an animal.

The rainy season had begun in the meantime, and as was the custom every year at this period all who were not directly fated to go out into the world to do business crept into their houses and caves. The rainy season, they knew, however advantageous it was for their few vegetable patches and the bushes and grazing of the desert, is equally detrimental to man and promotes those illnesses that are in any case so prevalent in their situation and place of habitation. Abdias too, with his few dependants, kept himself in almost complete seclusion.

The cistern filled and ran over, the only spring in the town that had flowed into a deep well and to which all inhabitants had recourse when the long drought reigned and every cistern had dried up, gushed and filled the well almost to the top, the bushes, grass and palm-trees dripped and when the unbearably hot sun looked on them again, the plants rejoiced, grew in one night unbelievably, shuddering and trembling as though in ecstasy when the frightful crash of the heavens rolled over them, repeated almost daily and hourly in varying degrees. The rubble turned to mud, the rock walls were washed clean or, like the bare sandy hills, became so covered with green as no longer to be recognisable.

After a time these manifestations gradually ceased. In the ruins they ceased all the more quickly because they were situated in the desert where the great quantities of sand round about usually turned the rays of the sun into such baking heat that it absorbed every cloud which was not overwhelmingly heavy and moist and dissolved it into invisible vapour. The dense, hanging, grey masses, only occasionally showing white, moist, gleaming patches and bringing the terrible jagged lightning of that part of the world, became gradually higher, divided up into individual clumps of cloud which became deeper and bluer, had white gleaming edges and let the clear air and the sun shine through for longer and longer periods – at last a completely clear sky stood over the ruins and the desert, except that out on the periphery for a few weeks more clouds and

cloud-banks of mingled dark blue and white, from which lightning flashed, moved past; until this too ceased gradually and the
new and now continuously clear sky and the bright sun stood
empty and swept clean over the sparkling gem that was the
rain-washed countryside.

The disc of the sun and the eternal stars now alternated daily.
The effects of the rain quickly vanished from the surface of the
ground and it was dry and sandy, so that to the inhabitants the
rain seemed a myth; only the deeper roots and wells could sense
how beneficial the huge quantity of water was, now sunk to be a
treasure worthy of conservation. And that too was diminished
constantly, the short-lived green hills became reddish and in
many places white showed through them, which made the always
clear sky look darker and bluer, the sun sharper and more fiery.

Abdias continued to live in his house as he had lived hitherto.
The moment for revenge did not seem to have come yet.

But when a long time had passed since the rains, when the flat
sandhills were no longer red but white, when the heat seemed to
hang dazzlingly over the sand and a reddish opaque glow
hovered over the horizon when the eye tried to look into the
distance, when every little breeze brought with it a soft
impenetrable cloud of sand like smoke, when the ruins, the
myrtle and palm-trees were grey and the air clear every day, as
though this must go on for ever, when the earth was dry as
though water were a commodity unknown in this country and
when the child Ditha was very healthy and strong, Abdias went
out one day behind his house, around the dessicated palm-trees
and the triumphal arch to a place near black scorched-looking
stones and dug with a trowel in the sand and earth in the
solitude of the rocks where he could hardly be watched. He
worked skilfully and several gold coins came to light and then
others. He counted them. Then he dug again and found more.
When he had counted them again, squatting, and seemed to
have found that he had enough, he stopped digging and
roughly smoothed the dry sand back over the smallish flat stone
under which the gold had been hidden, until the spot looked as
though someone had been here by chance and had scuffed up
the sand with his feet. He trod up and down a few times as
though someone had stood here, turning around and looking
out in various directions. Then he went off to another spot fairly

far away where he did exactly the same. At noon he went home to eat. He went out again immediately afterwards to find several more such places, each time doing the same as before. Where the sand had been blown in great heaps over his buried treasure, he went on digging no matter how long it took, he heaped mounds of loose earth beside him, knelt in the midst of it and searched – and each time the noble untarnished gold appeared, just as it had been when he entrusted it to the earth for safe-keeping. Towards evening he came back around that heap of rubble above his dwelling which we have often mentioned. He seemed to be finished with his task. He climbed up on the summit and looked around – and after he had looked long at the boundless emptiness, as though taking leave of a paradise, he climbed down, went into his cave and soon to bed.

Next day after dawn he said to Uram:

'Dear boy, go out into the desert and try to find the herds, count the sheep and other animals belonging to me and then come back and tell me how many I have.'

The boy got ready and left.

When he was out of sight, Abdias went into the room where Deborah had died and given birth to little Ditha. There he barricaded himself in as well as he could, to stop Mirtha coming in or a neighbour visiting him unexpectedly. Having made sure of this he went into the adjoining cave – for the vault was actually a double room – drew small pointed iron tools from his bosom, approached a corner of the room and began to chisel out one of the stones. When this had been done, a cavity was revealed in the masonry behind the missing stone containing a flat metal box covered with verdigris. He took it out and lifted the lid. Inside were some papers wrapped in silk and wool. He took them out, sat down and counted them out one by one onto his caftan; then he laid them all together, took a wooden container out of his pocket which held a powder made from a soft soapy silky stone, and rubbed each of the papers until it no longer rustled. Then he put each into a separate flat bag of fine, waterproof, waxed silk, and sewed these bags all over his caftan which was already covered with a large number and variety of patches. When this task was done, he put the flat box, the tools and the container of powder into the hollow in the wall and fitted back the stone he had taken out. He plastered the joint with a sort of quick-drying mortar, the colour of the wall, so that the spot looked indistinguishable from any other.

When these things were done, he opened the doors and went out. It was already almost noon. He ate a little and gave Mirtha some food. Then he went into the room where the donkey was and harnessed her for a journey. He explained to Mirtha that he intended to leave to find somewhere else to live and that she should get ready for the journey. The girl agreed and, because he said it was necessary, began at once to prepare herself and the child as well as possible. Abdias had sold the skinny camel a few days before so that his neighbours should not think he had money. So, after an hour, he led out the donkey, lifted Mirtha onto it when she was ready, gave her the child and led them away.

They went to and fro through various uninhabited parts of the ruined town, past high mounds from which plants and dry stems looked down until they finally arrived at the edge of the town. There Abdias led them over grey meadows and steppes, then over flat expanses and finally straight on into the plain, grassless and covered with innumerable small stones. He crossed this and soon the red-gold sandy air of the desert had swallowed them up so that they could no longer be seen from the ruined town, just as they could no longer see its grey line.

Abdias had tied sandals to his feet and pulled the donkey along by its leather bridle. For himself and Mirtha he had taken the tin of concentrated broth, as well as spirit and equipment for cooking; the animal carried water and its own fodder. Abdias carried the Arab cloak, originally white, now yellow with dirt on his shoulders and a bundle of dried fruit, so that the donkey should not be overloaded. On the other side of the donkey from Mirtha, a little basket was fixed to balance the saddle, with a little bed for the child, so that when it got too heavy for Mirtha and her arms ached, she could put it down. A cloth could be spread over the basket as an awning.

The donkey walked patiently and obediently through the sand which burnt her hooves. Abdias frequently gave her water and once she had to be milked for Ditha, for the milk they had brought with them began to go sour in the heat.

So they went on. The sun sank closer and closer to the horizon. Mirtha did not speak, for she hated Abdias for having killed

his wife. He was also continually silent, walking in front of the
donkey until the skin hung from his raw feet. Sometimes he
peeped into the basket where the child was sleeping to check
whether her face was still in shade.

When evening came and the sun like a huge blood-red disc lay
on the horizon, itself a perfect flat circle cut out of the sky, they
stopped to enjoy a night's rest. Abdias spread out a huge cloth
which lay on the donkey's back under the saddle, sat Mirtha on
the cloth with the baby's basket next to her and gave them the
white cloak as a cover for when night would fall and they slept.
Then he watered the donkey, gave her hay and kept a few
handfuls of rice ready to give her later. Then he unpacked his
cooking utensils, that is, a spirit lamp, a kettle and the concentrated soup. When he had lit the lamp, heated water and
prepared the soup, he gave Mirtha some, had some himself,
drank some of the stale lukewarm water in the skin and gave
Mirtha a drink. For dessert some of the dried fruit was taken out
of the bag. When all this was over, Mirtha lay down to rest,
soothed the child, who was crying for the first time that whole
day, and soon both were fast asleep. When Abdias had eaten, he
used what little was left of the daylight to sew some of the gold
coins he had dug up out of the sand the day before into the
pistol-holsters and the saddle, which had some little hollows in
the wood. He put the coins into the hollows where they could
not move and clink against each other and fixed old leather
patches on top or he pulled already existing patches apart,
pushed coins in and sewed them up again. When night fell
during these tasks, spreading the dense darkness of those
countries over the earth, he laid everything aside and got ready
to sleep. First he covered Ditha and Mirtha completely with the
cloak to protect them from the pestilential desert vapours. Then
he lay down on the bare sand, pulling the caftan he had taken
off for a covering over his face. He wound the donkey's halter
round one arm. The donkey was tired and had also lain down
on the sand. Near the other hand lay two pistols, each with four
rounds, which were in their holsters during the day and which
he took out as a precaution, although in this expanse of sand
there were no animals and scarcely any people to be afraid of.

The night passed quietly and at dawn the next day the journey continued. Abdias had got up as soon as the bottom edges

of the sky had grown red in the East, had gathered up and put away the hay and the cloths he had spread on the harness to stop it getting wet and splitting in the heat and then saddled Kola, the donkey, stowing everything in its right place. After he and Mirtha had eaten and Ditha had been given some donkey's milk, they set off.

After a short while, on this second day's journey, the blue mountains, Abdias's immediate goal, came into sight, very big and clear at the edge of the desert, but they stood for hours so clear and distinct that it seemed as though the travellers were only inching their way towards them. Abdias had purposely taken a route that was considerably longer than any other but that had the advantage of leading for only a short while through the desert since he was just crossing a spur of it on the way to the blue mountains. Abdias did this to avoid the desert air which Mirtha and Ditha had never breathed.

But although they were going straight towards them, the beautiful, blue, enticing mountains stood in front of them at the edge of the plain not merely for a few hours, looking as though one could touch them, they stood there for the whole day, changing neither in colour nor in size. Only when the short twilight of that region came did they reach, not the mountains themselves, but a green oasis, a sort of outskirts of them, where there was fresh vegetation for Kola and for all three a clear spring. When they had been to the oasis and enjoyed what it had to offer, especially the cold water, Abdias led them again into the desert, making a camp for the night at a place where sand and thistles and cacti were scattered at wide intervals. He did this on account of the dew which falls very heavily on oases and is unhealthy for those who sleep in the open. He made the same preparations as the night before, hiding the rest of the gold coins in those places in the saddle, reins and other tackle for the donkey which were there for that purpose. However, he hid some of the gold in various pockets in his clothing so that if they were robbed, the thieves would find it and not look further, thinking they had got all his money. As on the night before, he lay down to sleep on the bare sand.

At dawn, having slept much better than the night before, he was awakened by strange sounds. He thought he was dreaming of the time thirty years before when he used to put his head on his camel's head and listen to its breathing in the midst of the caravan sleeping round about. He rubbed his eyes, sore from the desert sand, and when he opened them he did indeed see a camel standing in front of him, snuffling in the morning heat of the desert and lifting its small head on high. He also saw a man, a sleeping companion, who must have arrived during the night. He lay on the ground fast asleep with the camel's halter wound round his arm as Abdias usually did. Abdias jumped up, went towards the two figures some little distance away and when he got to them, he could scarcely believe his eyes – it was Uram, terribly emaciated, lying on the ground in front of the camel. He slept on his back with his face turned up to the sky. This face, usually so young and cheerful, was now distorted as though the boy had aged ten years in the last two days. When Abdias woke him and Mirtha, who had got up in the meantime, had come up, they found out what had happened.

The boy had found the herd and among all the beasts belonging to the inhabitants of the ruined town had counted those belonging to Abdias the Jew, and, so as to make no mistake, had counted them again; then he had gone back home, eating on the way the bread and dates he had taken for his midday meal, constantly repeating to himself the number he had arrived at so as not to forget it. At home, where he arrived in the afternoon, he looked for Abdias, his master – he searched in all the caves, in the stable, where the hay was, at the cistern, at the aloe tree – and did not find him; only when he noticed that Mirtha and Ditha were missing and the donkey too did Abdias's departure become clear to him. So he stole a camel from the Jew Gad and hurried after them. At first he looked for the donkey's traces and found them in the paths between the rubble, from when they had made their detour towards the desert. At that point he took the camel, mounted it and rode with all speed towards the point where the tracks led into the desert. But however clear the hoof prints, whose small shape he knew so well, had been among the rubble and above all on the damp grass, in the soft sand of the desert they vanished. He saw nothing in the least like prints, only the fine ridges of blown sand, and here he had to dash constantly between the possible directions to see whether, on the pale shimmering expanse which showed many other little stars and twinkling spots, he could see a black speck which would be the travellers or their tracks. Then he became so hot and thirsty that he could see nothing, because the ground began to move before his eyes. Then he held on to the camel with both hands for it was much stronger than he – and the previous night the camel had run straight here. It must have sensed either the travellers or the spring, for before it went to sleep it had drunk a huge quantity of water from it.

Abdias stroked the boy's hair and cheeks and said he might stay with them. Then he prepared the broth and gave him some. He also gave him a small portion of fruit, saying he shouldn't eat much so as not to harm himself, for according to his reckoning the boy could not have eaten anything for about fifty hours. Then Abdias let the two animals, the camel and the donkey, eat as much of the vegetation on the oasis as he thought good for them, for they were more used to dry fodder. They then got a small portion of this fodder; it had to be eked out now because Uram had brought none with him and the country and the mountains where they could get more were still far away.

'Didn't you think the camel might weaken and be unable to carry you further?' asked Abdias.

'Indeed I did,' answered the boy, 'so I let it drink as much as it liked before I rode off and I gave it some of the grain you'd spilt at home.'

'Did you tell any of our neighbours that you thought I'd left?' asked Abdias again.

'No, I didn't say a word to anyone, in case they'd follow and find us,' said the boy.

'Good,' answered Abdias, as he continued to harness the donkey.

Meanwhile Uram had got the camel's scanty harness as ready as was possible. They agreed that Abdias and Uram should alternate on the camel as soon as one or the other grew tired. Mirtha and Ditha sat on the donkey as usual. When everything was ready, they left.

So the now augmented group of travellers went on in this way, and the ensuing days were just like the first two. Three whole days after they had left the oasis, they came to fertile countryside and reached the mountains advancing to meet them. Abdias led them into a single poor village to equip them with what they needed and what appeared to be about to run out. Then he turned into the wilderness again, here completely different from the desert but certainly no less beautiful, noble and terrifying. They went on, avoiding men, huts and villages, either through ravines or along lonely mountain ridges or towards gently climbing terraced terrain covered with pungent grass. Abdias had armed the boy too for he had many more weapons hidden in the desert. During the day he now carried four pistols in his belt and a dagger a foot long in a sheath at his waist. To the boy he also gave three pistols and a dagger. Every morning the weapons were checked and reloaded. At night the pistols lay near the sleepers; naturally, they did not undress. Now they made a fire every night to scare off lions and other animals, painstakingly collecting the materials for it during the day and carrying them on the camel. Abdias and the boy took turns to keep the fire going and to stand guard, so that one of them was always sitting by the fire, watching.

But none of the dangers they feared came to pass. The nights passed, still and soundless, with the clear fiery stars looking down out of the dark blue sky of that country; the days were brilliant and clear, each as beautiful and as cloudless, or even more beautiful and clear, than the one before. The members of the group were well, little Ditha was healthy and the air, flowing under the cloths covering her basket, put colour into her cheeks like that of a delicate apple. On the journey they had seen neither man nor beast, except for the solitary eagles that at times hung above them in the empty air as they travelled. Good fortune had accompanied them, as though a shining angel were travelling with them above their heads.

In the early morning of the twenty-ninth day of their journey, as they travelled over a scrubless, gently rising plain, the softly shining colour of the land that they had been looking at now for so many weeks broke off and far away against the pearly morning sky there lay an unknown immensity. Uram opened his eyes wide. It was a dark blue, almost black strip, cut off from the sky in a frightful, long, straight line, not like the straight line of the desert which lay against the sky in its soft beauty, often in an almost pink twilight; it was like a river and its breadth stood up vertically as though it must break over the mountains any minute.

'That is the Mediterranean,' said Abdias, 'on the far side of it is the country of Europe, where we are going.'

His two companions were amazed at the new marvel and the further they went, the more this originally narrow-seeming river became visible, colours and the play of light could be seen, and at noon on the same day, when they came to the edge of the plateau, the solid earth broke off abruptly, it fell away beneath them, and far below their feet lay the flat expanse of the sea. A dark richly-wooded belt of African coast ran along the water's edge, a white town looked up at them from it and the innumerable white dots of villas could be seen like sails gleaming in the green, resembling those other sails that gleamed out of the frightful dark blue of the sea.

Such is the beauty of the farewell greeting that the desolate sandy country calls after its son who is leaving it to seek the damp coasts of Europe.

Abdias climbed down into the town with his companions, not stopping in the town itself but further outside, where a white pier ran out into the blue waves and there were many ships, their rigging rising into the sky like the branches of a dried-up wood. Here he rented a little house to wait for a ship ready to go to Europe, and prepared to take him. He scarcely went out at all, except to make enquiries in the harbour, and Uram always stayed with him. They had sold the camel, since it was now useless to them, but they had to keep the donkey in the little house. So they lived very quietly for three weeks until one day a ship was ready to leave for Europe, and was even bound for the spot that Abdias had in mind. He had made an arrangement with the ship's master and in consequence embarked with the child, Uram and the donkey. Mirtha had left him on account of a lover she had found in the white town and could not be persuaded to follow him. He had not been able to get another nurse instead, for no matter what offers he made of what he would pay in Europe, not a single woman would go with him because they did not trust him. They would not even follow him onto the ship where he promised to pay the money and he did not think it wise to show that he had money while on land, he knew that it would only have resulted in the woman betraying him without going with him, for he knew these people and that they cling to their homes no matter how poor and will go to no other, least of all to untrustworthy and hated Europe where the infidels live. So he and Uram embarked alone.

At last, when the moment of departure had come and they were both standing on the floating house, the great iron anchors were pulled out of the water and the wooded coastline began to bob up and down before their eyes and to recede. As they moved further out, a line of coast appeared further down from which Melek's white house gleamed out. Abdias looked at it but as the coastline receded more and more, as land finally vanished like a foolish myth and nothing stirred around the entire ship except the waves, which were like innumerable shimmering silver scales, he sat down and let his eyes become absorbed in his child's face.

The ship travelled on and on – and he sat, holding the child in his arms. Whenever the other travellers looked at him they saw the same thing, a man who sat, holding the child in his arms. He only got up and moved away when he fed or washed it or adjusted the cloths in which it was wrapped to make it more comfortable. Uram lay between thrown down wooden tools beside a coil of rope.

There are people who love many things and divide up their love – they are attracted by many things: others have only the one thing and have to increase their feeling for it until they have learned to do without all the thousands of other soft silky threads of well-being that daily enwrap and pull at the hearts of the others.

Abdias and Uram stayed on deck all the time. The journey was very beautiful, the sky always clear with a soft breeze playing in the sails. Whenever a small cloud appeared in the sky, the travellers looked at it to see if it would bring a storm – but no storm ever came, the little cloud disappeared again, each day was as calm as the next, the waves were small as though their purpose were merely to bring variety and life to a surface that otherwise would be flat. Then one afternoon the shimmering, welcoming coast of Europe lay on the blue water, the country Abdias had once longed for. As the sun sank slowly towards the west, the kindly ocean waves bore the ship nearer and nearer to the northern country – one shining speck after another appeared out of the dark surface, shining lines rose up and when the sun had sunk at last behind the western horizon, a whole girdle of palaces encircled the black bay.

The ship now had to lie at anchor with its people and goods, until enough time had elapsed to show that it was not carrying any evil disease.

When this period was over and the people and goods had landed, some were surprised and others amused to see a gaunt, ugly Jew walk down the gangplank, carrying in his arms a child instead of bales of goods, with an almost naked, agile boy following, like a beautiful bronze statue, pulling a half-starved donkey behind him; to all three clung the same grey of the desert and of distant countries, just as a strange weathered colour can be seen on the animals of the wilderness. For a moment the crowds of onlookers stared at the strangers – the next moment they were swallowed up by the current of this crowded part of the world and carried off by its waves. Nothing could be seen but what could be seen any day: a restless, moving crowd, chasing its own advantage, its pleasure or other things, surrounded by the huge, calm, gleaming, often magnificently-built houses.

Let us hurry ahead of the strange arrivals for a moment to look at the spot where we shall find them again.

There is a very lonely valley in a distant, isolated part of our beautiful country. Few people will know the valley, for it does not even have a name and, as we have said, is so very isolated. No road runs through it with carts and foot-passengers, it has no river with boats, it has no riches or beautiful views to attract travellers, and so it can often lie there for decades without one wanderer crossing its meadows. But the soft charm of solitude and stillness lies over it, a kindly web of sunshine lies along the green surface as though the sun shone with especial love and mildness on this place, for it is protected from the north by a strong wide ridge and therefore soaks up the rays of the sun. At the period when what we have narrated here came to pass, the valley was completely uninhabited: now there is a neat white house with a meadow and some cottages around it, otherwise it is as lost and lonely as before. Once upon a time there was only the soft meadow-grass, almost completely treeless, just interspersed here and there with a big grey stone. The meadow swings round in a gentle hollow closed off to the north, as we have said, by a ridge, on the top of which a pine-wood runs along the sky-line like a dark band; to the east, however, the view is encircled by the blue of distant mountains. Otherwise there is nothing to be seen in the hollow except the green of the ground and the grey of the stones; for the narrow snaking brook that runs along the bottom of the hollow is not visible to the observer from a short distance away.

To the north of this valley, on the far side of the pine-wood, the regions cultivated by man begin again and the fields planted with the blue flax flower stretch in great strips. To the south also there are cultivated areas not too far away. Only the hollow had the reputation of being completely barren, as is often the case with such places, for indeed they present greater difficulties to the farmer. No one had ever tried to find out whether this reputation was well-founded, it was accepted from the beginning as true and so the hollow lay for centuries unused. Only a very narrow path went through the valley, mostly only recognisable by the trodden grass, and on this path in spring and autumn single inhabitants of a fairly distant village passed regularly on their way to a pilgrimage church far beyond the valley, for the barren valley was the nearest way to it.

On his wanderings in many European countries when he was looking for a spot where he could settle, Abdias had come by accident to the valley just described and decided at once to stay there. What had deterred most people from living in the valley, its solitude and barrenness, attracted him because it had a similarity to the beauty of the desert. The hollow we have described reminded him especially of the grassland of Mosul, where the valley curved around the place where according to legend the ancient town of Nineveh had stood. That valley like ours also consisted of grass without trees, except that in the valley of Mosul not even grey stones rose out of the grass to break up the single dusky colour and there were no such beautiful blue mountains as in ours.

Abdias had procured letters from several princes and lords which permitted him to travel and to stay in their lands. He also had a business friend whom he had never seen face to face and knew only through correspondence. He sought him out and agreed with him that, if he should want to acquire some land to build his future dwelling on, the business friend would lend him his name as though he himself had bought the land, as though he were going to cultivate it himself and build a dwelling and as though he were only letting the Jew use all these things in exchange for payment. To prevent any possible misuse of the deeds of sale, Abdias would bind his friend by means of a counter-demand of the same value which he could use against him. When he came to the solitary valley he resolved to stay there, to build a house, to cultivate some land and to settle down. He decided therefore to take the rest of the gold coins out of the donkey's harness and to cut out of his caftan the English papers which were so well hidden in the waterproof silk pockets. He wanted to have everything well organised and in train so that, when he went to Africa to drive a knife into Melek's heart, and if in doing so he was caught and killed, Ditha would be provided for. He would have to bring her up a little first until she was big enough to get along if he did not come back.

The inhabitants of the distant mountain village were surprised when one of their number went through the barren valley to the church and brought back the news that the ground was torn up in one part of the valley and that beams, stones and tools lay about as though the building of a house were under way. And when someone else went to the church again, walls were already standing and men were working. Another brought news of the further progress of the building, many went to the church only on account of this novelty, when otherwise they would perhaps have gone at another time. They talked about it until at last a plain white house of medium size gleamed against the green of the meadow and next to it the beginnings of a garden were being laid. To questions as to the why and wherefore of it, the answer was that a strange, foreign, peculiar-looking man was having it all built and had bought the land next to it.

When the white house had been standing for a while, when the garden was finished and the high, strong wooden fence stood around it, the rare passers-by got used to it as something which simply was, especially as the owner never came out to speak to them and they therefore had nothing to tell about him – and they regarded these things as they regarded the stones that stuck up here and there out of the grass or the objects that lay about by chance on the path.

When the building was ready and according to the builder's advice had dried out, Abdias went about equipping the inside of the house. He had double bolts made on the inside of every door, he had strong iron grilles put in front of the windows and in place of the former fence he even had a solid high wall built around the garden. Then there came objects such as were usual in Europe and among them he mixed in things he had had in Africa; for instance, he put carpets not just on the floors but also on things that were not meant for them, out of carpets and soft skins that he bought he made couches to rest on so that one could sit in the cool of the rooms. To create this coolness he had the rooms made with very thick walls as he had learnt to do in Africa, and in the rooms he had only a few small windows, widely spaced, which had double, hinged shutters of the kind with horizontal slats that can be made to overlap or opened to let in more light. He had got to know these shutters in Europe and used them instead of the myrtles that had surrounded and overgrown his upper window in the desert to prevent the burning rays of the sun there from coming in. The small windows of the rooms did not lead directly to the fresh air but to another room which also formed a sort of porch, which could be closed off by heavy doors and by hinged shutters to hold off the rays of the sun and the hot air from outside – all arrangements that were unnecessary in Europe.

What gave him most pleasure was a fountain which a builder had made for him in a corner of the courtyard which was always in shade; one had only to pull a metal knob in and out for crystal clear ice-cold water to flow into the stone basin. In the beginning he did not want to allow the knob to be pulled nor the water used too often, for fear that it would be used up too quickly, but when the water flowed for two years undiminished and always fresh whenever the knob was pulled, he realised that here was a treasure that could not be exhausted, that the people here were unable to appreciate and that in the ruined town was considered the highest good. Uram and he, in fact, during all the first period of their European wanderings, were constantly delighted by the wonderful springs and amazed that the people who lived there thought nothing of them; and often, when they were in the mountains and a really crystal clear stream burst from the stones, they drank from it for pleasure, even when they were not thirsty, in appreciation of the water. They preferred the mountain water to that of the plain even though they did not specially like the mountains, which closed them in, depriving them of the boundless space to which they were accustomed. In the garden, already encircled by a high wall, there was nothing yet except grass; however, with future shade in mind, Abdias had trees planted and decided to tend them himself and to take care of them, so that in a few years they would give shade to the grass and the white wall of the house. In future too he would arrange a section of the garden where vegetables and other useful things would grow; now, he thought, he should just complete the most essential things.

The inner rooms were all furnished now, the house was ready and protected from attack from outside. He had taken men-servants and maids from amongst his own race.

When the whole building was habitable, which had taken him three whole years, he moved in. He took Ditha from the wooden cottage, which had been erected with double walls as a temporary dwelling for himself and the child, and had her carried into the room specially arranged for her in the stone house. He came too, taking with him the very few things he had had in the wooden house. The cottage was now immediately torn down.

One of the goals he had been aiming at in Europe had now been achieved, namely a place to live. Here he now sat, all alone with Ditha; for Uram had languished and died in the European climate in the first year of their wanderings, in spite of the fact that thanks to his youth he had regarded everything that had happened to him with curiosity and often with delight. Abdias sat all alone with Ditha. He now intended to give her all his attention so that according to his plan she could be educated a little for while he had been building a dwelling for her, as hitherto, he had not had much time to see to her, and the servants who looked after her merely fed, waited on and protected her, and then let her lie as she wanted. However, her little body was healthy and flourishing. And so she now lay in front of him, a real mystery, a product of his own being, waiting for an unknown revelation.

With the same enthusiasm with which he had done everything up to now, Abdias set about paying attention to Ditha, although he did not really know what he should do to help her to develop and progress. He spent all his time in her room. He touched her, he talked to her, he sat her up in her cot, he put her down on the carpet, he stood her on her feet, he tried to see if she would walk a little if he held an attractive object in front of her, and many things of this kind: but very soon he saw that the girl was not as she should be. He blamed the two maids he had employed in Europe solely to wait on Ditha and who seemed only to have cared for her body, that it should be healthy and grow, but who had done nothing for the rest of her development.

The child was now around four years old, but she was not like a four-year-old child. Her face was inexpressibly sweet and beautiful and she became daily more like a charming replica of her father as he had been when still young and handsome; only the father's strength was softened by gentler traces of the mother which appeared in the formation of the face. The body was almost that of a four-year-old child, only it seemed more delicate and not strong enough for the movements that other children make at that age. But her limbs were not yet capable of these movements, her father did not know whether on account of neglect hitherto or because the movements had not yet come. She could not walk yet and showed no urge to do so, such as can be seen in other much younger children when they want to reach objects they like. She did not even crawl yet, as undeveloped children do as soon as they can sit up. If she was put down on the floor, she stayed sitting on the same spot, no matter what attractive objects or favourite sweets were placed near her. She could stand but if she was put on her feet she stood motionless, gripping the hand that held her, and if this was pulled away she stood alone in the air, and did not try to move in any direction, her little legs trembling and her face expressing fear and a plea for help. If a hand was then given to her and touched one of her fingers, she grasped it quickly, held it with both her little hands and showed an inclination to sit down. If she was prevented from doing this, then she stayed standing, holding onto the hand extended to her without attempting anything further. She seemed most contented when lying in her little bed. There she felt most secure, was very good, as she usually was, almost never cried, reaching out for nothing but liked to hold one hand with the other, feeling and playing with the fingers of one hand with those of the other. Neither did her little face show the animation that children usually exhibit when they are moved by their first and, on account of their help-less bodies, very strong desires. Not even when her father, whom she knew well, spoke to her, caressed or stroked her, did she show that animation which the smallest children usually have. The features of the inexpressibly lovely face always remained calm, the eyes of the loveliest blue so often admired by Abdias were open, did not move around and were empty and lifeless. Her soul did not yet seem to have entered the beautiful body. Her tongue did not speak yet, but when she felt very happy, she babbled strange incomprehensible sounds unlike any human language.

Abdias could not but think that Ditha was feeble-minded.

Now he really was all alone in his house, for Ditha was a non-person and Uram was dead. He had brought Ditha to Europe to save her. She was a cheat – always with the same motionless countenance and untroubled eyes. He thought to himself that he would spend many years in this way with her, then he would die, her face would not move, for she would not know that anyone had died – and when his face had stiffened, then the old, dead father would really resemble his young beautiful daughter, just as she now slightly resembled her gentle mother who had died years before.

He decided at least to develop the mindless body as much as possible. He thought that if he could make her body really healthy and strong, if he encouraged it in extraordinary exertions, then perhaps he could awaken a sort of soul in it, such as was not present now.

He brought Ditha into another room, for hitherto she had been in one of the cool rooms we have described. Her new apartment was airy and light and consisted of two rooms whose windows led out directly to the outside and whose doors opened onto corridors with many windows. He now let great currents of air in, let them move through the rooms and placed Ditha in them so that every part of her body could enjoy this soothing stream. He gave her her food himself and always determined what it should consist of. For he wanted it to be very light and nourishing and it had to be prepared in a very definite order. He also ordained what clothes she should wear; they should not confine any part of her body, should not be too warm nor too cool and should not impede the passage of air and sunlight too much. As often as possible in the uncertain weather of these parts, she was to be carried into the garden and often made to spend whole days there. He took her hand and led her around, not stopping until he noticed from the pull of her hand which got heavier and heavier that she had grown very tired and was only able to drag her body about. When the rays of the noonday sun shone, not vertically as happened in his homeland once a year, but still very warmly, she was placed, lightly covered, on the grass under the hot sun and left there for a long time, until huge drops stood on her forehead and neck and the fine linen that usually covered her began to stick to her. Then her clothing was changed, she was brought into the rooms and there he walked with her, holding her hand, often leading her out into the long corridor and walking her up and down there. Her legs – he soon saw – got much stronger. Her face was washed every day with soap and fresh water, her beautiful blue eyes were bathed every morning with pure well-water and her hair, as yellow and shining as golden flax, had to be combed and brushed and washed so that not a speck of dust or thread of dirt could be seen on her scalp and it shone as pure and smooth as the soft downward curve of the neck. Often, when he had been kneeling in front of her in the garden or elsewhere, calling until he was hoarse: 'Ditha, come here – Ditha, come here', then she was laid into a cold bath for which the water had just been taken from the well. Her naked limbs were dipped in the clear water which rippled in a very large marble basin, wet cloths rubbed her body and the clear drops hung like diamonds in her bound-up golden hair. Sometimes when she was too cold or if her hair was brushed too hard after she had been taken out, then her limbs trembled and her little face began to cry softly.

In this way some time passed. Abdias was almost constantly with her, observing her body's manifestations.

The strongest, indeed the only sign that she had a soul, he thought, was her reaction to sounds, for he spoke very frequently and about various things to her. He had a little fine silver bell – he would fetch this and let it ring near her ear. She listened, that could be seen clearly. And when the sound was repeated more often during the next days, she smiled – and this smile became clearer and sweeter the more often the pleasant sound was made for her. Later, she even asked for it herself, for she grew restive and uttered her incomprehensible words until it began: then she grew still and something like joy, even indeed like a very intelligent expression, glimmered in her face.

At this discovery, Abdias got an idea that flashed through his head like lightning, like a burning airy apparition: it occurred to him that the poor tortured child might simply be blind.

At once, as soon as he got this idea, he began to make experiments to test if it were true or not. He had the girl placed, lightly dressed, in her cot. Then he fetched a very long, very pointed needle and pricked her hand with it. Her hand twitched away. He pricked again and it twitched again. Then he merely touched her hand with the point of the needle and lo and behold, it also twitched away. If the child could see, she must now know the needle and must know that the fine tip of it was what gave pain. Now he brought the point of the needle close to the beautiful, large, blue pupil of her eye – closer still – and closer until it almost touched it: she did not move, the eye stayed open, calmly trusting. He now fetched a burning coal from the kitchen, held it in tongs and brought it near the eye – he waved it round silently in circles but close to her face so that it formed burning lines in the air: but no movement resulted in her face to show that the child had seen the fiery circle. The beautiful eye remained in the same speechless silence. He tried something else: he flicked the tips of his fingers very quickly but silently through the air just above her eye-lashes, which makes almost everyone, especially children, blink. But Ditha was completely unconscious of these movements going on so close to her eyelids.

It was now proved to him, and all he had previously observed was clear to him. She was blind. The young, misunderstood soul had been bound helpless in the everlasting night, ignorant of the nature of the world, not knowing what it was missing.

Just as soon as Abdias made this discovery, he sent to the distant town for the doctor. He did not come until the next day and confirmed from his knowledge what Abdias had suspected. At once a quite different procedure was adopted with the child. She was again banished into a room, a small chair was made for her so she could lean her head on the back of it in such a way that her eyes, her beautiful but useless eyes, were turned upwards, so that the doctor and her father could look into them. Abdias often looked into them but not the slightest thing, not the smallest trifle was to be seen that differentiated these eyes from those of other normal human eyes, except that they were more beautiful than others, that they were clear and gentle in a way that human eyes rarely are.

Although the doctor had said that he could hold out little hope, there now began various attempts to cure the eyes and these continued for a long time. Abdias did everything exactly as the doctor prescribed and Ditha put up with everything patiently, although the child could have had no idea what was intended and what treasure they were trying to give her. In the end, when the doctor declared that his powers were exhausted and that he had to repeat what he had said at the beginning, namely, that the child would probably never be cured but would have to remain blind all the days of her life, Abdias paid the doctor for his efforts and found a different one. However, after a time this one declared the same – and so there came a third, a fourth and more. Because they all agreed that the child could not be made to see, because the advice of the most diverse people who had heard of the misfortune and presented themselves had been tried in vain, with Abdias at each new unsuccessful attempt lowering his hopes, at last he gave up all hope, especially as there were no more doctors to be consulted and only rarely did anyone come who gave advice, or if he did, he was obviously lacking in sense. He got used to it and made the thought part of him that he had a blind child and that she would have to stay blind.

Instead now of beginning the sort of education that would have developed as much intellect and life as could be developed, Abdias took up quite another idea, which was to pile the child with such immense wealth that, when he was dead, she could buy hands to tend her and hearts to love her. He wanted to heap a great fortune on the child so that one day she could surround herself with every pleasure for her other senses, seeing that she had to do without the pleasures of one sense.

As a result of this decision Abdias now became miserly. He dismissed all the servants except one maid, Ditha's, and a watchman for the house. He denied himself anything and everything, he wore poor clothes, ate poorly, in fact, as he had

had to do in his fifteen-year apprenticeship, he now began to relearn in his old age how to acquire money and possessions, he began to push and bustle, he began to amass profits and interest, he began to be miserly, especially with time, and he did this with a kind of predatory fear, all the more so because he was pursued by the thought of his age and his approaching death. He therefore gave himself no peace – the business he knew and that had brought him riches in Africa, namely trade, he carried on as he had carried it on in Africa – and on many a night when the storm raged so that the dog crept into his kennel and the polecat into his den and no one was on the move, the black, bent shadow of the Jew passed over the fields, or when he had got lost, he knocked at a small window to ask for shelter for the night, which was often given him grudgingly, often refused; for now that he often came among people, they got to know him and he became an object of hatred and disgust. The misfortune that had overtaken his daughter was attributed to the just judgment of God punishing the boundless avarice of the father. The servants he had taken from among his race did not think it wrong to swindle him and if he had not been so sharp-sighted, they would have done it to an even greater degree.

When he was at home, he always sat in Ditha's room as soon as he had finished his accounts and his business. She had grown fond of the little chair with the headrest for her lovely head, she liked to sit in it now, although it had grown too small for her blooming, growing limbs. Then the Jew crouched on a small stool near her, speaking to her all the time. He taught her words whose meaning she did not know – she repeated the words and invented others from within herself which he did not understand and learned in his turn. So they conversed for hours and each knew what the other meant. She often stroked his hard cheeks and his homely, thinning hair with her delicate hands, after she had felt around a little in the air first. Sometimes he placed presents in her hand, a little piece of cloth for a dress whose fine quality she could feel and comprehend: above all linen which she was very fond of, whose smoothness, softness and purity she was particularly well able to judge and which was usually not just her inner but her only clothing, for she never went among people or needed to be dressed up. When she had put her outer linen dress over the inner one, to go around in the house, she arranged its folds so nicely and closed the buckle in the front so that sighted people would have thought she had done it in front of the mirror. Then she ran her hand down the fabric and taking it between thumb and index finger, said: 'Father, this is even softer than the other one.'

She placed her little feet in their shoes side by side on the footstool and felt its softness. Sometimes he gave her things to eat which he had brought, fruit and suchlike – and when she held the stone or anything that she wanted to put aside in her fingers, she felt for the nearby cup so that nothing should get dirty.

She gradually grew taller and when her white figure walked about on the grass in the garden or near the white wall, she gave the impression of a grown-up girl. Among sighted beings Abdias was loved the most by Asu, the dog. One day he had taken him and raised him when his mother had been killed and he was still blind. This dog, when he was full-grown, accompanied Abdias everywhere and when Abdias spent half the day in Ditha's room or sat with her in the garden on the grass, then the dog always sat with them, turning his eyes from one to another as though he understood what they were saying and as though he loved them both. When Abdias went to his room at night to sleep, he placed the dog's mat under the table and arranged it to make a soft bed for him.

A misfortune happened to Abdias with this dog, as though it always had to happen with this man that things conspired to form the strangest catastrophes.

It happened, at a time when there had been cases of rabies in many parts of the region, that Abdias was travelling home riding on a mule and accompanied as usual by Asu. In a wood only a few miles from home which gave all along its length onto the pine-wood mentioned above, he noticed a particular unease in the animal which forced itself upon his notice because he had not been looking much at him. The dog made involuntary sounds, he ran in front of the mule, jumping up and, when Abdias stopped, he turned suddenly round and shot back along the path in the direction from which they had come. If Abdias then rode on, the animal rushed in front after a few seconds and did the same again. All the while his eyes glittered more strangely than Abdias had ever seen before so that he began to grow fearful. After a while they came to a small shallow brook through which they had to ride. The dog did not want to go in at all. A slight foam could be seen on his lips, he stood in front of Abdias and with hoarse sobs snapped at the mule's hooves when the mule began to walk into the water. Abdias took one of his Arab pistols from the holster, stopped the mule for a moment and fired at the dog. Through the smoke he saw the dog stagger and bleed. Then in the confusion he rode through the water and on over the other side. When he had been travelling for half an hour he noticed suddenly that he no longer had a belt with silver coins which he always wore – and he realised the appalling error he had made when he had shot the dog. He had put the belt down in a place in the wood where he had rested for a while and now saw that he had forgotten it there. Immediately he rushed back. The brook was swiftly reached but Asu was not there, he was not lying on the spot where he had been shot but there was a trail of blood. Abdias hurried on and all along the path he saw blood. At last he came to the place in the wood, he found the belt there – and the dying dog lying in front of it. The animal made clumsy attempts to wag his tail for joy and fixed his glassy eye on Abdias. When Abdias dropped down beside the dog, said endearments to him and examined his wounds, the animal tried to lick his hand with failing tongue – but he could no longer do so and in a few moments had died. Abdias jumped up now and would have torn out his white hair – he howled, he screamed terrible curses, he ran towards the mule and tore the second pistol from the bridle, crooking his fingers around it. After a while he threw it into the grass of the wood. He picked up the belt ten times, threw it down ten times and stamped on it with his feet. At last when night had almost fallen, though he had shot the dog before the middle of the afternoon, he took up the belt with Ditha's money again and tied it round himself. He looked for the pistol he had thrown into the grass and put it into the holster. Then he mounted the mule and took the path for home again. When dawn was lighting the solitary valley he reached his home, all his clothes besmirched with the blood of the murdered animal, for he had held it almost on his lap when examining the wound. He had had little faith in being able to save him for he knew how well he had learned to shoot in the desert. He allowed himself to rest the day he arrived home, but on the next he hired two men, went out to the place in the wood with them and had them bury the dog in the earth in front of him.

Then he returned and carried on his business as he had done hitherto.

Some time after this he became ill. No one knows whether it was the excitement that resulted from this event or whether it was the region which was inimical to him that laid him low: suffice it to say that the illness was dangerous and he was unable to recover from it for a long time.

But it was precisely during this illness, when it was thought that everything would now proceed simply and calmly, that one of those twists in this man's fate, such as we have often had opportunity to remark on already in his life, came to pass. A wonderful event happened – an event that will remain a wonder until those great widespread forces of Nature have been fathomed in which our lives are floating and until we can easily bind and loose the bond of love between these forces and our lives. Hitherto they have been scarcely more than merely wonderful for us and their nature is not even vaguely known to us.

Ditha was almost fully grown – a slender girl with vigorous limbs which promised further development and justified the hope of great beauty. While he had been ill Abdias had not come to her in her room; but during this time she had not been well either. She had a strange trembling in her limbs which sometimes vanished and sometimes came to stay, appearing at different times, especially during hot, sultry weather. The doctor could not determine what it was and said it was the result of her growth, that her limbs had outgrown their strength, for latterly she had shot up. When her limbs had filled out, the trembling would stop. Abdias was at that stage of his convalescence when he could move around indoors and within the confines of the house but could not go further afield to pursue his business. One day, when he was sitting in his room in this condition, busy with accounts and plans, thinking especially how to compensate for the time he had been ill so as not to lose it completely, it happened that a thunderstorm blew up. He paid no attention to it for the thunderstorms he experienced here could in no way compare in ferocity and power with those he had seen in the ruined town and elsewhere in Africa. But suddenly, as he went on with his accounts and when the rain was scarcely beginning to trickle softly down the roofs, there was a great crash of thunder accompanied by a flash that lit up the whole house with dazzling brightness. Immediately Abdias realised that the lightning had hit the house. His first thought was for Ditha. Although his body was tired, he hurried at once to her room. The lightning had passed through it, had struck ceiling and floor so that there was thick smoke in the room, and had melted the iron bars of the blackbird's cage without injuring the bird, whose song Ditha loved so much, for it sat unharmed on its perch – and Ditha was also unharmed, for she was sitting up in bed where she had lain down because she had been affected particularly badly that day by the trembling. Abdias, as an inhabitant of the desert, well-versed in the weather, saw all this with one glance, quickly threw open a window to get rid of the strong, nauseating smell of phosphorus, then he looked towards Ditha – and as he looked more closely he noticed the most frightful excitement in her face, like horror, like the fear of death. When he went nearer to see what was the matter, she shrieked as though a monster had threatened to lay itself upon her and moved her hands as though to ward him off – it was the first time that she had stretched her hands towards something. – – A crazy premonition awoke in Abdias: he ran to the kitchen where a fire was burning, tore out a burning log, ran to Ditha's room and waved it in front of her eyes. She shrieked again, her face working strongly, as though she wanted to do something she was incapable of – at last, as though she had suddenly found out how to do it, she moved her eyes round as they followed the circles of the burning wood. The doctor was not present. Abdias ran for the night-watchman, telling him that he would give him a hundred gold pieces if he would ride as fast as a horse could ride and bring the doctor. The servant took a horse from the stable, saddled it with haste and rode off. Abdias watched from a window to see that he set off promptly. While the man had been saddling the horse, Abdias had had the idea to close all the shutters of Ditha's room and to draw the curtains as well, so that her eyes could remain for the present in the darkness which was so pleasant for them and thus avoid being injured by the sudden penetration of light. When this was done, with Ditha remaining silent all the time, he had torn open a window in the corridor, as we mentioned above, to

look after the messenger as he rode off; then he returned
quietly to her bed, sat down next to her and after a while began
to speak. His voice was what she knew best in him and it gradually
had its usual effect. The frightened child grew calmer after some
time and in the darkness forgot the first, frightful, wonderful
storm of seeing. After several minutes she even began to speak
herself and told him of the distant, penetrating sounds there had
been, of cutting, mute, vertical sounds which had hung in the
room. He answered everything she said, uttering very kind,
loving words. Sometimes when the conversation came to a short
stop, he stood up, ran his hands over his head in the darkness or
gripped them together as one grips wood or iron in order to let
out inner emotion. – Then he sat down by the bed again and
stayed sitting for a long time as he was able gradually to become
calmer. Ditha wanted to add another sign to that of his voice and
felt for his hands and when she had them, stroked them to
convince herself that it was really he whom she was holding. He
now stayed seated by her side all the time, and gradually she
began to talk of ordinary things such as happened every day. All
the while she seemed to be growing more tired, particularly since
in answer to his questioning she had told him that the trembling
had stopped completely, which was very good. After a while she
said nothing more, and when she had spoken a few more
trusting, disjointed words she arranged her little head on the
pillow and the eyelids closed in sleep over the new jewels she had
just received but not yet recognised. When she was sleeping
peacefully, Abdias softly withdrew his hand from hers and went
out into the garden to see what sort of day it was outside. It was
evening. The same thunderstorm that had made Ditha see had
smashed the roof of his house with its hail-stones and flattened
his neighbour's harvest, but he had noticed nothing of it. Now, as
he stood in the wet grass, it was all over. The region was very
quiet, the sun was just going down in the late evening and to the
south, the direction in which the thunderstorm had gone,
stretched a broad, shimmering rainbow over the whole dark
background.

After midnight the longed-for doctor came at last. He did not
recommend waking the softly-sleeping girl but decided to hold
the examination in daylight. However, he approved what Abdias
had done.

into the garden and not just into the garden but out into the country, into the valley. He showed her the sky, the endless deep blue in which the silver islands of the clouds were floating and told her that was blue, that white. Then he pointed to the earth, where the soft gentle hollow of the valley stretched out in front of them and told her that was the ground on which they were walking, the soft substance under their feet was the green grass, the dazzling thing that her eyes could not bear and that was more penetrating than the lamp had been yesterday was the sun, the lamp of the day, which always came after sleep, making the day and giving the eyes the power to see everything. Then he led her into the courtyard to the fountain, pulled the metal knob before her eyes so that the stream of water burst forth, and showed her the water which was so marvellous to him and let her drink from the bright, fresh crystal stream which he caught in a glass. The next day he showed her the trees, the flowers, he explained the colours to her, something completely new for her and which she not only mixed up when she was repeating them but also used quite incorrectly, especially when colours and sounds crowded together in her head. Among the grass there were often little creatures which he showed her and when a bird flew through the air, he tried to direct her eyes to it. He had to teach her to walk too and get her used to it when they wandered off from the garden onto the grass of the solitary valley; for it was as though she gripped the ground with feelers in her feet, not trusting herself to put her toe quickly and surely down on the grass because she did not know how big or how small the distance between this step and the next was, and this resulted in her walking much less surely now that she could see than when she had been blind, for then she had placed each foot in front of the other in the consciousness of the firm ground she had always been able to feel, not knowing what a huge number of objects lay at the next step. Ditha got pleasure from everything she saw, was always looking around and especially admired the house they lived in, the single most remarkable thing of its kind to be seen against the bare background of the grass. She scarcely wanted to go indoors so as not to lose the blue of the sky which she particularly liked and the green of the ground stretching out into the distance. She kept looking, unable to understand how a tree, a piece of the garden wall or the fluttering tip of her father's garment could at once remove such a large part of the world from her and how she could immediately cover everything, everything, with her little hand if she placed it under her forehead.

Evening came, as on the previous day, bringing exhaustion with it, and the father lulled his daughter to sleep, carrying on with the task they had begun on the morrow.

Abdias now gave up the trade he had been pursuing so zealously in recent times and occupied himself exclusively with Ditha, leading her on into the new realm of sight.

What other parents experience at long intervals, as though diluted in millions of moments, was now given him to a certain extent all at once. Ditha'a eyes had been veiled for eleven years. She had been in the world for eleven years, forced to wait for sight after having been given the world first from another aspect, that of the dark, lonely, restricted sense of touch: but just as we hear tell of that fabulous flower which as a bare grey plant takes many years to grow and then in a few days shoots up in a slim shaft and, as though with a bang, breaks into a magnificent tower of flowers, so it seemed to be with Ditha. Since the two flowers of her head had opened, a quite different Spring burst into flower all around her with lightning speed; but it was not only the outer world that was given her, her soul too began to grow. The fluttering wings of a young bird can be seen even when it is still sitting on the spot where it came out of the egg which held the wings folded for so long; in the same way Ditha's young inner life now spread the wings it had just received – for the seconds flew by laden with jewels, whole continents lay in the minutes and each day ended with a burden which it placed upon her. Light is so wonderful that in a very short time her body changed too: her cheeks grew red, her lips bloomed and after a few weeks her body was fuller and stronger. Abdias had lots of white hair, his face was black, criss-crossed with scars, and decay was engraved in his features. Thus he walked along at his daughter's side, she who could now walk slim and sure, for they were always in the open air which Ditha loved and he also.

But not only the girl's face became more beautiful, she also began to live and to display visibly the most beautiful thing of which man is capable, that is, a heart.

Now people no longer knew whether Abdias was still the

miser he had suddenly become several years before. He always
walked beside the girl. All those who hated the Jew looked with
visible pleasure on the innocent face of his daughter.

Her eyes, once such motionless, eerie things, were now
human, loving and warm, for they began to speak as human eyes
speak, displaying joy or curiosity or astonishment, love too,
when, talking and caressing, she looked at Abdias's face which to
her alone did not appear ugly; for he was to her heart what the
outside world was to her eyes – indeed he meant even more to
her than the world around, for she always believed that he was
the one who had given her this whole outside world.

In this way the summer passed, then the winter which was so
bleak to the girl, and another summer and winter. Ditha throve
all the time and grew more beautiful.

Two things made her strange and different from normal
people.

The first concerned a natural wonder which happened sometimes, though rarely. It had happened with Abdias too when he
was young, but had been gradually lost with age. Since the day
on which the flash of lightning had hit her room and had
changed her nervous system, it was noticeable that on thundery
days or even on days when thunder only threatened but then
moved away to the far horizon, Ditha was extraordinarily lively,
even gay and joyful, unlike other girls and women who are
usually afraid of thunder. She loved it and when a thunderstorm
could be seen anywhere in the sky, she went out to see if it was
coming. Once, in the twilight of a very heavy thundery night,
when she was standing at the open window looking at the distant
flashes, Abdias, sitting behind her in a chair, noticed that a
slight, pale radiance began to hover round her head and that
the ends of the ribbons round her hair began to move and stand
up straight. He was not afraid, for exactly this phenomenon had
frequently happened to him without cause in his youth and later
in manhood when he was strongly excited. His mother had told
him of it more than once. Usually at such times, his mother said,
he had either been very happy or very strong. The phenomenon
had never done his body any harm. Abdias stayed quite still
behind Ditha in his chair and told her nothing of what he could
see. In any case, after the day when the lightning had entered
Ditha's room, he had at once had her bed moved to another

room, and now, when he saw this manifestation, he immediately had lightning conductors put on the house such as he had seen in several parts of Europe. He now remembered too that in the East he had once been told that, when there was lightning in the night sky and a thunderstorm was unable to break, the flowers down below sometimes emitted a small flame from their calices or a strong, quiet glow even stood over them, not moving and yet not burning the leaves and tender stamens. Indeed, these flowers are at their most beautiful then.

From now on Abdias observed Ditha more closely and saw the manifestation twice more during that summer. Nothing was to be seen in the winter.

The second thing that made Ditha strange and different from other people was perhaps only a natural consequence of her circumstances, completely different from those that normal people encounter, a consequence of her early years and her solitary development. This was that ordinary life and dream-life, separate to other people, were for her all one. For others the daytime is the rule, the night the exception: for her the day was the exception. Her long night, now past but familiar, stretched over into her day and those whimsical images of her interior world not comprehensible to other people mingled with her exterior ones and in this way a dreamy meditative personality developed that seemed as strange to other people unacquainted with it as though a speaking flower stood in front of them. Just as she had once sat alone in her darkness, so now too she liked to be alone or with her father, who understood her very well. It was probably as a result of that long night too that she preferred cool, twilight colours to burning ones and again among those, blue. Once when they had been rather far from home, walking through the pine-wood mentioned above, and were standing on the far side of it on the edge of a large flax field in bloom, she exclaimed: 'Father, just look at how the whole sky is singing on the tips of those green upright threads!'

Whereupon she demanded a piece of it to take back home. Abdias brought her nearer, pulled out a few threads, showed her the delicate little flowers and explained to her that one could not just take away a piece of this blue. He promised her instead that they would soon have a similar blue field at home.

Similarly she spoke of violet sounds, saying that she preferred them to those that stood upright and were unpleasant like burning rods. Her voice, which in the latter part of her blindness she had preferred to use for singing rather than speaking, soon became a soft clear alto. So she lived in a world made of sight and blindness, like the blue of her eyes which, like that of our sky, is woven out of light and night.

When she had gained the use of her eyes and Abdias, as mentioned above, had ceased to devote his time to trade and travel, he took up something else. Together with the land on which the house and garden stood, he had acquired a not inconsiderable part of the barren valley. Hitherto he had let it lie fallow, merely thinking when he walked over it, this belongs to me. Now he began to cultivate it, intending to turn it gradually into fields, just as in the ruined town he had also had a field behind the dried-up palm-trees where he grew some vegetables and some sparse low maize. He employed labourers, bought the necessary tools and began. He employed a large number of day-labourers from distant parts for the first digging and clearing of the ground, to make it suitable for seed. At once he began to build barns and other buildings to take the harvest. When everything was in an acceptable state he dismissed the labourers from distant parts and carried on with his own workmen. After his arrival he had planted trees in the garden to give shade; now he added all kinds of shrubs, dug up a part of the ground that had previously just been covered with grass and put flower-beds there. On another side of the house the ground was prepared for vegetables.

Already, in the first spring in which Ditha could see, a beautiful green forest of corn waved in a spot where there had been only short faded green grass with grey stones sticking out of the ground. When the stalks had turned yellow, the blue cornflowers stood amongst them for Ditha. Abdias went about amongst all this and often when the gentle morning breeze was turning the ripening ears of corn into silver waves, his figure rose out of the cornfield with his white turban around his dark forehead, his black caftan moving in the wind and his great beard hanging down from his face even whiter than the turban.

Already in the first summer a piece of ground was prepared and sown with flax. When it was in bloom Ditha was led out and Abdias told her that the whole sky which was singing on the tips

of the green threads belonged to her. From now on Ditha often
stood in front of the blue cloth of the field, looking at it. On her
way back she would pluck a bunch of cornflowers from among
the corn.

Towards the middle of this summer a wagon laden high with
yellow corn belonging to Abdias drove into the new barn, con-
tradicting the opinion of his distant neighbours that the curving
green, stony valley was barren. A second and a third wagonload
followed the first and the wagon was laden until all that had
been sown was carried home as harvest. In another place digging had already commenced for an extension to the fields for
the next year.

In this way Abdias busied himself with another occupation
completely new to him, constant extension. After several years
he had cultivated all the land belonging to him and was already
contemplating writing to his business friend to procure through
him a new piece of land for cultivation. He had extended his
garden, surrounding the extension with a wall. The farm buildings he had erected grew too small and he extended them
constantly. He also contemplated new undertakings, and new
installations and buildings he intended to plan.

He had again taken on several servants and maids. He furnished the interior of the house almost as Esther's dwelling in
the ruined town had been. He laid down soft carpets, he made
niches by means of partitions and silk coverings, had couches
placed in them and yellow silk curtains hung in front of them
which could be drawn. In several compartments he placed
things for Ditha to find when he was dead and she had been
given the keys. In the courtyard and outside in the valley he
planted trees to give her shade when she was a matron. When, as
is the way with old people, he could not sleep or when the long
European dawn was too long for him, he got up and went to her
bed where she was usually asleep, flushed and healthy like a
rose. Then he could be seen walking around in the garden,
looking at this and that and making it fast.

He had never let Ditha learn to read or indeed learn anything, for it had never occurred to him. No stranger ever entered
Abdias's house and if a wanderer came to the valley, at the most
he could be seen drinking out of the brook from his hand
before going on. Abdias's labourers worked his fields, did as he

bade them, brought the corn to market and brought home the right money, which Abdias always knew beforehand, for he knew the market prices. Otherwise they spent most of their time with each other and in the servants' house which stood at the other end of the garden; although they were drawn from his own race, they still had a kind of fear of him and his strange personality. It was the same with the other servants. Ditha's maid always sat in the house, for she had been sent for from the town; she sewed clothes or read, for she hated the air and the sun. Abdias and Ditha were always outside. When he had planted trees for shade, he had not known the European skies or had not thought of them, for here they scarcely needed shade. When a hot sun shone so that everybody was exhausted and went indoors or sought the shade, Ditha usually sat on the sandy path in the garden in the midst of the fallen bean flowers and let the noon rays pour down onto her, while she sang a song she had made up herself. Abdias, however, in his wide robe, with his sparkling eyes, white head and beard, sat on the little bench in front of the house and shone in the noonday sunshine. In this way Ditha grew up, like the slender shaft of a desert aloe tree next to alders, junipers and other bushes. So they were alone and it was as though bleak African sunlight lay on the valley.

Abdias had wanted to go to Europe, now he was there. In Europe he was no longer beaten, his possessions were no longer taken from him, but he had brought his African soul and his desert nature to Europe with him.

Ditha often sat high up on the sloping cornfield where Abdias had extended his fields quite near to the pine-wood, looking at the corn-stalks or the grass growing amongst them or the clouds moving across the sky, or letting the grass seeds trickle over the grey silk of her dress and watching them trickling. Abdias liked to have her richly dressed and if she was not wearing the linen she was still very fond of, then she wore dark-coloured silk, either blue or grey or purple or light brown – but never black. The cut of her dresses was vaguely similar to European clothes, for they were made by her maid but they always had to be wide and full since she was not accustomed to tight clothing in her homeland and could not bear it. When she had been sitting for a long time at the edge of the corn, she often got up to wander alone along the edge of the field so that her figure could be seen

from far away in the valley, either gleaming white in her linen or
shimmering softly and indistinctly in her silk. Abdias then
usually went to meet her and they walked home together. He
thought he should speak comprehensibly to her so that she
could become comprehensible herself and be able to live on
after his death, and as they walked along he spoke to her. He
told her Arabian desert tales, painted southern pictures and
flung his Bedouin ideas like the vultures of the Atlas at her
heart. For this he usually used Arabic, his father's tongue. He
had learned the language of the country very quickly, something he had accustomed himself to in his youth, and had
spoken it with those he had been in trade with previously and
now spoke it with those in his service; but he preferred to speak
Arabic with Ditha. But because he sometimes also used another
Eastern language with her and since she learned the language
of the country from his mouth as well as from the servants, she
therefore spoke a mixture of all of them, expressing herself in
this and having a way of thinking to correspond.

Whenever Abdias thought of the future and how things
would turn out, whenever he thought of a future bridegroom,
he thought of the handsome, dark, friendly figure of Uram to
whom he would have given her, but since Uram was dead he
could think of nothing but that Ditha would become more and
more beautiful and so live on.

And indeed it seemed as though this wish would be fulfilled.
In the last while she had become considerably more developed.
Her body was stronger, her eye more beautiful, darker, more full
of longing, her lips fuller and her whole being more powerful,
just as in general she combined her mother's dreaminess with
her father's fire. She loved her father inexpressibly and often,
driven by this wild untamed love, she took his old hand and
pressed his fingers to her eyes, her forehead, her heart – she did
not know how to kiss, for she had no mother – and he never
kissed because he was so ugly.

Because Ditha had spent most of her time sitting when she
was blind and had only been able to move her legs weakly when
she walked, indeed because she had spent much the greatest
part of her time in bed, her development had been very slow
and although she developed more quickly once she had been
given sight, the period of maturity came later to her than it

usually does. She was already sixteen years old when she seemed to have reached this point. Her previous passionate personality became quieter, her eye more gentle and full of longing, her limbs were slender and full of life like those of every fully-developed being on this earth.

Abdias hurt himself on purpose or sacrificed something dear to him so that Fate should not demand something greater.

With all girls at this period great changes come about, and especially in Ditha's race a quiet slenderness of body and a tender shyness of glance are signs of the entry into maidenhood, and this was especially the case with Ditha. Her body indeed seemed to be in a sort of tension and although she was joyful and happy and almost as daring as before, yet it seemed as though an expression of sweet suffering had been poured over her.

It was summer and the time of harvest.

At this time, on an afternoon that to other people seemed very hot, Ditha went up over the hilly edge of the cornfield which her father had mown the day before. She walked until she arrived at the upper edge of it for there she had a flax field which she had sown late; she had had to make a detour to reach it while the corn was still standing, and it was about to flower any day now. She went up quite alone through the stubble and stood all alone, the highest figure, on the edge of the rise, if one excepted the pine-wood whose tips seemed to draw even nearer to the sky. Abdias's labourers had seen her going up through the cornfield as they were going home through the same field because they feared a thunderstorm. They paid no further attention to her. Only one who saw her father a little later, apparently looking for Ditha, said that if he was looking for his daughter she was up on the hill. Abdias had indeed been looking for her, for the delicate layer of cloud had grown thicker and spread over the sky, although most of it was still blue and the sun seemed to shine down more warmly than before. Having received this information from the labourer, he went up over the same cornfield already mentioned, saw Ditha standing at the edge of the flax field and went up to her. The field was completely covered with blue flowers and on the little trembling leaves, stirred by no breeze, was a large number of insects.

'What are you doing here, Ditha?' asked Abdias.

'I'm looking at my flax,' answered the girl. 'Look, yesterday not one single flower was open and today they are all there. I think the stillness and warmth have brought them out.'

'Don't you see the clouds in the sky,' said Abdias, 'they are drawing close and we must go home, otherwise you'll get wet and be ill.'

'I see the clouds,' answered Ditha, 'but they won't come so quickly, we still have time to go down. But if they do come sooner than seems likely, I won't get wet for I'll go into one of the houses they've made here out of sheaves and sit down there to watch the silver drops of rain running down the little chopped-off stems of the stubble. I'll be warm and dry in there.'

Abdias looked up at the evening sky and indeed the child's supposition that the clouds might come sooner than was likely seemed to be true; for the same lightly-coloured layer of cloud that had recently been standing in the evening sky had dissolved and separated into individual clouds whose white edges over-lapped and changed colour every minute. Towards the bottom, at the horizon, was a reddish grey.

Abdias realised that they would scarcely reach home before the rain and that Ditha's advice was perhaps best. But since he did not trust the flimsy house of sheaves in case of wind, he began to carry up more sheaves. When Ditha realised his inten-tion she helped him, until they had such a pile that the rain side was covered by a dense wall of sheaves and the whole was secure enough not to be easily torn down by the wind. He left an opening towards the south so that they could look out at the play of the rain and have a view of the thunderstorm as it passed over. At last the shelter was finished but there was still no breeze and no drop of rain fell. Then yellow stubble lay in front of them, the tender grass, exposed by the mown-down corn stalks, was motionless and a lark sang high in the air over the blue flax field, interrupted at times by the deep distant thunder.

Ditha was happy as usual in thunder, she turned towards the east and said: 'How wonderful it is, how inexpressibly wonder-ful. Because you're here now too, Father, I like it even better.'

They stood in front of their shelter of sheaves, looking at the clouds, ready at any minute, when the rain began, to sit down in the hut. The wind must already be blowing in the upper parts of the sky, for the grey veils of cloud that usually precede thunder moved visibly away, they had already overtaken the sun and were standing over the heads of the observers, hurrying southwards.

Inside the shelter Abdias had put several sheaves together for a seat and now sat down. Ditha sat down near him in the little yellow house with that love for cosiness peculiar to children. The opening they had left to the south was just big enough for them to see at their feet a bit of the stubble, then a little piece of flax and above, the grey airy veils moving across the sky, and they could hear the lark singing above the flax. The thunder was still distant, although the clouds had already covered the whole sky and not only over their heads, but had already spread far towards the south.

In this hiding place they sat, talking.

'Don't you think,' said Ditha, 'that the clouds are not at all thick and they will surely not let big heavy drops fall? I would be so sorry if they flattened the beautiful delicate flax flowers which only opened today.'

'I think that even heavy drops cannot batter the blue petals because they have only just opened and are still strong,' said Abdias.

'I love the flax flowers very much,' Ditha began again after a pause, 'a long time ago, when the sad black cloth was still in my head, Sara told me a lot about the flax in answer to my questions, but at that time I didn't understand it. But now I understand it and have observed it myself. It is man's friend, this plant, Sara said, it likes man. Now I know that that is true. First, the flax has the beautiful little flowers on the little green column, then when it is dead and is being prepared by the air and the water, it gives us the soft, silver-grey threads from which men make cloth, which, Sara said, is their real dwelling from the cradle to the grave. You know, that is true too: how wonderfully this plant can be bleached like the white, bright snow – then when the children are very small, as I was, they are placed in it and wrapped up – Sara gave her daughter a lot of linen when she went away to marry the strange man who wanted her; she was a bride and the greater the mountains of this snow that are given to a bride, the richer she is – our labourers wear white linen sleeves on their bare arms – and when we are dead, we are wrapped in white cloths, you know.'

She fell silent suddenly. He thought he had seen a soft light shining at the side of the sheaves. He thought, she has her shimmer again, for he had previously seen the tips of all her ribbons and hairs rise up. – But she did not have her shimmer. When he looked at her, it was all over already. After the brightness a short, hoarse crack had followed and Ditha leaned back against a sheaf and was dead.

Not a drop of rain fell, only the thin clouds trickled across the sky like quickly-drawn veils.

The old man made no sound but stared at the being before him and could not believe that this thing was his daughter. Her eyes were closed and her speaking mouth was still.

He shook her and spoke to her – but she sank out of his hands and was dead.

He himself had not felt the slightest movement. Outside it was as though there had been no thunderstorm. The succeeding cracks of thunder were distant again, there was no breeze and at times the lark still sang.

Then the man stood up, loaded the dead girl mechanically onto his shoulder and carried her home.

Two shepherds who encountered him were horrified to see him walking along in the wind that had arisen in the meantime, with the head and arm of the child hanging down over his shoulder.

The new marvel and the judgement, as they called it, flew immediately round the country. On the third day after the misfortune brothers of his race came and laid the lily in the earth.

The thunderstorm that had kissed the child's life away from her head with its soft flame poured down blessings on everyone and finished, as on that day when she had learned to see, with a beautiful rainbow far off to the east.

After this event Abdias sat on the little bench in front of his house, saying nothing but looking at the sun. He sat for many years, his labourers, on the orders of Abdias's business friend of whom we have often spoken, looked after the fields – out of Ditha's body grew flowers and grass – one sun after another passed away, one summer after another, and he did not know how long he had been sitting, for, according to reliable statements, he had gone mad.

Once he awoke again and wanted to go to Africa to stick a knife into Melek's heart, but he could no longer do it, for his servants had to bring him out of the house in the morning and in again at noon and evening.

Abdias still lived thirty years after Ditha's death. No one knows for how long after that. In old age he lost his dark colour and became pale again as he had been in his youth. Many people have seen him sitting on the bench before his house.

One day he no longer sat there, the sun shone on the empty spot and on his fresh grave mound, from which the tips of the grass already peeped out.

No one knew how old he had been. Many said that it was much more than a hundred years.

Since that day the barren valley has been fruitful, the white house is still standing, since that time it has even been improved and extended and the whole is the property of the sons of Abdias's business friend.

So ended the life and career of Abdias the Jew.

Brigitta

1. Journey in the Steppes

There are often things and relationships in human life which are not at once clear to us and whose basis we are unable speedily to lay bare. These then affect our souls with the soft and beautiful charm of the mysterious. The face of an ugly person often has for us an inner beauty, which we cannot relate then and there to any intrinsic value, while the features of another, of which everyone says that they possess the greatest beauty, appear to us cold and empty. In the same way we sometimes feel ourselves drawn to someone whom we really do not know at all, his movements please us, his manner pleases us, we are sad when he has gone and have a certain longing, even a love for him whenever we think of him in later years. Yet we are unable to reach an understanding with someone else, even though his sterling qualities have manifested themselves to us in many actions and we have known him for years. There is no doubt that ultimately there are moral reasons which the heart senses, though we cannot always weigh and examine them consciously and with calculation. Psychology has illuminated and explained many things, but there is much that it still finds dark and impenetrable. We believe therefore that it is not too much to say that there exists for us a bright and unfathomable abyss in which God and the spirits move. In moments of ecstasy the soul often soars over it, poetry in its childlike innocence sometimes reveals it; but science with its hammer and its spirit-level mostly only stands at the edge and in many cases is unable even to approach it.

I have been led to these observations by an event that I experienced in my extreme youth on the estate of an old Major, at a time when I still had a great wanderlust which led me to set off here and there into the world, hoping to experience and to investigate God knows what.

I had got to know the Major on my travels, and already at that time he repeatedly invited me to visit him in his native country. I took this, however, for a mere conventional polite phrase such as travellers customarily exchange, and should probably not have followed the matter up at all if a letter had not arrived from him in the second year after we had parted in which he took the opportunity to inquire after my well-being and finally to reiterate his old request that I should pay him at least one visit and spend a summer, a year, or five or ten years with him, just as I liked; for he was now finally of a mind to stick to one tiny point on this earth and to let his foot touch no soil other than that of his homeland, in which he had now found a goal that he had looked for elsewhere on the globe in vain.

Since it was spring and I was curious to learn what his goal was and since I did not know at that time where I should travel to next, I decided to accede to his request and accept his invitation.

He had his estates in Eastern Hungary. For two days I debated plans as to how best to travel, on the third day I was sitting in the mail-coach rolling eastwards, already gazing at heathland and forest scenes, for I had never seen this country – and on the eighth I was already walking on a puszta as magnificent and desolate as only Hungary can provide.

At first my whole soul was filled with the immensity of the scene – the way in which the boundless air caressed me, the fragrance of the steppes. and the way the shimmer of solitude spread everywhere and over everything. But when it was the same the next day and again the day after – nothing but the fine round in which heaven and earth met in a kiss – then the spirit became accustomed to it, the eye began to succumb and to become as sated by nothingness as though it had loaded itself with masses of material and to turn inwards and, while the rays of the sun played and the grass shimmered, various stray thoughts moved through my soul, old memories came thronging over the heath and among them was the image of the man I was now walking to meet: I gladly took up this image and in that solitude I had enough time to collect in my memory all those things I had found out about him and to give them a new freshness.

It was in Southern Italy, in almost as majestic a wilderness as the one through which I was walking, that I had first set eyes on him. At that time he was fêted everywhere in society and, although already almost fifty, he was still the cynosure of many beautiful eyes; for never was there a man whose face and figure could be deemed more handsome, nor one who bore himself more nobly. There was, I should say, a soft majesty that surrounded all his movements, so simple and so winning that more than once he bewitched men too. But, so legend had it, his influence over women's hearts had once been truly disturbing. There were rumours of victories and conquests he had made and these were wonderful enough. But he had one fault, so it was said, which made him really dangerous, which was that no one, not even the greatest beauty on earth, had succeeded in captivating him for longer than suited him. He behaved to the end with that charm which won him all hearts and filled his chosen lady with the joy of conquest, then he bade farewell, went on a journey and never came back. But this fault, instead of frightening women off, attracted them all the more, and there was many a Southern lady who burned to fling herself, her heart and her happiness at his breast, and as soon as possible. Another great charm of his was that no one knew where he came from and what his position in society was. Although it was said that the Graces played around his mouth, yet people added that on his forehead the marks of some sorrow could be seen, the indication of a significant past – but the most seductive thing ultimately was that no one knew what this past was. He was said to have been involved in affairs of state, he was said to have made an unhappy marriage, he was said to have shot his brother – and many more such rumours. One thing everyone did know, however, which was that he was now very much engaged in scientific pursuits.

I had already heard a great deal about him and recognised him immediately when I saw him one day on Mount Vesuvius, first hacking out specimens and then going to the newly formed crater and looking down smilingly at the blue curls of smoke that still rose gently from the opening and out of the cracks. I walked across the yellow shining rocks and spoke to him. He answered readily and one word led to another. We were at that moment in the midst of a frightfully disrupted, dark, desolate landscape which appeared all the harsher because of the indescribably pleasant deep blue Southern sky above it, to which the little puffs of smoke rose gently sideways. On that occasion we spoke for a long time together, then went our separate ways down the mountain.

Later we again had occasion to meet, we then visited each other frequently, and in the period before my departure we were almost constantly together. I found him not really responsible for the effect caused by his exterior. From within him there sometimes broke forth something so spontaneous and primordial as though he had kept his soul in reserve until now because, although he was nearly fifty, he had not been able to find the right outlet for it. When I spent time with him over a longer period I recognised that his was the most ardent and poetic soul I had ever encountered, which also perhaps accounted for its childlike, unconscious, simple, even naive qualities. He was not aware of these gifts and expressed naturally the most beautiful things I had ever heard from anyone's lips. Never in my life, not even later when I had the opportunity to associate with poets and artists, have I encountered anyone with such a sensitive feeling for beauty, which could be irritated to the point of impatience by deformity and crudeness. It may have been these unconscious gifts that won him the hearts of all members of the opposite sex, for this kind of lustre is altogether rare in men of advanced years. Perhaps that explains why he liked so much to associate with such a very young man as I; I for my part did not really know, at that time, how to judge these things correctly and only penetrated them fully when I was older and beginning to put together the story of his life. I was never able to discover the extent of his legendary success with women, for he never spoke of such things and I never had any opportunity to observe it. Neither was I able to discern anything of that sorrow which was supposed to mantle his brow, just as I never found out more of the events of his previous life than that he travelled constantly, had now been in Naples for years and was collecting lava and antiquities. He told me himself that he had estates in Hungary and, as I said above, invited me repeatedly to stay with him there.

For quite a long time we lived side by side and finally separated, on my departure, not without emotion. But all sorts of images of lands and people thronged afterwards through my memory, so that it would never have occurred to me even in a dream that I should one day be journeying to this man across a Hungarian plain as I was now. I painted a mental picture of him in ever greater detail and became so absorbed in it that I often had difficulty in believing that I was not in Italy; for the plain on which I was walking was as hot and as silent as Italy and the blue haze in the distance was like a mirage of the Pontine marshes.

I did not make straight for the Major's estate which he had indicated in his letter but made a detour in order to see the country. In the same way that the image of my friend had previously always been interwoven with that of Italy, so now it emerged more and more clearly and specifically as something independent and entire. I crossed a hundred rivulets, streams and rivers, I often slept among shepherds and their shaggy dogs, I drank from those solitary springs whose high jets shoot towards the sky, and I ate under many a low thatched roof – there the bagpiper rested, there the carter flew over the plain, there the white cloak of the mounted herdsman shimmered – and I often asked myself how my friend would look in this country; for I had only seen him in society and in the sort of hubbub in which all men are as like each other as pebbles. There his exterior had been that of the polished, sophisticated gentleman; but here everything was different, and often when I had seen nothing for whole days but the distant reddish-blue glow of the steppe and the thousands of little white dots on it which were cattle, when I saw the deep black earth at my feet and so much wildness, so much fertility and, in spite of its long history, so much that was primitive and primordial, I asked myself how he would behave here. I wandered around the countryside, I settled in more and more to its ways and its peculiarities and it was as though I could hear the hammer-blows that were forging the future of this people. Everything in this nation is prescient of future times, those things that are about to be superseded are lacking in vitality, those which are emerging are fiery, and for that reason I liked to look at its endless villages, at its vineyards, its marshes and reed-beds and far away its soft blue mountains.

After wandering around for months I thought one day that I must be very near to my friend's estate and, rather tired of so much looking, I decided to give my pilgrimage a goal and to head straight for the estates of my future host. I had walked the whole afternoon through a hot field of stones; on the left distant blue mountain peaks rose against the sky – I took them to be the Carpathians – and on the right lay uneven country with that peculiar reddish colouring such as is often seen on the steppe, but the two never met and between them stretched the picture of the boundless plain. Finally, as I was climbing out of a hollow which contained the bed of a dried-up stream, a chestnut wood and a white house leapt into sight; a sand-dune had concealed both from me until now. Three miles, three miles – that's what I had heard almost the whole afternoon whenever I had asked for Uvar, which was the name of the Major's residence. Three miles. But, as I knew the Hungarian miles from experience, I had walked for at least five of them and therefore hoped intensely that this house might be Uvar. Not very far away the field rose up towards an embankment on which I could see people. Intending to question them, I went through one spur of the chestnut wood. Here I saw that what I had immediately suspected, made wiser by the many optical illusions of that country, was true, namely that the house did not lie directly next to the wood but beyond a plain which extended from the trees, and that the house must be a very big building. However, I saw a figure dashing on horseback over the plain towards the fields on which the people were working. All the workmen gathered round the figure when it arrived, as though around their master – but it did not look in the least like my Major. I walked slowly towards the embankment, which was also farther away than I had thought, and arrived just at the moment when the whole glow of the sunset was burning round the dark waving fields of maize and the groups of bearded labourers and round the rider. The latter, however, was a woman, about forty years old, wearing, strangely enough, the wide trousers of that country and sitting on horseback like a man. Since the labourers were already moving away and she was almost alone on the spot I put my question to her. Supporting my pack on my stick and looking up at her, and as though brushing the slanting rays of the sunset out of my face, I said in German to her:

'Good evening, Mother.'

'Good evening,' she answered in the same language.

'Please be so good as to tell me whether that building is called Uvar.'

'That building is not called Uvar. Are you expected in Uvar?'

'Indeed I am. I am supposed to visit my friend the Major there, at his invitation.'

'Then walk a little way beside my horse.'

With these words she urged her horse to a walk and, so that I could follow her, rode slowly between the tall green ears of maize up the slope. I walked behind her and was able to direct my gaze at my surroundings – and indeed there was more and more cause

to be amazed. As we went higher, the valley behind us opened
out visibly, a huge plantation of trees ran from the house off into
the mountains that began behind it; avenues stretched towards
the fields, one area of cultivation after another was revealed,
each appearing to be in excellent condition. I had never seen the
long juicy fresh maize-leaf before, and there was not a blade of
grass between its stalks. The vineyard, the edge of which we had
just reached, reminded me of those on the Rhine, only I had
never seen on the Rhine such a robust growth of leaf and grape
as here. The plain between the chestnut trees and the house was
a meadow, as pure and soft as if velvet had been spread out on it;
it was bisected by fenced-in paths, along which the white cattle of
the country were moving, but smooth and slender like deer. The
whole contrasted wonderfully with the stony region through
which I had walked that day, and which lay now behind us in the
evening air and, hot and dry in the red shimmering rays, looked
across to this cool green freshness.

In the meantime we had reached one of those little white huts
of which I had seen several scattered among the green of the
vineyards. The woman said to a young man who, in spite of the
hot June evening, was wearing his shaggy sheepskin and working
away alone in front of the door of the little house:

'Milosz, this gentleman wants to go to Uvar today. Perhaps you
would take the two bays which are at pasture, give him one and
lead him as far as the gallows.'

'Yes,' replied the lad and stood up.

'Just go with him now, he will guide you correctly,' said the
woman and turned her horse in order to ride back the way she
had come with me.

I took her for a sort of steward and wanted to give her a
sizeable coin for the services she had just rendered me. But she
only laughed, showing a set of beautiful teeth. She rode off slowly
down the vineyard, then we soon heard the quick hoof-beats of
her horse as she flew across the plain.

I put my money away again and turned to Milosz. In the
meantime he had put on a wide hat in addition to his sheepskin
and led me some way through the vineyards until we entered a
bend in the valley and came on some farm buildings, from out of
which he led two of those small horses such as are to be found on
the heathland of that country. He saddled mine, mounted his

just as it was, and we rode off immediately into the twilight
towards the dark eastern sky. It must have been a strange sight:
the German wanderer on horseback with his little pack, his
gnarled walking-stick and his cap, by his side the slender Hungarian with his round hat, his moustache, his shaggy coat and
flapping white trousers, both of them riding off into the night
and the wilderness. Indeed it was a wilderness that we entered on
the other side of the vineyards, and the settlement was like a
phantom in it. In fact, this wilderness consisted again of my old
stony field, which looked so similar to its old self that I would
have thought we were riding back the same way I had come if the
dirty red that still burned in the sky behind me had not informed
me that we were really riding east.

'How far is it still to Uvar?' I asked.

'Another mile and a half,' answered Milosz.

I accepted this answer and rode along behind him as well as I
could. We were riding past the same innumerable grey stones
that I had been counting in their thousands the whole day. They
glowed behind me on the dark ground with a false light, and
because we were actually riding on dry, very firm heathland, I
could not hear the hoof-beats of our horses, except when a shoe
struck one of the stones accidentally, something the horses, used
to such paths, were usually able to avoid very well. The ground
was always flat, except for the fact that we climbed up and down
into two or three hollows, in each of which lay a motionless
stream of pebbles.

'Who owns the estate we have just left?' I asked my companion.

'Maroshely,' he answered.

He spoke the words so quickly as he rode along in front of me
that I did not know if this was the name of the owner or if I had
understood him correctly at all; for the motion made both
speaking and listening difficult.

Finally a blood-red segment of moon rose and a slender
scaffold, which I took to be the end of my companion's journey,
was visible in its weak light.

'Here is the gallows,' said Milosz. 'Down there, where you can
see something shining, is a brook, near it is a black shape, make
for that, it is an oak-tree on which miscreants used to be hanged.
That's not allowed any more, because now there's the gallows. A
made-up path lined with young trees begins at the oak tree.

Proceed along that path for rather less than an hour, then pull the bell-rope at the gate. Now listen carefully. Even if the gate is not locked, do not go in on account of the dogs. Just pull the bell-rope. Now, dismount and button up your coat better so that you do not catch a fever.'

I dismounted and, although my attempt to tip the stewardess earlier had not succeeded, I again offered Milosz money. He took it and put it into his coat. Then he made a grab for my horse's bridle, turned and flew hastily away, before I had time to say that he should convey my thanks to the owner of the horses, who had allowed me to ride off so unconditionally into the night. Obviously he was keen to get away from that place. I looked up. There were two pillars with a beam across them which loomed up in the yellow moonlight. On top lay something that resembled a head. But in fact it was probably some sort of protruberance. I went on and it was as though the grass of the heath whispered behind me and as though something moved at the foot of the gallows. Not the faintest sound could be heard from Milosz any more, as though he had never been there. I reached the death-tree immediately. The brook shimmered and gleamed and meandered around the reeds like a dead snake. Next to it was the black structure of the tree. I walked round it and on the far side was a straight white path lit up by the moon. The path was trodden hard and lined with ditches and rows of young poplars. I was glad to hear the ring of my own foot-steps, as on the paths back home in our country.

I walked slowly onwards. The moon rose ever higher and finally it stood clearly visible in the warm summer sky. Beneath it the heath stretched away like a pale disc. Finally, when a good hour must have passed, black shapes rose before me, like a wood or a plantation, and after a short time the path arrived at a gate set in the wall which ran round the outside of the wood. Behind it stood enormous treetops, stretching up motionless into the silvery night air. There was a bell-pull at the gate. I pulled it and it rang from inside. Straight away there sounded not a barking but two of those deep, decisive and inquisitive grunts produced by noble dogs – the dull sound of a leap – and the biggest and most beautiful dog I have ever seen in my life was standing on the other side of the gate. He stood on his hind-legs, grasped the iron bars with his fore-legs and looked out at me without the slightest sound, in the solemn manner of these animals. Soon two smaller and younger examples of the same breed of smooth-haired mastiffs came up growling and chasing, and all gazed fixedly at me. After a while I heard footsteps approaching and a man in a shaggy coat appeared and asked me my business. I asked if I was in Uvar and mentioned my name. He must have had his instructions, for he immediately spoke soothingly to the dogs in Hungarian, and then opened the gate.

'The Master has received letters from you and has been expecting you for a long time,' the man said, as we walked along.

'I did write that I wanted to take a look at your country,' I answered.

'And you've been looking at it for a long time,' he said.

'Indeed,' I answered. 'Is the Major still awake?'

'He's not at home, but at a meeting. He'll ride over early tomorrow morning. He's had three rooms prepared for you and said that we should take you to them if you came in his absence.'

'Then take me to them.'

'Yes, of course.'

These were the only words we exchanged on the long walk through what appeared to me to be more primeval forest than a plantation. Huge pine-trees stretched up towards the sky and branches of oak-trees as broad as a man reached out. The larger dog walked quietly beside us, the others sniffed at my clothes and then chased each other from time to time. When we had walked in this manner through the glade, we came to a treeless rise on which stood the Major's seat, which, as far as I could see, was a large square building. Wide stone steps, lit by the most beautiful moonlight, led up the rise. At the top of the steps was a somewhat flatter space and then a large iron gate, which served as the gateway into the house. Once we had arrived at the gate, my companion spoke a few words to the dogs, whereupon they shot back into the plantation. Then he opened up the gate and led me into the building.

A light was still burning on the stairs and lit strange tall statues of figures wearing wide boots and trailing robes. They might have been Hungarian kings. Then on the first floor we came to a long corridor covered with rush matting. We traversed this and then climbed another set of stairs. Here there was another similar corridor and, opening one of the double doors that led off it, my

companion told me these were my rooms. We entered. After he
had lit several candles in each of them, he wished me good night
and departed. After a while someone else brought me wine,
bread and cold meat, whereupon he, like his predecessor, wished
me good night. From this, and from the self-contained nature of
the rooms, I realised that I should now be left alone and went
therefore to the doors and locked myself in.

Then I ate, and examined my apartment. The first room, in
which the food had been placed on a large table, was very
spacious. The candles burned brightly and illuminated everything. The furnishings were different from what is usual in our
country. In the middle was a long table, at one end of which I ate.
Oak benches were placed round the table, not really very comfortable in appearance, more as though meant for meetings.
Otherwise there were only chairs here and there. Weapons from
various periods of history hung on the walls. They must once
have been used by the Hungarians. There were still many bows
and arrows among them. Apart from the weapons there were
also garments there too, Hungarian ones, which had been
preserved from earlier days, and also loose silk ones, which might
have belonged to Turks or Tatars.

When I had finished my supper, I went into the two adjoining
rooms. They were smaller and, as I had seen at first glance on
being led in, furnished more comfortably than the big room.
There were chairs, tables, cupboards, wash-stands, writing
materials and everything a solitary wanderer could wish for in his
lodgings. There were even books on the bedside-tables, and they
were all in German. There was a bed in each of the two rooms,
but on each bed, instead of a coverlet, was spread that wide folk
garment which they call a 'bunda'. This is usually a fur mantle,
with the hairy side turned in and the smooth white one out. The
latter is often decorated with all kinds of coloured thongs and
with appliquéd patterns in coloured leather.

Before I went to sleep, I went, as was always my custom in a
strange place, to the window to see how it looked outside. There
was not much to see. But one thing I could make out in the
moonlight was that the landscape was not German. The dark
patch of the wood or plantation lay spread out on the steppe like
another, enormous bunda – beyond it gleamed the grey of the
heath – then there were all kinds of bands, I didn't know whether

they were objects on the ground or layers of cloud.

After I had let my eyes wander over these things for a while I turned away again, closed the window, undressed, went to the nearest of the beds and lay down.

As I pulled the soft fur of the bunda over my tired limbs and as I was almost closing my eyes, I thought: 'Now I am curious to know what I shall experience in this house, pleasant or unpleasant.'

Then I fell asleep and everything already in my life and all that I wished most earnestly would enter into it was dead.

2. House in the Steppes

I do not know how long I slept but I do know that I did not sleep deeply and well. My over-tiredness must have been at fault. The whole night long I was walking about on Mount Vesuvius, seeing the Major now in his travelling dress sitting in Pompeii, now standing in his frock-coat among the cinders looking for stones. Into my early morning dreams entered the neighing of horses and the barking of dogs. Then I slept deeply for some time and when I awoke it was broad daylight in the room and I looked out into the chamber in which the weapons and the clothes were hanging, lit up by the sun. Down below the park was ringing with the sound of the birds and when I had got up and had stepped over to one of the windows, the heath outside was shimmering in a web of sunbeams. While I was not yet fully dressed, there was a knock at my door and my friend entered. All these days I had been curious to know how he would look, and he did not look any different from how he could look, that is, so in keeping with his entire surroundings that it seemed as though I had always seem him like this. On his upper lip he wore the usual moustache which made his eyes seem even more sparkling, his head was covered with a broad round hat and from his hips fell the wide white trousers. It was quite natural that he should be like this, I suddenly could not even think how he looked in a tail-coat, his costume appeared charming to me, so that my German coat of coarse wool, which lay dusty and battered on a bench under the faded silk garment of a Tatar, seemed almost pitiful to me. His coat was shorter than is usual in Germany but fitted in well with the whole ensemble. My friend seemed indeed to have aged, for his hair was mixed with grey and his face was full of those short, fine lines which finally show the toll of years in well-formed people who keep their youth for a long time, but he seemed as pleasant and winning as ever.

His greeting was very friendly, very hearty, indeed even intimate, and when we had chatted for half an hour, we were as well acquainted as we had been before. It felt as though we had not been apart at all since our Italian journey. As I was getting dressed, I remarked that a suitcase with my other things was on its way and he suggested that until then or, if I liked, for the whole period of my stay I should wear Hungarian costume. I agreed and the necessary garments were soon provided. He remarked that he would arrange for a change of clothing during the next few days. As we came down into the courtyard to the menservants wearing the same costume as ourselves, and as they looked so approvingly at us from out of their dark moustaches and bushy eyebrows and led up the horses for our morning ride, there was something so noble and so soothing in the spectacle that I felt myself inwardly refreshed by it.

Accompanied by the great quiet mastiff we rode around the Major's estates. He showed me everything, issuing occasional orders and words of praise. The park through which we rode first of all was a pleasant wilderness, very well tended and maintained and dissected by paths. When we came out onto the fields they were undulating with the darkest green. I have only seen their equal in England; but there, it seemed to me, the green was softer and more tender, while here it was stronger and more sun-soaked. Behind the park we rode up a gentle hill, with vineyards extending from the ridge which gave onto the heath. Everywhere a dark broad leaf was seen, the plantations made a wide band, everywhere pear trees were scattered and in their due places there shone out, as in Maroshely, the shimmering white dots of the herdsmen's huts. When we reached the heath we saw his cattle, a large, scattered herd, almost impossible to take in at a glance. An hour's ride then took us to the stud-farm and the sheep-breeding station. As we came over the heath, he pointed to a narrow black strip which dissected the grey of the steppe very far to the west and said: 'Those are the vineyards of Maroshely, from where you had the horses yesterday.'

We went back another way and here he showed me his gardens, his fruit-plantations and his glass-houses. Before we got to them we rode past a very insignificant-looking piece of land, on which a considerable number of people were occupied. In answer to my question he said that these were beggars, tramps, scaff and raff, whom he had got to work for him by giving them prompt payment. They were draining a marshy strip and building a road.

At midday, after coming home, we ate with all the servants, male and female, in a sort of anteroom or rather under a huge jutting-out roof, beside which stood an enormous nut-tree. Some gypsies who were passing by played by the wooden surround of the well. A stranger appeared at table too, a youth in his earliest years. He struck me because of hisextraordinary beauty. He had brought letters from the neighbourhood and rode off again after the meal. The Major treated him very attentively, even tenderly.

We spent the hot afternoon in the cool of our rooms. In the evening my host showed me the sunset over the heath. We rode out especially for that purpose, after he had advised me to do as he did and put on a fur coat against the malarial air of the plain, even if the air, which was still warm, would seem to make it superfluous. After we had ridden out we waited at the point indicated by him until the sun had set. And indeed, a magnificent sight followed. The huge dome of the burning, flaming yellow sky was so placed over the entire black flat disc of the heath, surging to such an extent into the eyes and dominating them, that everything on the earth appeared black and strange. A blade of heath grass stands out like a post against the background of this conflagration, an animal passing accidentally by represents a black monster on a gold ground, and spindly juniper and sloe bushes depict distant cathedrals and palaces. Then, after a few minutes, the damp cold blue of night begins to rise in the east and with its mournful opaque vapour dissects the true radiance of the dome of the sky.

This spectacle lasts longest during June when the sun is high. After we had gone home, after we had had our supper and had spent some time in conversation, when I stood at the window in my bed-room and it was already almost midnight, a dreary piece of yellow light still stood in the west, while the red crescent of the moon was already burning in the blue of the east.

I decided this evening that, on the morrow or on the day after or whenever there was an opportunity during the succeeding days, I would ask the Major about that goal which, so he had written to me, he had found at last and which would attach him to his homeland for all time.

Next morning he woke me before sunrise and asked if I would like to spend the day on my own or if I wanted to share it with him. Both were open to me during my stay. If I wanted to take part in the activities and the aims of the house, then I needed only to get up on the day on which I intended to do this at the sound of the bell in the courtyard which was rung every morning and present myself at the common breakfast. But if, on a particular day, I had other plans, then his people had been given instructions, if he was not there himself, to assist me with horses, with companions or with anything else that was necessary. He would take it as a kindness if I would inform him of such plans beforehand, especially if they involved long distances away from the house, so that he could spare me detours, difficulties and perhaps even minor dangers that could ensue. I was grateful to him for his helpfulness and declared that I wanted to take part in his activities that day and the next and indeed until I changed my mind.

I rose, therefore, dressed, and went down to breakfast under the outdoor roof. The servants were already almost finished and had separated in order to go to their various tasks. The Major had waited for me and stayed until I had finished breakfast. Then the saddled horses were led up. I did not ask what he was going to do, but followed him wherever he rode.

This day we did not just ride generally around, so that he could show me his estates and occupations overall, but he said he intended to do what was necessary on that particular day and I could watch, if it would not bore me.

We came to extensive meadows on which they were making hay. The handsome Hungarian chestnut the Major was riding danced over the beautiful soft mown green of the grass. He dismounted, and, while a groom held his horse, examined the various hay-stacks. The groom remarked that they intended to bring the hay home that afternoon. The Major ordered several drains to be dug, while the meadow was mown, to drain superfluous water and in other places to collect it. From the meadow he turned onto the path to the glass-houses, which were not, as is usual in other places, near the house but in a suitable place on a gentle earthy bank, from which their roofs were visible to the east and the south. Next to these houses a small clean stable had been erected in which the Major and his companions, if he should by chance have any, could put their horses; for it happened frequently that he had to spend a long time here and, if there were visitors who wanted to see the green-houses, this often took several hours. We put our horses still saddled into the stable and he went first to inspect several plants that were being sent off in response to requests, then he went into the office where there were papers to be dealt with and spent quite a long time at the table engaged on them. In the meantime I looked at the things around me, of which, however, I understood as much and as little as a ceaseless traveller who has visited countless glass-houses can understand. But when I went through the books and illustrations on the subject a little later in his library, I recognised how little I actually knew of its essentials.

'If one really wants to get results from these charming pursuits in which one can easily get carried away,' said the Major one day, 'one has to study them from scratch and try to go far beyond what others have achieved in the same field.'

On coming out of the office he watched several women for a while who were occupied in dusting and cleaning the green camellia leaves. At that time this plant was rare and expensive. He examined those which had already been cleaned and made some observations. From there we went past the many clean white sand-filled beds of the glass-houses, in which were the very young plants, then past all the flowers and shrubs to the breeding of which he had devoted himself. Our horses were waiting for us at the opposite entrance to the glass-houses, for a gardener's boy had led them round in the meantime. Here was where the soil was prepared and mixed, brought by donkeys in panniers from various regions and often from very distant pine-forests the whole year through. There were even special places where the earth was burnt and, nearby, oak logs were piled up which were used in winter for the heating system.

Since, as I had already noticed the day before, it was not far from the glass-houses to the heath, we now rode out onto it. The good pace of our slender horses soon carried us so far onto the

monotonous plain, fragrant in the morning air, that we could
only see the house and the park as a dark patch in the distance.
Here we came upon his shepherds. Some poles, so slender that
there was no question of their providing shelter, formed a hut, or
perhaps only a sign which could easily be seen and located in the
midst of the steppe. Under these poles a fire was burning or
rather glowing, kept alive by the tough branches or roots of the
juniper, sloe and other ungainly bushes. Here the shepherds,
who took their midday-meal at eleven o'clock, were preparing
their food. Tanned figures, dressed in dirty white trousers and
shirt sleeves, whose fur coats lay about on the ground, surrounded the Major, answering his questions. Others, who had realised
from far out on the plain that he had arrived, came dashing up
on small, insignificant horses, without saddle or saddle-cloth,
and often with only a piece of rope instead of bridle and halter.
They dismounted, held their horses and surrounded the Major,
who had also dismounted and given someone his horse to hold.
They did not just talk about their work for him but also about
other things, and he knew almost all their names. He was as
affable with them as though he had been one of them and this, I
think, awakened a sort of rapture among them. Here, as in our
mountains, the animals spent the whole summer outdoors. They
consisted of those white, long-horned cattle which are to be
found in that country, and which feed off the plants of the
steppes which have a spicy fragrance and a perfume that we
Alpine dwellers would scarcely credit them with. The men who
tend these animals also stay outdoors and often have nothing
else to cover them but the sky and the stars and often, as we had
just seen, only a few poles or a hut dug out of the earth. They
stood in front of the Major or the Master, as they called him here,
and listened to his instructions. When he mounted again, one of
the men, whose flashing eyes looked out of a dark face and
brows, held his horse and another with long hair and a bushy
moustache bent down and held his stirrup.

'Goodbye, children,' he said as he rode off. 'I will visit you
again soon and, when our neighbours come over we'll spend an
afternoon on the heath and eat with you.'

He had said these words in Hungarian, translating them into
German at my request.

As we rode off he said to me: 'If it would amuse you to see

working life on the heath more closely and if you wanted to come out here alone some time, as it were to live with these people, then you must watch out for the dogs they have. They are not always as tame and patient as you saw them today, but would treat you savagely. You must tell me beforehand, so that I can escort you, or if I cannot, so that I can send a shepherd with you, whom the dogs know well and love.'

Indeed, while we were near the shepherds' fire I had admired the unusually large, thin, shaggy dogs such as I had not encountered on my entire journey, which were sitting so quietly near and among us at the fire, as though they understood the discussion and were taking part in it.

As we rode on, we turned towards the house, for the time for the midday-meal was already approaching. As we were passing near the same place as the day before where the men were draining the marsh and marking out a road, he said, pointing to a wheatfield not far off on which the crop was unusually beautiful: 'These good acres, if they do what they should, must provide the money for us to achieve something in other places. The men work over there in the wilderness the whole year through. They have their day's wages and cook right next to their work in the open air. They go into those wooden huts you can see to sleep. In the winter, when it is icy, we move to the deeper places, which we cannot get to now because of the excessive softness of the ground, and fill them in with gravel and stones which we take from the vineyards.'

Indeed I saw, as I looked at the unusual place, the wooden huts of which he had spoken and, in various places on the ridge of the heath, thin smoke rising, which must indicate the simple hearth on which these people were cooking their midday meal.

As we were riding into the park with the big and the little dogs leaping round us, the bell was just ringing at the house to call us and the other people to dinner.

That evening I did not ask my friend about his goal, as I had resolved so firmly to do on going to sleep the day before.

The afternoon passed as usual at home, except that at about five o'clock the Major drove off, I do not know where, along the smooth path lined with poplars by which I had arrived the previous night, while I examined the increasing number of books he had had brought to my room from his library.

The next day the Major had a lot of writing to do and I spent almost the whole day looking at the horses he had at home and getting to know his people.

The next day I went to his sheep-breeding station with him, two hours' ride away, where we spent the whole day. He had some men there who showed that they had considerable training and who seemed to want to penetrate with him to the root of their beloved occupation. Here I saw too that all the branches of his operation had their own finances, for he advanced the sheep station a sum that had been taken from another area. This was noted very exactly and correctly in the books. The station was very extended and the breeding was organised according to its needs.

Another time I saw the stud-farm, and we went to the pastures on which his foals and the younger ordinary breeds of horse were looked after by herdsmen, just as the cattle were elsewhere.

In this way I gradually got to know the whole extent of his activities, which was not inconsiderable. I was surprised that he should be devoting such attention and care to these things, for I had known him earlier rather as a dreamer, writing and researching in the sciences.

'I think,' he said once, 'that one must begin in this way with the soil of our country. Our constitution, our history is very old, but there is still much to be done; we are preserved in it, like a flower pressed in an album. This broad country is a greater jewel than one might think, but it still needs a setting. The whole world has entered on a struggle to make itself fruitful and we must go with it. The body of this country is capable of great flowering and beauty, and both must be cultivated. You must have seen it, on your way to me. These plains consist of the finest black arable soil, in these hills, full of glittering stone as far as those blue mountains you see to the north, sleeps the fiery stream of the wine, and the gleam of metal shimmers, veiled by the earth. Two very noble rivers flow through our land, but the air above them is still dead, as it were, and is waiting for countless colourful flags to flutter in it. There are all manner of people in our land, many of them still children who have to be shown what to do. Since I have been living in the midst of my people, over whom I have more rights than you think, since I have been going around with them in their costume, taking part in their way of life, and since I have

won their respect, it seems to me as though I have gained many a
happiness I had looked for in various distant spots in vain.'

I did not ask this man now about the goal he had mentioned
to me in his letter.

He devoted his attention above all to the different kinds of
grain. And they were growing in such richness and beauty that I
was already curious to see when these ears of corn would ripen
and when we should harvest them.

The solitude and the strength of these occupations reminded
me frequently of the strong ancient Romans who had loved
agriculture so much and who, at least in the earlier period, had
also liked to be solitary and strong.

'How beautiful and how primeval,' I thought, 'is the vocation
of the farmer, if he understands and ennobles it. In its simplicity
and variety, in this first coexistence with nature, which is without
passion, it borders above all on the myth of paradise.'

When I had been on the Major's estates for a longer period,
when I had an overview of its parts and had learned to understand them, when everything grew in front of me and I took an
interest in its good growth, the gentle succession of these days
and occupations wrapped me round so that I felt myself well and
evenly stimulated and forgot our cities, as though what was done
in them was trifling.

When we had been once again among the horses on the heath,
and when their herdsmen were joined by those who looked after
the cattle, so that by chance a large crowd of these people had
gathered on the heath with us, the Major said to me as we were
driving home – for this time he had harnessed a beautiful team
to a carriage, which rolled safely over the heath-grass with its wide
axle: 'I should even be able to lead these people into battle, if I
placed myself at their head. They are unconditionally attached to
me. Even the others, the menservants and the workmen whom I
have at home, would let their limbs be crushed before one of
them allowed a hair of my head to be injured. If I add those who
are bound to me in the feudal relationship and who, as I have
had many opportunities to observe, are attached to me from the
bottom of their hearts, then, I think, I should be able to assemble
a fairly large number of people who love me. – Just think, and I
only came to them when my hair was already grey and I had
forgotten them for years. How would it be to direct hundreds of

thousands like that and lead them towards the good, for mostly, when they trust someone, they are like children and follow him for good and ill.'

'Once,' he went on after a while, 'I thought I would become an artist or a scholar. But I saw that such people have to have a deep, serious message for mankind, which would stir it and make it nobler and greater – or at least the scholar must reveal and invent things that would increase man's earthly possessions and advance him. But in both cases it is necessary that such a man should himself possess, first of all, a great and simple heart. But since I do not possess such a thing, I let it all drop and now it is all over.'

It seemed to me, when he said these words, as though a gentle shadow passed over his eye and as though at this moment it was still looking into the distance with the same dreaminess as in the past, when we sometimes sat idly on the Epomeo, a whole sea of blue sky rejoicing around us, the ocean shining below and he spoke of all the wishes and dreams of young hearts. Suddenly, therefore, the thought came to me that the happiness that he told me he had found might nevertheless not yet quite exist.

This was the only time during our acquaintanceship that he referred to his past, and in our previous intercourse he had never done so. Nor had I ever asked about it, just as I never asked later. Anyone who travels a lot gets to know his fellow-men and lets them be in that inner sanctum of their lives, which does not open unless by their volition. I had now been at Uvar for a considerable time and liked being there. I took an interest in the occupations of the place and was later often to play a real part in them, and at other times I went on with the diary I was writing of my travels and experiences. But I thought I could perceive that there was some sort of sediment in the pure busy life of the Major which did not allow it to be completely purified, and it seemed to me as though there was some sadness there which in a man only expressed itself in a quiet seriousness.

Otherwise he was very simple in his life-style and in his intercourse with me, and there was not the slightest question of reserve or pretence. Thus, on the table in his study, which I entered often and in which we often chatted about various things on hot afternoons or in the evening by candlelight, there stood a portrait – it was a miniature of a girl of perhaps twenty or twenty-

two in a beautiful gold frame – but the strange thing was that, no
matter how the painter concealed it, it was not the portrait of a
beautiful girl but of an ugly one – the dark colour of her face and
the shape of her forehead were strange, but there was something
in them, a strength and a power, and her gaze was wild, like that
of a strong-willed being. It was clear to me that this girl had
played a role in his earlier life and it occurred to me to wonder
why he had not married, just as it had occurred to me during our
friendship in Italy; but in accordance with my principles, I had
not asked then and did not ask now. Indeed, he could leave the
picture freely on the table, for none of his people came into his
study, instead, if they had something to say to him, they had to
wait in an anteroom, where a bell rang if someone entered. None
of his acquaintances or visitors entered the room either, for he
always received them in his other apartment. It represented,
therefore, a degree of intimacy that I was allowed to enter and
see everything that stood and lay about. I probably had the fact
that I never inquired or speculated to thank for this intimacy.

In the meantime the harvest had come and I shall never forget
this cheerful joyous time.

Now and then the Major had to undertake short journeys in
the neighbourhood and invited me to accompany him. There is
no country in which the distances are so great between the
populated points as here, but one covers them in a relatively
short time on the speedy horses or driving in the light carriages
over the heath. Once the Major put on the close-fitting Hungarian costume. He was richly dressed with his sabre at his side. This
suited him very well. He was making a speech in Hungarian at a
meeting of local officials on matters of common importance.
Since it had always been my custom to learn as much of the
language as I could in every country I visited, I had already
learned some Hungarian from the Major's people and from
everyone I met, and therefore I understood much of his speech,
which drew passionate admiration from some and passionate
criticism from others; on the way home he translated it for me
completely into German. In the afternoon I saw him at table in a
frock-coat such as he used to wear in Italy, for most of those
present had put off their folk costume and wore the common
European frock-coat.

I accompanied him on other visits he made in the neighbourhood. Here I discovered that there were four estates like the Major's. A few years previously they had formed a federation to raise the level of agriculture and the exploitation of natural resources primarily by doing it themselves to the highest standard on their own estates and so providing others with an example, especially when they should see that prosperity and a better life were the results. The federation had its rules and the members held agricultural meetings. Apart from the four big model farms which up to now had been the only members of the federation, a few smaller owners had already begun to imitate their bigger neighbours without actually joining the federation. All farmers and others who wanted to listen or occasionally to ask for advice could attend the meetings, if they had announced the fact beforehand. And not a few did take part, as I could see at a meeting held four hours' ride away on Gömöri's estate. At this meeting only the Major and Gömöri were members but there were quite a number of others present.

Afterwards I visited Gömöri twice by myself and the last time I even spent several days with him.

As the harvest was coming to an end and there was less work, the Major said one day to me: 'Because we shall now have a little leisure, we'll ride over to my neighbour Brigitta Maroshely next week and pay her a visit. In my neighbour Maroshely you will meet the most wonderful woman on this earth.'

Two days after this speech he introduced to me Brigitta's son, who had ridden over by chance. It was the same young man who had dined with us on the first day of my stay and who had struck me at that time because of his extraordinary good looks. He stayed the whole day with us, going with us to various places on the estate. As I remarked the first time, he was in the earliest years of his youth, scarcely past the boundary between boyhood and youth, and I liked him very much. His soft, dark eye spoke so beautifully to me, and when he sat on horseback so full of strength and humility, my whole being turned towards him. I had had a friend like him who had gone to the cold grave in the earliest years of his youth. Gustav, as Brigitta's son was called, reminded me vividly of him.

Since the Major had made his speech about Brigitta and since I had got to know her son, I was very curious to see her in person also.

I had heard a little about the Major's past from Gömöri, when I had been with him. Gömöri, like many of his friends whom I met at his house, was open and friendly in his speech and told me what he knew without being asked. The Major had not been born in the area. He came from a very rich family. Since his youth he had almost always travelled, no one really knew where, just as it was not really known in what service he had won the rank of major. In all his earlier life he had never visited his estates at Uvar. He had come there a few years ago, settled in Uvar and joined the federation of agriculturalists. At that time there were only two members: Gömöri himself and Brigitta Maroshely. Indeed, it was not a federation at all, for the meetings and the rules came later. Two neighbours, he and Brigitta, agreed together to begin to cultivate their estates in this wild region better. In fact, it was Brigitta who started it. Because one would have to call her ugly rather than pleasing, her husband, a young, frivolous man, to whom she had been married at a young age, had left her and had not returned. At that time she appeared with her child on her estate at Maroshely, began to make changes and to cultivate it like a man and until now had always dressed and ridden like a man. She kept her servants together, was active and worked from morning till night. It could be seen here what ceaseless work could achieve; for she had almost worked miracles on the stony ground. Once Gömöri had got to know her he had become her imitator and had introduced her ways on his estates. He had never regretted it to the present day. In the beginning, when he settled in Uvar, the Major had not visited her. Then one day she fell mortally ill, the Major rode to her across the heath and made her well again. From that day on he often visited her. At that time people said he used the healing powers of magnetism that he possessed, but no one really knew the rights of it. An unusually intimate and friendly bond had developed – the woman was indeed worthy of the highest friendship – but whether the passion that the Major had for the ugly and already ageing Brigitta was natural was another question – and that it was a passion, anyone could see who came to visit. The Major would certainly marry Brigitta if he could – he was obviously deeply unhappy that he could not; but since no one knew anything of her husband, neither a death certificate nor a certificate of separation could be produced. This fact spoke very much in

Brigitta's favour and against her husband, who had once upon a time left her so frivolously, when now such a serious man longed to possess her.

Gömöri had told me these things about the Major and Brigitta, and I had met her son Gustav a few times when we were on a visit to neighbours, before the day dawned that had been set aside for our ride to see his mother.

On the evening before this day, when the voices of a thousand evening crickets were chirping in my sleepy ears, I was still thinking of her. Then I had all sorts of dreams about her, above all I could not shake off a dream in which I was standing on the heath in front of the strange female rider who had given me the horses that time, who was putting a spell on me with her beautiful eyes, so that I must always stand there, unable to move a foot, unable all the days of my life to move away from that spot on the heath. Then I fell into a deep sleep, woke the next day fresh and revived, the horses were led in and I looked forward now to seeing face to face the woman who had been with me so much in my dreams of the past night.

3. The Steppes in the Past

Before I describe how we rode to Maroshely, how I got to know Brigitta and how I often visited her estate afterwards, it is necessary to tell the story of her earlier life, for without it what follows is not comprehensible. How I came by such a deep knowledge of the circumstances described here will emerge from my relationship with the Major and with Brigitta and will reveal itself by the end of this story without my having to disclose prematurely what I did not discover prematurely but only in the natural course of events.

There exists in the human race the wonderful quality of beauty. We are all drawn to the sweetness of this vision and are not always able to say in what the charm resides. It is in the universe, it is in an eye, and then again it is not in features that are formed according to all rational laws. Often beauty is not perceived because it exists in the wilderness or because the right eye never comes: often it is adored and idolised and is not there at all – but it may never be totally absent when the heart beats with passion and delight or when two souls are mutually inflamed; otherwise the heart stops and the love of these souls is dead. The soil from which this flower springs is different a thousand times in a thousand cases; but if it is there, one can deprive it of every point from which it might sprout and it will still burst forth at another where it was least expected. This beauty belongs to man alone and ennobles man so that he kneels before it – and everything in life that is worth having and praising is poured by it alone into the trembling blissful heart. It is a sad thing for whoever does not have it or does not know it or in whom the eye of a stranger cannot find it. Even the mother's heart turns away from the child when she is unable to find in it even a single glimmer of this ray of light.

This was what happened to the child Brigitta. When she was born she did not appear to her mother as a beautiful angel, which is how a mother usually sees her child. Later her unpleasantly dark, gloomy little face lay in the beautiful little golden cradle amongst the snow-white linen as though a demon had breathed on it. Her mother, unknown to herself, turned her eyes away and directed them to the two beautiful little angels playing on the rich carpet. When strangers came, they neither criticised the child nor praised her, and asked after her sisters. And so she grew. Her father often passed through the room, as he went about his business, and when her mother sometimes caressed the other children as though with a despairing ardour, she never saw Brigitta's black staring eye fixed in her direction, as though the tiny child already understood the wrong being done her. When she cried, no one saw to her needs; if she did not cry, she was left to lie there, everyone was busy with his own business, and she fixed her big eyes on the gilding of the cradle or on the arabesques in the wall-paper. When her limbs had grown strong and she no longer lived in the narrow cradle, she sat in a corner, played with pebbles and made sounds that she had heard from no one. When she had advanced in her games and had become more agile she often rolled her great wild eyes, as boys do when they are inwardly playing at dark deeds. She hit her sisters when they wanted to interfere in her games – and when her mother folded the little creature in her arms and bedewed her with her tears in a rush of belated love and kindness, the child showed not the least joy but wept and pulled free of the enfolding hands.

This made the mother simultaneously more loving and more embittered, because she did not know that the little roots that had once looked for the warm soil of a mother's love and had not found it had no choice but to take root in the rock of the child's own heart and there grow obstinate.

So the desert grew bigger and bigger.

When the children grew and beautiful clothes were brought into the house, Brigitta's were always right, but her sisters' were altered many times until they fitted. The others were given rules of conduct and praise, she was not even given blame, even when she dirtied or crumpled her dress. When they began their lessons, which filled the morning hours, she sat at their feet and stared at the corner of the distant book or at the map with the only beautiful thing she had, with her truly beautiful dark eyes; and when the teacher put a rare quick question to her, she was startled and did not know what to answer. But on long evenings or at other times when the others were in the drawing-room and did not miss her, she lay on the ground poring over a muddled collection of books or over pictures and torn maps which the others no longer needed. She must have been hatching a fantastic and deformed world within her heart. She had read almost half her father's books without anyone knowing it, for the key was always in the bookcase. She was unable to understand most of them. They often found pages in the house with strange wild drawings on them, which must have been by her.

When the girls became young ladies, she stood amongst them like a strange plant. Her sisters had grown soft and beautiful, she was merely slender and strong. That there was almost a man's strength in her body was proved when she simply calmly brushed one of her sisters aside with her slender arm when the sister wanted to murmur playful endearments to her or caress her, or when Brigitta put her hand to rough man's work, which she liked to do, until sweat stood on her forehead. She never learned to play a musical instrument, but she rode well and daringly like a man, often lay on the lawn in her best dress and spoke half-finished speeches and exclamations into the bushes. It came about now too that her father began to admonish her about her obstinate and silent character. Then, even if she had just been speaking, she stopped suddenly and became even more silent and obstinate. It was no use for her mother to give her hints and to wring her hands to demonstrate her displeasure in bitter despair. The girl did not speak. When her father so far forgot himself as to administer corporal punishment to her, his grown-up daughter, because she simply would not go into the drawing-room, she just looked at him with hot, dry eyes and still would not go, let him do whatever he like to her.

If only there had been one person who had an eye for her hidden soul, who could see her beauty so that she did not despise herself. But there was no such person. The others could not and she herself could not either.

It was her father's habit to live in the capital city, where he gave himself a glittering social life. Once his girls had grown up, the report of their beauty spread throughout the land, many people came to see them and the gatherings and soirées at his house became more numerous and lively than they had been before. Many a heart beat fast and tried to gain possession of the jewels this house contained – but the jewels took no notice, or they were still too young to understand such homage. They gave them-selves up all the more to the pleasures that such gatherings could bring with them, and a gala dress or the arranging of a party could keep them occupied for days in the most gripping and intense way. Brigitta, as the youngest, was not asked her opinion, as though she did not understand these things. Sometimes she was present at these gatherings and then she wore a full, black silk dress which she had made herself, or she kept away, sat in her room and no one knew what she did there.

A few years passed in this way.

Towards the end of this time a man appeared in the city who excited attention in various circles. He was called Stephan Murai. His father had had him educated in the country in order to prepare him for life. When his education had been completed, he had first to travel, and then he was supposed to make the acquaintance of the most exclusive society in his homeland. This was the reason he came to the capital. Here he soon became almost the sole topic of conversation. Some praised his under-standing, others his manners and his modesty, others again said that they had never seen such a handsome man. Several main-tained that he was a genius and, since there was no lack of calumnies and slanders, many said that there was something wild and shy about him and that you could see by looking at him that he had been brought up in a wood. Others thought too that he had pride and, if it should come to that, certainly falsehood as well. Many a maiden's heart was at least curious to see him once. Brigitta's father knew the new arrival's family very well, and he had often been on their estates in his earlier years, at a time when he still made short journeys; it was only later when he lived all year round in the capital and they never did that he had lost touch with them. He enquired about the condition of their estates, which had formerly been excellent, and found out that it was now better still, and was improving all the time because of the simple life-style of the family, and he thought that, if this man was personally to his taste as well, he could prove a desirable bridegroom for one of his daughters. Since, however, several other fathers and mothers thought the same, Brigitta's father made haste to get in ahead of them. He invited the young man to his house, he accepted and had already been to several soirées. Brigitta had not seen him because at that period she had avoided the drawing-room.

Once she went to her uncle's, who was holding some kind of party and had invited her. In previous times she had sometimes visited her uncle's family not ungladly. On that evening she was sitting there in her usual black silk dress. On her head she wore a decoration that she had made herself and her sisters said was ugly. At least, it was not the custom anywhere in the town to wear such a thing, but it suited her dark colouring very well.

There were many people present and once, when she looked through a group of them, she saw the two dark soft eyes of a young man fastened upon her. She looked away immediately. When she looked in that direction later on, she saw that the eyes were again turned towards her. It was Stephan Murai who had looked at her.

About a week after that her father gave a ball. Murai had been invited too and came when most people were already there and the ball had already begun. He looked on and, when partners were being taken for the second dance, he went up to Brigitta and asked her modestly to dance. She said that she had never learned to dance. He bowed and mingled with the observers. Later on he was seen to dance. Brigitta sat down on a sofa at a table and looked on. Murai spoke to various girls, danced and joked with them. On this evening he was especially friendly and civil. Finally the entertainment was over, people scattered in all directions to go home. When Brigitta reached the bedroom she inhabited alone, a concession she had wrested from her parents by means of many requests and threats, when she got undressed she shot a glance at herself in the mirror as she passed and saw her brown forehead and the raven-black hair encircling it slide through the glass. Then she went to her bed, for she did not tolerate a maid either when dressing or undressing, pulled back the snow-white linen from her couch, which she always had made up very hard, lay down, put her slender arm under her head and looked at the ceiling with sleepless eyes.

As there were frequent soirées after this and Brigitta attended them, Murai noticed her again, he greeted her very respectfully, and when she had left he brought her her shawl, and when she had gone, his carriage was heard immediately rolling away below taking him home.

This lasted for a good while.

Once, she was at her uncle's again and on account of the great heat in the drawing-room had stepped out onto the balcony through the doors which were always open. Thick night air lay round her. She heard his footsteps approaching her and could then see in the darkness that he had positioned himself near her. He said nothing more than commonplaces but if one listened to his voice, then it seemed as though there was something fearful in it. He praised the night, saying that people did it an injustice when they decried it, for it was so beautiful and so gentle and it alone veiled, soothed and calmed the heart. Then he was silent and she was silent also. When she stepped into the room again he went in too and stood for a long time at a window.

When Brigitta got home that night and had gone to her room and had removed her party clothes garment by garment, she stood in front of the mirror in her night-dress and looked into it for a long, long time. Tears came into her eyes which did not dry but gave way to more which welled up and ran down. These were the first tears of her whole life. She wept more and more, and more and more passionately, it was as though she had to make up for her whole wasted life and as though she would feel much lighter when she had wept her heart out. She had sunk onto her knees, as she often did, and was sitting on her heels. By chance there lay on the floor next to her a little picture. It was a child's picture, depicting how one brother sacrifices himself for another. She pressed this little picture to her lips so that it became crumpled and wet.

When the well-springs had finally dried and the candles had burned down, she was still sitting on the ground in front of her dressing-table, thinking, like a child that has cried itself out. Her hands lay in her lap, the bows and ruffles of her night-dress were damp and hung down without allure round her chaste bosom. She became quieter and more motionless. Finally she drew a few fresh breaths, passed her open hand over her eyelashes and went to bed. As she lay there and the night-light, which she had placed behind a little shade after the candles had burned out, was still glowing dimly, she wrote the words: 'It is just not possible, it is just not possible.'

Then she fell asleep.

When she met Murai again in the future, things were as before. He merely distinguished her even more but otherwise his behaviour was shy, almost hesitant. He said hardly anything to her. She herself did not make a single, not the smallest move in his direction.

When an opportunity presented itself to speak to her alone, after several previous such opportunities had passed by unused, he took courage and addressed her and said that it appeared to him that she was averse to him – and if this was true, then he had a single request, that she should get to know him, perhaps he was not wholly unworthy of her attention, perhaps he had qualities, or could acquire them, which would win her respect, and that there was nothing he wished for more sacredly.

'Not averse, Murai,' she answered, 'oh no, not averse; but I too have a request to put to you. Do not do it, do not do it, do not court me, you will regret it.'

'But why, Brigitta, but why?'

'Because,' she answered softly, 'I can demand no other love than the very greatest. I know that I am ugly, therefore I demand a greater love than the most beautiful girl on this earth. I do not know how great, but it seems to me as though it must be without measure and without end. Look – since this is impossible, do not court me. You are the only person who has asked whether I have a heart, I cannot be false towards you.'

Perhaps she would have said even more if people had not

come up to them; but her lips trembled with pain.

It is understandable that Murai's heart was not calmed by this speech, but even more inflamed. He adored her like an angel of light, he lived quietly, his eye passed over the greatest beauties who surrounded him in order to seek hers with a soft entreaty. And so it went on immutably. In her too the dark night and the immensity of her feelings began to tremble in her impoverished soul. In both of them this was obvious. The people around them began to sense the incredible and were openly amazed. Murai displayed his soul clearly in the face of all the world. One day in a deserted room, when the music they had gathered to hear sounded from afar, when he stood before her and said nothing, when he took her hand and drew her gently to him, she did not resist and when he bent his face down towards her and she felt his lips suddenly on hers, she pressed sweetly back. She had never felt a kiss until now, for she had never been kissed even by her mother or her sisters. Murai said many years later that he never again experienced such joy as at that moment when he felt those lonely untouched lips on his mouth for the first time.

The curtain between the two was now torn and fate went its way. In a few days Brigitta was the declared bride of the fêted man, for the parents of both parties had agreed. Friendly social intercourse now resulted. A warm life now emanated from the depths of the heart of this hitherto unknown girl, insignificant and unimportant at first, then developing richly and serenely. The instinct that had drawn the man to this woman had not deceived him. She was strong and chaste, as no other woman was. Because she had not enfeebled her heart prematurely with thoughts and images of love, the breath of an undiminished life was in her soul. Her society too was charming. Because she had been constantly alone she had constructed a world for herself alone, and he was initiated into a new, strange kingdom which belonged only to her. As her being then unfolded in front of him, he recognised in addition her heartfelt and passionate love which surged like a golden stream between full but lonely banks; for other people share their hearts with half the world, while hers had remained intact and, since only one single person had recognised it, it was now the property of this single person. So he lived through the period of his engagement in elevated joy.

Time passed on rosy wings and with it fate with its dark pinions.

The wedding-day came at last. When the sacred act was over, Murai folded his silent bride in his arms on the threshold of the church, lifted her into her carriage and brought her to his house, which, since the young people had decided to remain in town, he had had furnished in the handsomest and most glittering manner from his father's means, the latter having put all his savings at his disposal. Murai's father had come to the wedding from the country seat he had chosen as his permanent residence. His mother was unable to share in the joy, for she was long since dead. From the bride's side her father and mother, her sisters, her uncle and several close relatives were present. Murai and Brigitta's father had wanted to celebrate the day publicly and with great magnificence, and so it had been.

When the last guest had finally left, Murai led his wife through a series of lit-up rooms, where they had always had to be satisfied with one up to now, back to the living-room. They were still sitting there when he said these words: 'How well everything has gone and how wonderfully it has all turned out. Brigitta! I recognised you. When I first saw you I knew that I should not be indifferent to this woman; but I did not yet see that I should either have to love you infinitely or hate you infinitely. How happily things have worked out that it is love.'

Then they ordered the rest of the celebration to be cleared away, the host of superfluous lights to be put out and the rooms for the party turned into a normal dwelling. This was done; the servants went to their rooms and night fell for the first time on the new dwelling and on the new family which consisted of two people, and which was only a few hours old.

From this time on they lived in their house. As they had made each other's acquaintance only at social gatherings and as they had only met in public during the period of their engagement, now they always stayed at home. They did not consider that any external thing was needed for their happiness. Although their house had all that was necessary in general, yet there still remained details to be improved or beautified. They pondered this, they considered what could be installed here and there, they supported one another in word and deed, so that the space became more and better ordered and those who entered were received with straightforward comfort and simple beauty.

A year later she bore him a son, and this new miracle kept them at home even more. Brigitta tended her child, Murai looked after his affairs, for his father had made a part of the estates over to him, and he administered these from the town. This meant many things had to be done by indirect means, and affairs piled up in a way that would otherwise have been inadvisable.

When the boy had grown enough to make constant care no longer so necessary and when Murai had ordered his affairs so that they ran smoothly, he began to take his wife more frequently to public places, to parties, on walks, to the theatre, than had been his wont previously. On these occasions she noted that he treated her more tenderly and more attentively in front of other people even than at home.

She thought: 'Now he knows what I lack', and clutched her stifling heart to her.

Next spring he took her and his child on a journey and when they came back towards autumn, he suggested that they should live permanently in the country on one of his estates. For in the country, he said, it was much pleasanter and more agreeable than in the town.

Brigitta followed him to his country estate.

Here he began to manage the estate and to make changes and to spend his spare time hunting. And here fate put quite a different woman in his path than he was accustomed to seeing. He saw her on one of the lonely hunting trips he now frequently took, during which he walked or rode through the countryside alone with his gun. Once when he was leading his horse slowly down a slight slope through a willow swamp, he suddenly saw two beautiful startled eyes through the bushes, like those of an exotic gazelle, and next to the green leaves the sweetest dawn blush of the cheeks was visible. It was only an instant, for, before he could see properly, the creature who was sitting on her horse in the bushes had turned the horse and flown over the plain between the sparse bushes.

This was Gabriele, the daughter of an elderly count who lived in the neighbourhood, a wild creature, who had been brought up by her father in the country, where he allowed her every freedom, because he thought that only in this way could she develop in the most natural manner, without turning into the sort of doll which he could not stand. Gabriele's beauty was already well known far and wide but it had not come to Murai's ears because he had never been on this estate of his before and had recently been on his extensive journey.

Several days later the two met again in exactly the same place, and then more and more often. They did not ask who they were or where they came from, but the girl, like a chasm of unrestrained naturalness, joked, laughed and teased him and challenged him to daring, foolhardy races in which she flew beside him like a divine, crazy, glowing mystery. He joked with her and usually let her win. But one day, when she was breathless with exhaustion and could only indicate by repeated grabs at his bridle that he should stop and when she murmured languishingly as he lifted her down from her horse that she was beaten – then, when he had repaired the strap of her stirrup in which something was broken and saw her standing near a tree, glowing – then he pulled her suddenly to him, pressed her to his heart and before he could see whether she was angry or joyful, leapt onto his horse and fled away. It had been done out of high spirits, but a chaos of indescribable delight was in him at that moment, and as he rode home he saw before his soul the image of the soft cheek, the sweet breath and the mirror-like eyes.

They never met on purpose after that day, but once when they encountered one another for a moment in the drawing-room of a neighbour, the cheeks of both of them were flooded with a deep scarlet.

Then Murai went to one of his more distant estates and changed everything he found there.

But Brigitta's heart was destroyed. A ball of shame, as big as the world, had grown up in her bosom, as she said nothing and moved round the rooms of the house like an over-shadowing cloud. But finally she took her swollen, screaming heart in her hand and strangled it.

When he returned from his alterations on his distant estate, she went to his room and asked him in gentle words for a divorce. He was extremely shocked and entreated her, he made representations to her and when she always said the same words: 'I told you you would regret it, I told you you would regret it', he leapt up, took her by the hand and said in a heartfelt voice: 'Woman, I hate you inexpressibly, I hate you inexpressibly!'

She did not say a word but merely looked at him with dry, inflamed eyes, and when he had packed his bags and sent them off, when he had ridden off himself towards evening dressed for a journey, she lay, as she had once done long before when she shouted the poetic compositions of her heart into the garden bushes, in pain on the carpet of her room, and the tears that ran from her eyes were so hot, it seemed as though they must burn her dress, the carpet and the wooden floor – they were the last tears she shed on the departure of her dearly-beloved; there were no more. Meanwhile he rode along the dark plain and intended a hundred times to blow his boiling brains out with the pistol at his saddle. During his ride, while it was still light, he passed by Gabriele's house; she stood on the balcony of her residence but he did not look up and rode on.

Six months later he sent his consent to the divorce and gave up the boy to her too, whether this was because he thought he would be better off in her hands or whether it was his old love which did not want to deprive her of everything, for she was now all alone, while the wide world lay before his gaze. With regard to his fortune, he had made the most generous provisions possible for her and the boy. He sent her the papers that contained these provisions too. This was the first and last sign Murai gave of his existence, after that came none and he did not appear either. The sums of money he needed were transferred to an Antwerp bank. This was what his steward said later; he knew no more than this.

At this time Brigitta's father, her mother and her two sisters died one after another. Murai's father, who had anyway been very old, died shortly afterwards.

Thus, in the strictest sense of the word, Brigitta was all alone with her child.

Very far from the capital she had a house on a barren heath where no one knew her. This estate was called Maroshely, which was where the name of the family came from. After her divorce she reverted to her original name of Maroshely and went to this house on the heath to hide.

Just as once upon a time when someone had given her a beautiful doll probably out of sympathy and she threw it away after a short period of pleasure and took simple things into her bed, such as stones, little pieces of wood and similar things, so now she took the greatest treasure she had with her to Maroshely, namely her son, and tended and guarded him, and her eye was fixed solely on his cradle.

As he got bigger and his little eye and his heart expanded, so too did hers; she began to see the heath around her and her spirit began to work in the wilderness round about. She took men's clothes, got up on horseback, as she had done in her youth, and appeared among her workpeople. As soon as her son could sit on a horse, he came everywhere with her, and the active, creative, commanding soul of his mother gradually flowed into him. This soul spread more and more around her, the heaven of productivity came down upon her; green hills swelled, springs flowed, deer whispered, and in the barren field of stones a strong, progressive heroic song was being composed. And the poem, as it does, brought its blessing. Many imitated her, the federation of agriculturalists was formed, people far away became enthusiastic and here and there on the barren blind heath a human free activity began, like the opening of a beautiful eye.

After Brigitta had lived at Maroshely for fifteen years, the Major came, and moved into his estate at Uvar, where he had never been before. From this woman, as he told me himself, he learned activity and effectiveness – and he formed for this woman that deep and belated affection of which we have spoken above.

Now that we have narrated this part of Brigitta's earlier life, as we mentioned at the beginning of this section, let us go back to where we left matters and tell how they developed.

4. The Steppes in the Present

We rode to Maroshely. Brigitta was indeed the female rider who had given me the horses. She reminded me with a kindly smile that we had already met. I blushed, because I remembered the tip. There were no other visitors except the Major and myself. He introduced me as someone he had met on his travels, someone with whom he had once spent a great deal of time and of whom he flattered himself that he was about to turn from an acquaintance into a friend. I had the joy – and it was indeed no insignificant one for me – of seeing that Brigitta knew almost everything that related to the earlier time I had spent with the Major, which meant that he must have told her a lot about me, that he must like to dwell on those days and that she thought it worth the trouble of remembering these things.

She said she did not want to give me a guided tour of her house and of her fields, for I would see these things in the course of our walks and if I came over to Uvar often enough, which she politely invited me to do.

She reproached the Major for not having come over for such a long time. He excused himself by mentioning how busy he had been, but principally by saying that he had not wanted to ride over without me and that he wanted to see first how compatible I should be to his friend.

We went into a large chamber where we rested a little. The Major took out a writing tablet and asked her several things, which she answered clearly and simply and some of which he noted down. Then she asked various questions with regard to some of the neighbours or to the affairs of the moment or to the forthcoming regional parliament. Thus I had the opportunity to see with what a deep seriousness she treated things and what attention the Major paid to her opinions. If she was uncertain about something, she admitted her ignorance and asked the Major for the right answer.

When we had rested and the Major put away his tablet, we got up to take a walk around the estates. There was much talk here of the changes that had been made in her house only recently. When she touched on things in the course of this that related to his house, it seemed to me as though there was a kind of tenderness in the way she was concerned about them. She showed him the new wooden colonnade on the ground floor of the house and asked if she should grow vines up it; a similar arrangement could be built on to his courtyard windows, she said, where one could sit out very pleasantly in the late autumn sun. She led us into the park which ten years earlier had been a wild oak wood; now there were paths through it, streams flowed between well-built banks and deer wandered about. By means of immense persistence she had managed to have a wall built round it against the wolves. She drew the money for this from her cattle herds and the maize-fields, whose cultivation she had very much improved. When the enclosure was finished, the park was hunted over piece by piece to see if a wolf, which could breed in future, had not been enclosed too. But there was none. Only then were deer introduced into the enclosure and other arrangements made. The deer, so it seemed, knew all this and were grateful; for, when we saw some of them on our walk, they were not shy but looked at us with dark shining eyes. Brigitta liked to take her guests and friends through the park because she loved it. At the top we reached the pheasant pens. As we were walking along these paths and white clouds were peeping in between the tips of the oak trees, I had an opportunity to look at Brigitta. Her eyes, so it seemed to me, were blacker and more shining than those of the deer and shone especially brightly today, perhaps because the man walking at her side was the one best able to understand her activities. Her teeth were snow-white and her figure, still supple for her years, exhibited indomitable strength. Since she had been expecting the Major she was in women's clothes and had put her affairs aside, in order to devote the day to us.

During conversation of the most varied kind – on the future of the country, on the raising and improvement of the lot of the ordinary man, on the preparation and exploitation of the soil, on the strengthening of the banks of the Danube, on the more remarkable personalities among the Hungarian patriots – we went through the greatest part of the park, for she did not intend to guide us around her estate, as I said above, but just to give us her company. When we came back to the house it was time to eat. Gustav, Brigitta's son, also appeared for the meal, with fairly sun-burned cheeks, a delightful slim youth, the picture of health. Today, in his mother's place, he had inspected the fields and had distributed the tasks, and now he reported various things to her briefly. At table he sat at the bottom, listening modestly; in his beautiful eyes there was enthusiasm for the future and endless goodness for the present. As at the Major's, the servants sat at table with us, so I noticed my friend Milosz, who greeted me as a sign that we knew each other.

The greater part of the afternoon passed in inspecting various changes which were new to the Major, in a turn around the garden, and a walk through the vineyard.

Towards evening we took our leave. As we were gathering up

our coats Brigitta reproached the Major with having ridden away from Gömöri recently lightly dressed – did he not know, she said, how treacherous the dewy air of these plains was, to which he was exposing himself?! He did not defend himself and said he would be more careful in future. But I knew very well that he had pressed his bunda on Gustav on that occasion, for Gustav had come without one and the Major had pretended to him that he had another one in the stable. But this time we left provided with everything adequately. Brigitta herself saw to everything and only went back into the house when, wearing our heavy outer garments, we were sitting on horse-back and the moon was rising. She gave the Major another few commissions and took her leave then with simple, noble friendliness.

The conversation of these two people had been calm and cheerful the whole day, but it seemed to me that a secret depth of feeling tried tremulously to come through, which both were ashamed to make way for, because they already thought them-selves too old. But on the way back the Major said to me, when I could not restrain myself from uttering some heartfelt words in praise of this woman: 'Friend, I have often been passionately desired in my life, whether I have been as passionately loved I do not know. But the company and the respect of this woman have become a greater happiness to me in this world than any of the other things in my life that I thought were happiness.'

He said these words without any passion but with such a calm certainty that I was completely convinced of the truth of them in my heart. At this moment something almost came over me that was not typical of me, that is, I envied the Major this friendship and his domestic activities; for at that time I had no real fixed point in the whole world to hold on to, apart perhaps from the walking-stick with which I set off to see this or that country, but this was hardly anything lasting.

When we came home the Major proposed to me that I should spend the summer and winter with him. He had begun to treat me with great intimacy and to let me see deeper into his life and his heart, so that I had formed a great love and affection for the man. So I accepted. And when I had done this, he said that he would like to entrust a branch of the business of the estate to me which I should be permanently in charge of – I should not regret this, he said, and it would certainly be useful to me in the future.

I agreed and indeed it was useful to me. I have to thank the Major for the fact that I now have a household, that I have a dear wife to work for and that I now draw estate after estate, deed after deed into our sphere of influence. When I became a part of that harmonious activity which he had developed, I tried to play my part as well as I could and, as I gained practice, I was able to do it better and better, I was useful and took pains – and when I learned the sweetness of activity, I saw too how much more valuable this was than my previous strolling existence, which I called gathering experience, and I accustomed myself to activity.

So time passed gradually, and I was infinitely glad to be in Uvar and its surroundings.

Under these circumstances I often came to Maroshely. I was respected and became almost like a member of the family, and I got better acquainted with the situation all the time. There was no trace of a sinister passion, of a feverish desire or even of the magnetism I had heard of. Yet the relationship between the Major and Brigitta was of a peculiar kind, whose like I had never previously seen. Without any doubt it was what, between people of opposite sexes, we should call love, but it did not appear as such. The Major treated the ageing woman with a tenderness, with a reverence, which was reminiscent of an attachment to a higher being. She was filled with visible, inner joy at this, and this joy bloomed on her face like a late flower and laid a breath of almost unbelievable beauty on it, but also planted there the firm rose of cheerfulness and good health. She returned her friend's respect and reverence, only that sometimes a trace of anxiety for his health, for his minor needs and suchlike was mingled with it, which was part of the woman and of her love. The behaviour of the pair did not transgress these limits by a hair's breadth – and in this way they lived on side by side.

The Major once said to me that they had decided, in one of those moments when they were talking intimately together about themselves, as people seldom do, that friendship of the most beautiful kind, honesty, equal striving and communication should obtain between them, but nothing more; they intended to go no further than this altar of firm virtue, happy perhaps till the end of their lives – they did not intend to put any further questions to fate, lest it should wound them again and be malevolent. Things had been like this now for several years and would remain so.

This was what the Major told me – however, some time later fate, unasked, gave its own answer, which solved everything quickly and in an unexpected manner.

It was already very late in the autumn, one could say it was at the beginning of winter, and a thick mist lay over the already frozen heath one day as I was riding with the Major along the newly-built poplar avenue; we were intending perhaps to hunt a little, when suddenly through the mist we heard two dull shots.

'Those are quite certainly my pistols,' cried the Major.

Before I could understand and put a question to him, he was already spurring his horse down the avenue, at a pace more frightful than I have ever seen a horse gallop. I had a premonition of some disaster, and when I caught up with him I came upon a spectacle so terrible and so magnificent that my soul shudders and rejoices at it now. At the spot where the gallows stands and the reedy brook glints, the Major had found the boy Gustav defending himself with the last of his strength against a pack of wolves. He had shot two, with his sword he was holding off one that had leaped at his horse from the front, he was keeping the others momentarily at bay with the anger in his eyes, blazing with fear and wildness, boring into them; but waiting and slavering they stood around him, waiting for a turn, the blink of an eye, a trifle, to give them a reason to fall on him as one – then, in the moment of greatest need, the Major appeared. When I arrived, he was already in their midst like a mortal miracle, like a meteor – the man was almost terrible to behold: with no thought for himself, almost like a beast of prey himself he leaped upon them. I had not seen him descend from his horse, for I arrived too late; I had heard the crack of his double-barrelled pistol and, as I appeared on the scene, his hunting-knife flashed out at the wolves and he was on foot. It may have taken three or four seconds, I only had time to let off my hunting-rifle amongst them and the sinister animals had vanished into the mist as though they had been swallowed by it.

'Load again,' the Major shouted. 'They will be back directly.'

He snatched up the pistols he had flung down and shoved in the cartridges. We loaded up also, and in that moment in which we were relatively quiet, we heard an uncanny padding round the gallows-tree. It was obvious that the hungry frightened animals were encircling us, until perhaps their courage should have grown for another attack. Actually, these animals, when they are not spurred on by hunger, are cowards. We were not equipped for a wolf-hunt and the accursed mist lay thick in front of our eyes, so we took the path to the house. The horses shot along it in deathly fear, and as we rode along thus, more than once I saw something like a shadow chasing beside me, grey in the grey mist. With extraordinary patience the pack hurried beside us. We had to be in constant readiness. Once there came a shout from the Major to the left, but we could see nothing, there was no time to speak, and so we reached the park gate, and as we pushed inside, the noble, beautiful mastiffs broke out past us and in the same moment their angry howling could be heard out of the mist as they chased after the wolves in the direction of the heath.

'Mount, all of you,' the Major cried to the men, as they hurried up to us, 'let out all the wolf-hounds, so that my poor dogs do not suffer. Call up the neighbours and hunt for as many days as you like. I'll give a double bounty for every dead wolf, apart from those lying at the gallows – for we killed those ourselves. And perhaps one of the pistols I gave Gustav last year is lying at the gallows too, for I only see one in his hand and the saddle-holster is empty. See if it is so.'

'For five years,' he said, turning to me as we rode on through the park, 'no wolf has dared to come so close to us and it has been quite safe here. It must be a hard winter, and it must have begun already further north, since they are already pressing so far south.'

The men heard their master's orders and in less time than seemed credible to me a group of huntsmen were ready, and those beautiful, shaggy dogs, peculiar to the Hungarian heathland and so indispensable there, were beside them. They discussed how to fetch the neighbours and then they went off to set a hunt in train, from which they would not return for a week or two, or even longer.

We three, without dismounting, had watched the greater part of these arrangements. But when we had turned from the farm buildings to the house, we saw that Gustav had indeed been wounded. For as we arrived under the archway from where we intended to go to our rooms, he was suddenly overcome by faintness and almost slipped from his horse. One of the men caught him and lifted him down, and we saw that the flanks of his horse were red with blood. We took him into an apartment on the ground floor which gave onto the garden; the Major had a fire lit instantly in the grate and the bed made ready. Meanwhile the sore spot was exposed and he examined the wound himself. It was a light bite in the thigh, not dangerous, only the loss of blood and the foregoing excitement left the youth struggling not to swoon. He was put into bed and one messenger sent immediately for a doctor and another for Brigitta. The Major stayed by the bedside and took care to prevent any of the fainting-fits from becoming too serious. When the doctor came he administered a strengthening medicine, pronounced the wound not to be in the least dangerous, and said that the loss of blood was a curative in itself, as it would lessen the inflammation that often resulted from bites. The only bad aspect of the illness was the powerful emotional shock, and a few days' rest would remove the fever and the exhaustion. We were pleased and reassured and the doctor left with the thanks of all, for there was no one who did not love the boy. Towards evening Brigitta appeared and, as was her decisive way, did not rest until she had examined her son's body limb by limb and had assured herself that, apart from the bite, there was nothing that threatened any malady. When the examination was over, she stayed sitting on the bed and gave Gustav his medicine according to the doctor's orders. A hastily-prepared bed had to be put up for her in the sick-room for the night. Next morning she was again sitting near the boy, listening to his breathing, while he slept, and slept as sweetly and refreshingly as though he would never wake. – Then a heartrending scene came to pass. I can still see that day before my eyes. I had gone down to ask after Gustav's condition and stepped into the room adjoining the sick-room. I have already said that its windows gave onto the garden. The mist had lifted and a red wintry sun was shining through the branches into the room. The Major was already there, standing at the window, his face turned towards the glass, as though he was looking out. In the sick-room, through whose door I was looking and whose windows were slightly darkened by very light curtains, Brigitta was sitting, looking at her son. Suddenly a joyful sigh forced itself from her lips, I looked more closely and saw that her eye was resting with great sweetness on the boy's face and his eyes were open; for he had woken up from a long sleep and was looking brightly around. But from the spot where the Major had been standing I heard a sound too, and as I looked, I saw that he had turned half round and that two frozen tears hung on his lashes. I went towards him and asked what was wrong. He answered softly: 'I have no child.'

With her sharp hearing Brigitta must have caught these words, for she appeared at this moment in the doorway between the rooms, looked very shyly at my friend and with a look which I cannot describe, and which, as though filled with the most timorous fear, scarcely dared to utter a wish, she said nothing except for the single word: 'Stephan.'

The Major turned round fully – they stared at each other for a second – only a second – but then stepping forward he lay with one bound in her arms, which wrapped themselves round him with boundless passion. I heard nothing but the soft sobbing of the man, during which the woman embraced him even tighter and pressed him ever closer to her.

'No separation any more, Brigitta, for now and all eternity.'

'None, my dear friend!'

I was in the greatest embarrassment and tried to go silently out, but she lifted her head and said: 'Stay, stay.'

The woman whom I had always seen serious and severe had been weeping on his neck. Now she lifted her eyes, still shimmering with tears – and so wonderful is the most beautiful thing of which poor erring man is capable here below, that is, forgiveness, that her features were radiant with inimitable beauty and my spirit dissolved with deep emotion.

'Poor, poor wife,' he said with anxiety, 'I had to do without you for fifteen years and you were a victim for fifteen years.'

But she folded her hands and looked beseechingly into his face: 'I was wrong, forgive me, Stephan, the sin of pride – I never imagined how good you are – it was only natural after all, there is a gentle law of beauty which attracts us.' – –

He put his hand over her mouth and said: 'How can you talk like that, Brigitta – yes, the law of beauty does attract us, but I had to wander the whole world until I learned that it lies in the heart and that I had left it at home in a heart that had had the best of intentions towards me, which is staunch and true, which I thought to have lost and which accompanied me all those years through all those lands. – O Brigitta, mother of my child! Day and night you were before my eyes.'

'I was not lost to you,' she answered, 'I spent sad, remorseful years! – How good you have become, now I know you, how good you have become, Stephan!'

And again they fell into one another's arms, as though they could not have enough, as though they could not believe the happiness they had won. They were like two people from whom a great weight had been removed. The world had opened up to them. A joy such as one finds only in children was in them – in that moment they were innocent, as children are; for the most purifying, the most beautiful flower that love, but only the highest love, produces is forgiveness, and therefore it is always to be found in God and in mothers. Beautiful hearts often forgive – bad ones never.

The man and wife had forgotten me again and turned into the sick-room where Gustav, who sensed the whole thing, lay like a glowing, blooming rose, waiting breathlessly for them.

'Gustav, Gustav, he is your father, and you never knew it,' cried Brigitta, as she stepped over the threshold into the darkened room.

But I went out into the garden and thought: 'O how sacred, how sacred must married love be and how poor are you who have never realised it hitherto and have merely let your heart be touched by the dim flame of passion.' – –

I only went back into the house when it was late and found everything resolved and revealed. Busy joy, like cheerful sunshine, moved through all the rooms. I was received with open arms as the witness of the beautiful scene. They had been searching for me everywhere, for I had vanished from their eyes when they were too taken up with themselves. They told me everything that had happened and that I have narrated above, partly straight away in broken sentences and partly during the ensuing days connectedly.

So, my travelling companion had been Stephan Murai. He had travelled under the name of Bathori, the name of one of his female ancestors. This was how I had known him, but he always used the title of Major, a rank he earned in Spain, and indeed everyone called him the Major. When he had seen the whole world, he went under the same name to his desolate estate at Uvar, drawn by his inner self. He had never been there, no one knew him and, as he well knew, he would be the neighbour of his estranged wife. He did not come to visit her straight away, she who was so capably administering Maroshely already, until rumour brought the news of her mortal illness to his ears. Then he set out, rode over and went to her, though she did not recognise him in her fever, stayed day and night at her bedside, watched over her and tended her until she recovered. At that time, moved by seeing each other and drawn by gentle love, yet still fearful of the future, because they did not know each other and because something terrible could happen again, they made that strange pact of mere friendship, which they kept to for years and which neither of them dared to be the first to tamper with, until fate severed it by the sharp cut made in both hearts in order to join them together again in a more beautiful, more natural bond.

All was now well.

In two weeks it was announced to the whole neighbourhood and then irksome visitors came from far and near to give their congratulations.

But I stayed on for the whole winter with them at Maroshely, where we all lived for the time being. The Major never intended to take Brigitta away, for she was in the midst of what she had created. Gustav almost felt the most joy, for he had always been so attached to the Major and had always called him passionately and single-mindedly the most wonderful man in the world; he could now revere as a father the man on whom his eye rested as though on a divinity.

During that winter I became acquainted with two hearts that had now opened in a full, even if delayed flower of happiness.

I shall never, never forget those hearts!

In the spring I put on my German costume again, took my German walking-stick and set off on foot towards my German homeland. On my way I saw Gabriele's grave; she had died twelve years before at the peak of her youthful beauty. Two big white lilies stood on the marble.

With sad, gentle thoughts I moved on until I had crossed the Leita and the beloved blue mountains of home shimmered before my eyes.

The Forest Path

I have a friend who, although he is still alive and it is not the custom in these parts to tell stories about living people, has allowed me to narrate an incident that happened to him, so that it may be of use and benefit to all who are great fools; perhaps they may derive a benefit from it similar to his.

My friend, whom we called Tiburius Kneigt, has now the prettiest country villa to be found in our part of the world, he has the most magnificent flowers and fruit trees around the house, he has a more beautiful wife than can ever have existed on earth before, he lives year in, year out with his wife in his country house, he has a cheerful expression, everyone loves him and he is twenty-six years old again, although a short while ago he was over forty.

My friend has become all this through nothing more nor less than a simple forest path; for Mr Tiburius was previously a very great fool and no one who knew him at that time could have believed that he would end up like this.

The story is really very simple and I only tell it to be useful to many a poor confused person who may find an application for it. Many a reader who has travelled in our country and in our mountains, if he reads these lines at all, will immediately recognise the forest path and recollect many of the feelings the path inspired in him when he wandered along it; though no one has been altered so radically by it as Mr Tiburius Kneigt.

I have said that my friend was a very great fool. He became one from several causes.

First, his father was a great fool. People relate various things about this father; I will cite only a few of them which I can vouch for because I saw them myself. At the very beginning he had many horses, all of which he wanted to tend, groom and ride himself. When all of them were unsuccessful, he sent the head groom packing and because the horses could never remember anything of the rules and exercises he taught them, he sold them for a tenth of their value. He subsequently once lived for a whole year in his bedroom, during which time he kept the window-curtains down so that his weak eyes could recover in the gloom. In answer to the representations of those who said that he had always had good eyes, he proved how much in error they were. He opened the peephole he had in the dark wooden passage next to his room and gazed out for a while at the sunlit gravel path of the garden, whereupon he was able to maintain with a good conscience that his eyes were paining him. Snow was of course quite unbearable. He refused to accept any other remonstrances. In the last stage of these goings-on he sat in the darkened room with a blindfold on his head. When a year had passed, he gradually began to criticise those doctors who recommended him to spare his eyes, and to reject all medical science and its practices. Finally he persuaded himself that the doctors had forced him into this whole procedure, he heaped contumely on the profession and prophesied that he would now cure himself. He drew back the window-curtains, opened all the windows, had the wooden passage torn down – and when the sun was especially hot and glaring he sat without a hat in the middle of the blaze of light in the garden, looking at the white wall of the house. By this means he developed an inflammation of the eyes, and when this was over, he was cured. – Of his other doings I will only add that, having for many years occupied himself very busily and very successfully with the wool trade, he suddenly gave up this business. He possessed a great number of doves at this time, by cross-breeding which he hoped to obtain certain colour markings, and then he intended to start a collection of all possible types of cactus.

I relate these things in order to establish Mr Tiburius's family background.

Secondly, there was his mother. She loved the boy inordinately. She kept him warm so that he should not catch cold and be torn from her by some sudden illness. He had very beautiful knitted vests, stockings and sleeves which, quite apart from their usefulness, all had lots of very beautiful red stripes. A knitting woman was employed the whole year round on behalf of the child. In his little bed there were fine leather undersheets and leather pillows and, as a protection against the draught from the windows, there was a screen. His mother saw personally to the suitability of his food and would not let it be prepared by any of the servants. When he was bigger and could walk around, she chose his clothes most judiciously. To occupy his imagination and so that it should not be distressed by unpleasant ideas, she brought him home all kinds of toys and tried to make the latest one always exceed the previous one in beauty and magnificence. But in this she experienced a certain contrariness on the part of the boy which she could never have imagined; for he laid everything aside after a short inspection and after playing with it for a while, and as, because of a peculiarity which no one understood, he always preferred girls' games to boys', he took his father's boot-jack, swathed it in clean wrappings and carried it around, caressing it.

Thirdly, there was the tutor. For he acquired a tutor. He was a very orderly man and always wanted things to happen in a seemly manner, whether the unseemliness did any harm or not. Seemliness was an end in itself. For this reason he did not allow the boy to tell anything at length or by means of irrelevant metaphors, because he, the tutor, was in this regard of the opinion that everything must be told only in those words which were strictly necessary, with not a single one more or less – and least of all should secondary matters be brought in, or the naked object swathed in wrappings. Since the boy could not speak as children and poets do, he spoke almost like a formula, which is short and complicated and which no one understands. – Or he was silent and thought all sorts of things to himself which no one could know of, simply because he told no one about them. He hated all knowledge and all learning and could only be brought to it if the tutor made a long and conclusive speech, tormenting to the boy, about the use and excellence of the learned disciplines. When, after many days of application, the latter then wanted to recite it all at once, dams and barriers were put up and only the thin trickle of the principal subject was allowed out. Since the tutor, according to the principles of Tacitus, had taken no wife, he stayed for a very long time in the house.

Fourthly and lastly, there was the uncle. He was a rich unmarried merchant in the town; for the boy's father and mother lived outside the town on an estate. Although the boy's parents were rich enough themselves, the uncle's property was still expected to come to the boy and the old bachelor had confirmed this himself often enough in express terms. He therefore authorised himself to educate the boy. He shouted practical instructions at him and explained clearly to him, when he came out to his sister on the country estate, how one should go about tree-climbing – a thing the boy never did – so that trousers were torn as little as possible.

Before I go further with the story, I must also say that my friend was unfortunately not called Tiburius at all. His first name was Theodore; but however much he might write 'Theodore Kneigt' under his exercises when he was growing up, or 'Theodore Kneigt' in visitors' books when he went on his travels later on, on however many letters that came to him might be written 'To the Honourable Theodore Kneigt, Esq' – it was no good; everybody referred to him as Tiburius and most of the strangers who stayed in the town gradually came to think that the lovely country house on the North Road belonged to the father of Mr Tiburius Kneigt. It is such a queer-sounding name, and is in no calendar. The matter came about, however, like this: because the boy was very often so thoughtful and meditative, it happened that he absent-mindedly did things that were ridiculous. When, in order to get something from the high clothes-cupboard, he pulled up his toy drum as a stool – when he brushed his cap in order to go for a walk and then laid down the cap and went off with the brush – when, on a grey day, he cleaned his shoes on the doormat before going out – or when he sat in the middle of the lettuce-bed, talking to cats and beetles – then his uncle used to call: 'Oho, Mr Theodore, Mr Turbulor, Mr Tiburius, Tiburius, Tiburius!' And because this name was repeated by others as the easiest way to pronounce, it came into the family, spread by accident to the neighbourhood and, because the boy was a rich heir on whom all eyes were fixed, it crept from there like bind-weed over the land, round the country and finally sent its roots into every distant forest hut. So the name Tiburius came to be used, and as often happens when someone has an unusual or even ludicrous Christian name, no one calls him by his surname any more, so it happened here: all the world called him Mr Tiburius and most people thought he had no other name. This could not have been stamped out even if his real name had been written on all the border posts in the country.

Under the influence of his educators Tiburius grew up. No

one could say what he grew into because he never revealed himself and because, amidst all the commotion of his upbringing, only the bringers-up were discernible, not what was to accrue to the boy from it.

When he was almost a man, all his educators gradually fell away. First his father died, then very soon afterwards his mother, the tutor went into a monastery and the last one he lost was his uncle. He had inherited the family fortune from his father, from his mother the dowry she had brought with her on her marriage, and from his uncle what had been amassed in thirty years in business. His uncle had retired shortly before his death; he had converted his business into cash and intended to live on the interest from it. However, this he was never in a position to enjoy, because he died and it fell to Tiburius. Mr Tiburius was, therefore, on account of these circumstances, a very rich man and rich primarily in cash, whose fruits can be gathered with the least possible trouble; one has only to wait quietly till they are ripe, send someone for them and then consume them. What he had received from his father did in fact consist partly of the estate on which he was living, but on it there had lived since time immemorial a bailiff who usually handed over very large rents from it. So it remained under Mr Tiburius. He had, at least at the time that he became the sole member of the family, nothing to do except to consume his extremely large income. He had been abandoned by all who had hitherto been with him and was quite helpless.

Since his circumstances were known over an extensive area, there were many girls who would have married Mr Tiburius, and he always found out about this; but he was afraid and did not do anything about it. On the contrary, he began to enjoy his riches for himself. He ordered first of all a great many utensils and saw to it that they were beautiful. Also handsome clothes, both underwear and top-clothes, both linen and fabric, then curtains, carpets, mats and all kinds of things were brought into the house. Finally, everything that was thought good to eat and to drink was stored in abundance. Mr Tiburius lived on for a time amidst all these things.

After this period was over, he began to learn the violin and once he had begun he always fiddled the whole day long, only taking care that the pieces he played should not be too difficult so that he could play on unperturbed.

When he had given up the violin, he painted in oils. In the apartment that he had fitted out for himself on the estate hung the pictures he had finished, and he had had very handsome gold frames made for them. Later on, many of them did not get finished and the paint dried up on the numerous palettes.

Other things happened in between and other objects were acquired.

Mr Tiburius read the lists of new books in the newspapers very eagerly, sent for a bale of them and spent many hours cutting the pages. He had had a fine wide leather chaise-longue made so that he could lie on it to read, and he also had a wing chair for this purpose; or he could stand at his reading desk, which could be screwed up and down so that when he had stood for long enough he could sit down. He had started a collection of famous men whose heads, all in uniform black frames, he intended to decorate the whole building. He also had a collection of pipes which he intended later putting into fine pine cabinets, but which still lay on the tables. His metal mounts, pipes, little chains, tinder-boxes, tobacco-jars and cigar boxes were all beautifully worked. He had sent for a very fine mastiff from England who lay on his own specially-made leather pillow in the valet's room. He had four horses for his own exclusive use in case he should go for a drive some time; among them were two greys which were really excellent animals. The coachman loved them very much and tended them well. Several things combined to cause disquiet. The new chaise-longue could not be put anywhere because the old ones were taking up the available space and the new, very finely-worked chests he had ordered could not be unpacked out of their cases when they came, because no one could find a place for them to stand. Mr Tiburius had got to the stage of having twelve dressing gowns, and his watchkeys had become innumerable; and if he had wanted to take a different stick for every day of the year when he went out, he could have found one. Sometimes on a beautiful summer evening, when he looked through the glass of his tightly-shut window down into the courtyard and saw the farm hands coming in with a load of hay or a waggonful of sheaves, he became quite irritated that this type of person could live on in thoughtless, rough gaity, worrying about nothing and shaking hay-forks and shirtsleeves under the gateway.

Finally, he had to admit to himself that he was ill. Strange symptoms were present. Besides even the trembling limbs, the blurring of the eyes and the sleeplessness, there was something else out of the ordinary. When he came home in the twilight from a walk, it happened every time invariably and without exception that a strange shadow like a cat climbed over the stile beside him. Only over the stile, nowhere else. This affected his nerves to an uncommon degree. He had read enough, he had books in which both old and new wisdom was to be found; but what two bodily eyes see must truly be there. And the more incredible the idea appeared to the people around him, the more seriously and calmly he insisted on the thing to their faces, smiling at their foolishness when they did not grasp it. Because of this he never went home in the evening again, but always earlier.

After some time he no longer went out of the house at all and walked about the rooms and passages in down-at-heel yellow leather slippers. It was at this time too that in a compartment in the floor under his bed where no one could come across it, he carefully hid a volume of poems which he had composed while his parents were alive and neatly written out. He watched his servants more and more strictly to see that all his orders were carried out as exactly as possible and he always fixed his eyes on them when they were with him.

In the end, not only did he not leave the house any more, but he did not even leave his living-room. He had a large cheval-glass carried into it and contemplated his figure. Only at night did he enter his bedroom, which was adjacent, to go to bed. Whenever a visitor chanced to come from a long way off or from the town, Tiburius was impatient for as long as he stayed, almost drove him away and locked the door behind him. He did indeed look worse: he had even developed wrinkles in his face, and when he walked up and down in this way, he usually had long stubble on his chin, the hair on his head was tousled and he wore a dressing-gown like a penitent's shirt round his loins. He eventually had strips of flannel nailed to the window-frames and the doors padded. He mocked the advice and urging of his friends, quite a number of whom Mr Tiburius could not avoid having still, and gave them plainly to understand that he regarded them as stupid and that it would in fact be for the best if they never appeared at his house again. This eventually came to pass and no one visited him any more. The man could now be compared to a tower that is so cleanly whitewashed and plastered all over that the housemartins and woodpeckers that previously flew to it from all sides must leave it. The flock is gone and the tower stands there alone. But Mr Tiburius was delighted at this outcome and rubbed his hands for the first time in a long while, for he could now proceed undisturbed to something he had often wanted to do but that he had never got around to. The fact was that although his sickness was proven to exist he had never done anything for it; he had neither sent for a doctor nor had he taken any other measures against it. Now he decided to treat himself. Just as the bailiff was already taking care of the management of the estate, the valet now had to take over the wardrobe, the steward the furniture and equipment, the trustee the income and he, the master, had nothing to do except to cure himself.

In order to attain his goal, he immediately sent for all the books that dealt with the human body. He cut the pages and laid them in piles in the order in which he intended to read them. The first ones were naturally those that dealt with the nature and organisation of the healthy body. Not much could be got out of those, but as soon as he came to the diseases, it was quite clear that the symptoms described fitted him exactly – and moreover, signs he had not previously observed in himself but that he now read in the books, he found clearly and recognisably developed in himself and could not understand how they had escaped him earlier. All the writers he read described his disease, even if they did not all give the same name for it. They only differed in that the one he read last described the matter even better and more correctly than the one he had read before. Because the task he had set himself was very extensive, he remained involved in it for a considerable time and had no other pleasure, if pleasure it might indeed be called, than that of sometimes finding his condition as extraordinarily and unbelievably accurately described as if he had dictated it to the writer himself.

He treated himself for three years, having to change the course of treatment every so often as his insight gradually deepened. At last he got so bad that he had all the symptoms of all

the diseases at the same time. I'll just mention a few. He now had
shortness of breath; when he followed the precept of one of his
books and went into the garden on a summer's day, he could not
walk far without getting tired and over-heated. Sometimes his
right temple throbbed, sometimes his left. If his head was not
buzzing, with spots before his eyes, then his chest was constrict-
ed or he had a stitch in his side. He had the sporadic shivers and
dragging feet of the nervous diseases, sudden flushes pointed to
dilation of the blood-vessels – and there was much more. He
could not now get properly hungry as he had once done so
deliciously in his childhood, although instead he had a false
craving which incited him to eat all the time.

This is how bad Mr Tiburius was. Many people had sympathy
for him and many an old lady even prophesied he wouldn't last
much longer. But he did last. Eventually no one spoke of him
any more, because he still couldn't die, but accepted him as
being what he was; or he was spoken of as someone possessing
some unusual feature such as a crooked neck or a frightful cast
in his eye or a wen. Many a passer-by, seeing the country house
with the closed windows, looked up and thought of how differently from the addled owner he would spend the fortune that
was up there, if he had it. Boredom and desolation had spread
their banner over the house of Mr Tiburius. In the garden stood
the uniform rows of medicinal herbs that he had begun to have
planted and some wag maintained that the cocks crowed more
mournfully inside the boundaries of his farmyard than
elsewhere.

We have now got to the stage of being able to understand Mr
Tiburius's misery – let us proceed to the happier event by which
he came out of this slough of despond again and became everything that we praised him for at the beginning of this story.

There was a man in the neighbourhood of whom people also
said that he was a great fool. A rumour suddenly went about that
this man was treating Mr Tiburius. The man was indeed a doctor
of medicine but he cured no diseases, although many had seen
his written licence to do so; he had simply come to the neighbourhood one day, bought a run-down farm-house whose owner
had failed through bad management, together with its garden,
fields and meadows, rebuilt the house and engaged in agriculture and fruit-farming. If, however, someone who was ill did

come to him, he gave him no medicine but sent him off, pre-
scribing lots of work, a better diet and the opening wide of all his
windows. Since the people now saw that he was making a mockery out of doctoring and that instead of medicines he prescribed
only natural things, no one came to him any more and they left
him alone. Behind his house he had a whole field full of stick-
like trees of which he took great care and in a glass-house there
were also saplings with green, shiny, leathery leaves which no
one recognised. As one fool attracts another, they said, so Mr
Tiburius had trust in this one man and took medicines from
him.

But in fact this was not true. Here is how things were. Since Mr
Tiburius took a great interest in all that had to do with medicine,
his servants thought to please him by telling him about the new
doctor who had bought the Querleithen house and was now
living there. Mr Tiburius's valet spoke of him a few times without
Mr Tiburius taking special notice of it, but, as providence sometimes has wonderful ways of making people's fate come about, so
it happened here that Mr Tiburius had come on a passage in the
writings of the already long-deceased Haller that contained an
obvious contradiction, that is, obvious to anyone learned in
medicine – for anyone else the passage was comprehensible
neither with the contradiction nor without it – but on the other
hand not quite obvious in so far as it was uncertain whether
anyone might be learned in medicine or not. Amidst these doubts
tormenting Mr Tiburius, surprisingly enough the newly-arrived
doctor occurred to him, although his valet had not spoken of him
for a long while. Here, however, we must honour the historical
truth and confess that he occurred to Mr Tiburius only because
people called him a fool; for Mr Tiburius had his own ideas about
foolishness and the man seemed to him therefore remarkable.
Only, when people like Mr Tiburius think of things, it usually gets
no further than a thought. It must have stayed like that with Mr
Tiburius for a while until one day he suddenly ordered his closed
carriage to be put to, he was going to go over to the doctor at the
Querleithen house. His people were amazed that with his serious
illness he should dare to go into the air and be shaken around in
the carriage, since he was rich enough to send for this doctor, and
ten more, to come to the house. However, Mr Tiburius got into

the carriage and drove over to the Querleithen.

He found the doctor in the garden working industriously, in shirt-sleeves with a wide yellow straw hat on his head. The doctor was a not very large man, dressed in rough, loose, unbleached linen. He stopped a little in his work when he saw the carriage arrive at his garden and looked at it with dark, fiery eyes. Mr Tiburius, protected from the air by a very thick suit, stepped out of the carriage and went towards the expectant man. He said, when he stood before him on the garden path, that he was his neighbour, Theodore Kneigt, and that he spent a lot of time on the sciences, especially medicine. Several weeks previously he had come on a passage in Haller which he, with his resources alone, could not completely master. Therefore he had come over to the man whom rumour reported to be knowledgeable in these things and begged him, by sacrificing a few minutes of his time, to assist him in this matter with some advice.

To this speech the little doctor replied that he never read out-of-date works such as those by Haller, he did not practise any more, he could give reliable cures in only a very few cases and he used the knowledge he had of the human body in order to prescribe a life-style for himself which would be by far the most useful and healthful for his body. For this reason he had left the capital and had gone so far into the country as to be able to lead the healthiest life and reach the greatest age that was possible given the harmony of the elements of his body. Still, if his neighbour had the Haller with him, they could have a look at the passage and see what could be deduced from it and what not.

At this speech Mr Tiburius went to his carriage, pulled out the Haller from the inner compartment and came back again with it to the little doctor. The latter led his neighbour into the summer-house, the men stayed there some time and when they came out again, Mr Tiburius had the satisfaction that the strange doctor said the same about the passage in Haller as he did. The doctor said to Mr Tiburius, after their main business was over, that he had a young and very beautiful wife, and that it was the usual custom to introduce a guest and neighbour, the first time he called, to the lady of the house; however, he did not know if his neighbour might not be objectionable to his wife.

For it was the foremost of his principles that his wife, like himself, must have absolute freedom of action in everything not actually to do with the marriage. He would ask his wife about it and if his neighbour came again, he would be able to tell him if he could bring him in to her or not.

To this Mr Tiburius replied that he had come over on account of the Haller, that had been dealt with and all was well.

Regardless of this, the doctor quickly showed him his plantations, where he had his camellia houses, where he grew his rhododendrons, azalias, verbena, heather and other plants and where he mixed and burnt the different kinds of earth. Not much could be seen yet of the fruit or other things.

Then Mr Tiburius climbed into his carriage and drove away. The doctor had a wooden implement, a pair of clappers, which made a very loud noise, which he sounded when he wanted to call his people, when they were all scattered around doing different jobs, together to eat or work or to make an announcement. As Mr Tiburius drove down the slope of the Querleithen, he heard the clapping of this implement, which meant that the strange doctor was already in communication with his people.

Mr Tiburius visited this man again after some time and then more often, and so it went on, either because, as happens with such people, he had got into a rut and couldn't get out of it, or because he wanted to learn something from the doctor. Thus the two men whom people called fools sometimes stood in the garden together, one of them in a straw hat and a rough linen suit, so that the air could enter at the openings and touch all his limbs, and the other with a felt cap on his head pulled down over his ears, a long coat almost sweeping the ground buttoned up over his other clothes and in addition, on top under his collar, a huge bunched-up scarf to keep his neck warm, and finally big wide boots, inside which he had on two pairs of stockings so that his feet should not get cold. On these visits the doctor said nothing more about taking Mr Tiburius in to see his wife and the latter never requested it either.

Because, therefore, Mr Tiburius visited no one except this man and because he did not leave his room at all except when he went to the doctor's, it was natural that people should think he was being treated medically by the foolish doctor and that both had dreamt up medicines that were remarkable and had to be kept secret, which was why they were always meeting and putting their heads together.

However, as we know, this was not the case. But as popular acumen always has a few grains of truth and foundation for its baseless rumours, so it was here too, because from this doctor came at least the first impulse, which continued to take effect, as a consequence of which Mr Tiburius was transformed completely. Like the caterpillar of the peacock butterfly which, having lived monotonously on a nettle, has hung itself up and shrunk into itself, suddenly jumps up one day, pushes back its horrible black thorny body and shows the horns and feelers of the beautiful pupa in which the future, colourful, shimmering, shining wings already lie wrapped, so Mr Tiburius suddenly asked the doctor one day something that he must have had on his mind for a long time. He said: 'If you, my revered Doctor, as you yourself said to me exactly five weeks ago today, know a reliable cure for just a few cases, perhaps then you might have one for me?'

'Certainly, my dear Mr Tiburius', answered the doctor.

'Well then – for God's sake – speak!'

'You must marry, but before that you must go to a spa where you will find your wife.'

That was too much for Mr Tiburius! He pressed his lips together and said with an incredulous and sneering smile:

'And to which spa should I go then?'

'In your case that is all one,' answered the doctor, 'only a mountain spa would probably be the best, perhaps the one in our mountains where so many people go now. Uncles, aunts, fathers, mothers, grandmothers, grandfathers are there with very beautiful girls and among them will be the one who is meant for you.'

'And so, finally, if you can describe the treatment so well, what is my disease?'

'I won't tell you that,' replied the doctor, 'because once you know it, no medicine is any good any more, because you won't take any more – or you won't need any because you will already be cured.'

Mr Tiburius inquired no further; after this conversation he said not a word but went slowly to his carriage and drove home.

'The crazy doctor is right,' he said to himself in the carriage, 'he's not right about marrying, that is rubbish – but a spa! – a spa! That is the one thing I haven't yet thought of – it's incomprehensible that it didn't occur to me. I'll consult all the books that deal with spas and try to find out which spa in our part of the world could be considered for my condition.'

And the whole way home he pondered this idea. The doctor had stirred Mr Tiburius considerably. He must even have thought a little about getting married, because he cut the beard he had let grow all over his face to a certain length with scissors, then shaved it over and over again very cleanly and stood in front of the mirror to contemplate himself.

'No, no,' he said, 'that is rubbish, there is no sense in that at all and it cannot be.'

Nonetheless that evening he sent to the town for a very good toothpowder because he had noticed in the mirror that he had been greatly neglecting his teeth.

With regard to the spa, he began next morning to make the necessary arrangements very seriously. He wrote to the town for all the books dealing with spas, in order to find out to which he should go; then he would make the rest of the arrangements. But the thought of the spa had so gripped him that he did not follow his usual procedure up to now, which had been to read all possible books first of all, which would have resulted in his not getting to any spa at all that summer; on the contrary, he decided at once on the spa the doctor had suggested. The first thing he now did was to order his travelling carriage to be put into a travelworthy condition. His servants were startled by this order but they carried it out. He had never used a travelling carriage in his entire life because he had never gone farther from his estate than the town. His household therefore believed that he had either now gone completely mad or else that he was at the beginning of a recovery. They pulled the travelling carriage out of the container in which it had stood since Mr Tiburius had had it made into the courtyard and inspected it to see if it was in good condition all over; they then fitted it out with all things that a traveller such as Mr Tiburius might need on his journey. He sent for all the books that existed on this particular spa so that he could take them with him and read them there. Then he himself wrote on a sheet of paper the things his servants must take, among them his greys and his driving carriage, which were to be sent on ahead so that he would have them at the spa on arrival. Finally, work had to be started on all the necessary clothes, cushions and other equipment to be taken. He did these things with a fair amount of skill.

To the doctor, whom he visited twice during this time, he said not a word. The doctor seemed also to have completely forgotten their conversation about the spa.

After some time had passed in this way, four post-horses arrived one day on Mr Tiburius's estate and, to the wonder of everyone, pulled the master off to strange parts in his travelling carriage.

I cannot allow myself to describe his journey, as it has no essential connection with the purpose of these lines, but I must just say this, that it seemed to Mr Tiburius that he had already travelled many, many miles, that he was already extremely far away when he had been driving for one day, when he drove for a second day and when finally even a third day had come.

On the afternoon of this third day, as an indescribable summer heat reigned, he was travelling along a long, narrow mountain valley towards a lovely green, gushing, mirror-clear steam. Where the valley widened, a cloud of white steam could be seen rising out of a big hut, and the valet said to Mr Tiburius that this was the stream rising out of the brine that was boiled there, and that they were quite near the end of their journey. Shortly after these words, Mr Tiburius drove into the streets of the resort in his completely closed carriage. It was very quiet there on account of the great heat, no one was out, the hinged shutters and the curtains were closed; at the most, a pair of eyes looked out through a slit or a crack to see who this new arrival was.

Mr Tiburius drove up to the inn in which his valet had reserved a room for him by letter. He alighted and was led up to the little room. There he sat down at the small yellow-painted table which stood in it. His servants and the people from the inn busied themselves in unpacking and bringing up the things from the carriage.

Mr Tiburius could now reassure himself that he had arrived. The mocking words of the little doctor had become a reality. The previous day, while he was still driving through the plain, Mr Tiburius had thought that if only he did not die before he arrived, then everything would be all right; now he had arrived and was already sitting there at his little table. The people had almost filled the room with the things they had found in the carriage. Through the green slats of the shutters fragrant mountain slopes looked in – he was almost ecstatic and mentally ordered his travel impressions. There were the endless fields and meadows and gardens he had driven through, and the houses and church spires that had all flashed past him, then the mountains had come even nearer, then a long green lake which he had crossed in his travelling carriage flickered through his mind, and then there was the rushing stream in the valley and the frightful glare of the sun on all the mountains.

But Mr Tiburius could not concentrate too much on all this because quite different things now needed to be done; for instance, his apartment had to be arranged as befitted his illness and the resort doctor had to be called very soon so that he could get to know him and they could arrange a plan of treatment together and begin to carry it out without delay.

Above all, a bigger table had to be sent for, on which he could lay all the piles of books that his servant had unpacked, so that at the first opportunity he could cut the pages and start to read. Then the bed, whose components he had brought himself, must be set up in the little room adjoining his living-room. The steel frame of it was erected in the corner where there would be least draught. The uprights of the screen he had also brought with him had to be screwed apart, and silk fabric, on which there were innumerable red Chinamen, stretched over them. Because so many cloakbags, carriage trunks and other leather receptacles lay around, the landlord had to have another cupboard brought up, which was put in the anteroom where the servants slept, to accommodate the linen, dressing-gowns and clothes. Finally, draught-excluders had to be fitted to the windows and door frames, and the empty suitcases and leather bags stowed in the luggage compartment of the carriage.

When everything was in order, Mr Tiburius sent for the resort doctor. It could not be put off and it was indeed uncertain whether all the movement he had suffered on the long journey would not be followed by a severe illness.

The doctor was not at home and could not be found anywhere. Mr Tiburius had to wait till the evening. He sat in his room and waited. In the evening the doctor came and the two men conversed for over an hour and set out the whole plan of treatment to be followed.

The next day, Mr Tiburius began to put the plan into operation. He was seen going to the pump-rooms in a long grey buttoned-up overcoat and disappearing inside. He took his first bath there. And later he could also be seen in the places where whey was drunk or where people sat in the sun and strolled a little. He did this every day, going conscientiously wherever the plan demanded. In order to take the amount of exercise prescribed by the doctor in the form of walking, he had worked out his own method. He drove for a stretch with his greys along the road that led deeper into the mountains, until he came to a certain big stone which he had discovered on the very first day. Near this stone there was a fairly large, dry clearing which consisted of freshly-laid sand. At this spot he got out and walked up and down for as long by his watch as the prescribed time for exercise lasted, then he got into his carriage again and drove home. The people in the resort got to know him fairly quickly, saying to each other that that was the gentleman who had recently arrived in the closed carriage.

The season was in fact already fairly advanced, but, because the last months of summer are the hottest and driest in these mountain valleys, there was still a great crowd of brilliant and select visitors. Among them were many very beautiful girls. Mr Tiburius, who could not avoid seeing one sometimes, fleetingly remembered the doctor's words about marriage – but he thought the doctor a sly fellow and concentrated only on what was directly necessary to his health. He gradually read a good way down his mountain of books, he performed all that the resort doctor had prescribed for him exactly, adding many other things he had learned and prescribed for himself out of books. He had screwed a telescope onto his window-ledge and often looked through this at the silly mountains which stood around bearing rock on their peaks.

It was strange that here too, at this great distance from his home, and indeed in a very short time after Mr Tiburius had arrived, the name Tiburius became common in the mouths of the people, although in the Visitors' Book it said 'Theodore Kneigt' and although no one knew him. Probably his servants so named him in secret.

There were all kinds of people and families at the spa. There was a count with a limp who was seen everywhere and into whose weathered face there almost shone a reflection of the great beauty of his daughter, who patiently accompanied him everywhere, walking quietly at his side. Two beautiful young girls often drove about in a carriage with two fiery black horses, their eyes even fierier than the horses and with usually green veils floating about their red cheeks. They were the daughters of a mother, still beautiful herself, taking the waters and who sat leaning back in the carriage wrapped in a rich shawl. Then there was a fat, childless couple who had brought a niece with them who gazed dreamily around, sometimes looked oppressed and who had blond curls as lovely as it is possible to see. In one house with lots of windows there was always the sound of a piano and many curly-headed young girls and boys were to be seen looking out of the windows or rushing past them on the inside. Then there were many lonely old men, here in search of health, with no one except a servant; then many an old bachelor who, past the summer of his life, went around without a companion. Mention must also be made of two blond blue-eyed girls. One of them liked to turn her blue eyes to the not far distant forests from a secluded balcony and the other fixed hers on the depths of the running stream. She often went walking on the banks of this stream when she passed it, accompanying her sick, depressed mother. Then there were also the lovely, blushing cheeks of the country girls accompanying an invalid father, mother or benefactress – not to mention all the others who came every year to enjoy the beauty of the surroundings or merely to pay homage to the prevailing fashion, trying hard to lord it over everything, discussing every new arrival or shy person and gloating over it. Tiburius lived on almost timidly among these people. He never mixed with them and if he was about to meet some of them on the walks prescribed for him by the doctor, then he preferred to make a detour to avoid them. They talked about him because he stood out on account of his strangeness; but he did not know that they spoke of him or what they called him. He stayed on amidst the constantly changing crowd, for at that time there were indeed always new people coming and others going.

It is impossible for us to say what the use of the baths did for Mr Tiburius, since he himself said nothing to anybody and went on bathing. He declared to the doctor, in answer to every question as to how he was, that it was all going according to the nature of things. We should probably in the end have been in a position to give definite information about the success of his bathing if something had not happened that changed everything and made every estimate of secondary causes impossible.

We said above that Tiburius always drove out to take his exercise and walked up and down by a solitary stone. He was very assiduous and had already done this many, many times. One day, after a good length of time had passed since his arrival, when an almost steel-hard dark-blue sky stood over the valley, he drove farther than usual because the day was doing him so much good. He saw quite unfamiliar mountains, and dark firs and lighter beech-trees came almost to his carriage. No one knows whether his receptivity to the beneficial quality of the day was a result of his bathing or whether it was the uncommonly pleasant clear mildness of the air that affected everyone and therefore him too. Near his carriage was a sunny glade with firm heathery ground; it was surrounded by protective stone cliffs so that no rough wind could blow in, and it reached back in this way into the still wood. This enticed Mr Tiburius out of his carriage in order to walk about a little and enjoy the soft, vertically-falling midday rays.

'I'll take my exercise here, not at the stone,' he said to his servant and the coachman. 'It's all the same; you wait here at this glade until I come back and get in again.'

Whereupon he took off his overcoat as he always did, threw it back into the carriage, climbed down the steps his valet let down for him and went forward towards the dry glade. Tiburius had never seen the inside of a wood. In his homeland there were only small groves of trees, in which he had never been anyway, and he had only observed the great forests that lay on the mountains around the resort from his windows through the telescope. Here he was almost in a wood. Although the place he had chosen for his walk had no trees, they were nevertheless so near, and on many of the neighbouring hills besides, that it could have been said that Mr Tiburius was in a woodland clearing. Everything delighted him. No human being could be seen or heard all around – that was just what he liked. The glade went inwards from the road into the depths of the region. When Mr Tiburius had traversed its entire length and was going to turn round, in order, according to his idea of a walk, to go up and down, he saw that there was an even more beautiful glade farther in. On the left was a rock-face of considerable height, on the right stood trees some distance away, and farther back the glade was shut off by woodland. It was even stiller here and the midday heat streamed so pleasantly down the rock-face that it was as if one might almost be able to hear it trickling. This in itself was already very beneficial for the body, as the season was now the middle of autumn and some of the foliage was already shimmering yellow. The ground was very dry on account of the long preceding spell of fine weather.

Mr Tiburius decided immediately to walk on to the second glade and to make it his place of exercise. He thought that even if he went straight ahead for a slightly longer time, he could still turn back according to his watch and all told take exactly the prescribed amount of exercise in the same way as if he had walked up and down. It would certainly not be harmful. Owing to the reflective power of the rock, the mild sunshine did him so much good that he felt extremely cheerful once he had gone half-way across the new glade. Also, everything he saw around him was new, he liked everything and he had never thought that he could be so happy in a wood. A wide white stone lay along the ground and different plants grew along its length. On the left at the rock-face were various stones that had broken off from it, white, yellow, brown and all sorts of others. Among them stood rust-coloured brambles, single saplings and various other things. Sometimes a butterfly sat on a stone, to open and sun shimmering wings such as Mr Tiburius had never seen where he came from. Sometimes one flew silently past him like the silent air and became immediately invisible. Mr Tiburius also noticed that there was a very pleasant fragrance here.

He went on. Sometimes he held up his cane, turning it slowly between his fingers and delighting in the sparkle of the gold knob in the dark, quiet, solitary air. After a while he came to some mutilated tree-trunks with resin flowing out. He had never seen that and stood still. The transparent liquid welled out of the bark in the sunshine and the drops stood like pure molten gold hanging in a little skin. Then he went on again. He met a crowd of wonderful blue gentians, he looked at them and even picked a few stalks.

At last he had arrived at the very end of his chosen

promenade. The woodland, which he had seen from a distance as a termination, consisted of fairly widely-spaced trees. Tiburius stood for a while to look at them and to consider if he should go in amongst them or not. – Lizards slipped past in the midday glare, a little stream went unheard towards the fir-trees, and between the trunks airy shiny autumn threads were stretched, just as Mr Tiburius had often seen them in the garden at home. Before he went any farther he must just first find out what kind of peculiar hoarfrost that was on the distant pine needles and how the cloud looked that peeped in between the green of the trees from far outside, and whether it meant rain. He took out his pocket telescope, put it together and looked through it. But the hoarfrost was only the inexpressible glow of the sun on the smooth side of the pine needles and the cloud was a distant mountain such as stand one behind the other for miles in this part of the country. He decided therefore to go on, especially since the rock-face still continued and at the beginning only one and then only a few beech-trees stood between him and it. Also a very well-beaten black path led into the trees. When he stepped onto this path, Tiburius thought involuntarily of the little foolish doctor who had to burn different materials to make this earth for his rhododendrons and heathers, and here it lay of its own accord; and he saw various kinds of heather under the trees, much more beautiful than the ones the doctor grew in pots. He planned, when he came home, to tell him about this fact.

Tiburius went on along this path which was bordered by all manner of things. Sometimes the cranberries lay like red corals near him, sometimes the bilberries stuck up their foliage and held similar clusters of little red-cheeked balls in their shining leaves. – The trees became darker all the time and now and then the trunk of a birch-tree stood out like a line of light among them. The path always looked the same, the places in front were like those he had left behind. Gradually it changed, the trees stood very thickly, they constantly became darker and it was as though a colder air descended from their branches. This warned Mr Tiburius to turn back, for it might even be harmful to him. He pulled out his watch and saw what a dark premonition had already told him when he was attentive, that he had gone farther than he thought and that, counting the return journey, he had taken more exercise than usual that day.

He turned round on the path, therefore, and went back.

He went back more quickly, since he did not want to look at things so closely and since he was concerned, after he had looked at his watch, to reach the carriage as quickly as possible. He went along the path which was just as black as before and which ran along by the trees just as on the way out. But after he had been walking for a fairly long time, it did occur to him that he had not yet reached the rock-face. On the way out he had had it on his left, now he had turned round and consequently it must now appear on the right – but it did not appear. He thought that perhaps he had been lost in thought at the entry to the wood and that the path was longer than he now thought it; he was patient therefore and went on – but he walked rather more quickly.

But the rock-face did not appear.

Now he became anxious. He did not understand how there could be so many trees on the way back – he walked much more quickly and finally hurried along, so that, even by making a large addition to his calculations, he should have been at the carriage long before. But the rock-face did not appear and the trees did not come to an end. He now went a considerable distance off the path both to the right and to the left to orientate himself and to see if the rock-face was not somewhere near – but it was nowhere, neither to the right nor to the left, neither in front nor behind – there was nothing, except the trees into which he had let himself be enticed, all beeches, only more numerous than those he had seen on the way out, it even seemed as though they were increasing all the time – only he could not find the single tree that had stood at the beginning between him and the rock-face.

Tiburius now began to run, something he had not done since his childhood, and ran in great haste a good way along the path, but the path, which he could not lose, always stayed the same, trees, nothing but trees. He stopped now and called as loudly as he had strength for and as his lungs would allow, to see if he would be heard by his servants and get an answer back. He shouted several times in succession, waiting in between a fairly long time. But he got no answer, the whole wood was still and not a leaf moved. The human voice sank into the many branches there as into straw. He thought that perhaps the direction in which he had run might be leading away from the road on which his carriage was and not towards it, since with all his searching he could perhaps have turned round without realising it. Consequently, his intention was now to run back again in the same direction. He first threw away the gentian he was still holding in his hand and which was now looking at him so strangely with that terrible blue, and then ran back. He ran until the sweat stood out on him, and did not know if what he now saw was the same as what he had seen when running the other way. When he had gone as long a stretch back as he had earlier gone forward and as far again, he stopped and shouted again – but again he got no answer once his voice had died away, everything again became quite still. Here it was also quite different from the place where he had been before, and everything he saw was strange. The beech trees had stopped; there were fir-trees and their trunks stretched up higher and wilder all the time. The sun was slanting already, it had become afternoon, on many a mossy stone lay a frightful glistening gold and innumerable little streams ran past, each like the next.

Mr Tiburius could no longer deny that he was well and truly in a forest and who knew how big it was? He had never been in a position where he had had to find his way out of such situations and his distress was great. Other things also contributed to this. In his to-ing and fro-ing in the grass, when he had gone off the path to find the rock-face, he had got his feet wet, he was perspiring and had only one thin coat on as the other one lay in the carriage, he dared not sit down to rest however inviting the stones looked, since he would catch cold – and finally, the container with the medicine he had to take that afternoon was at home. One thing he did realise, and that was the most essential thing here, that instead of to-ing and fro-ing, he should go along the path always in the same direction; for the path must lead somewhere, it was so well trodden. It was indeed a great piece of good fortune that at least there was a path, for what a catastrophe it would be to be standing in this condition in a trackless wood.

Mr Tiburius decided therefore to keep going along the path in the direction he had last taken.

He tightly buttoned up the coat he had on, turned up the

lapels, pulled them close around his face and walked on very briskly. He walked on and on and on. The heat of his body increased, his breath became short and his tiredness grew. Finally, the path went uphill and became an ordinary forest track. But Tiburius did not know what forest tracks were like. Broken stones of the largest and most terrifying kind lay to the right and to the left along the path, which often went over them. Some were shrouded in moss which showed various greens he had never seen before, others lay naked, showing their sharp violent fractures. Large-fingered fans of fern stood there, and the high thick trunks of the fir-trees, towering up above everything or lying prone, were moist when Tiburius touched them. – For a while the path consisted of nothing but small sticks which lay across it, sometimes almost awash in water, moving with every step or even, if they themselves were firm, making him slip. – Then a steep mountain appeared. The path climbed to it unperturbed and Tiburius went on along it. When he reached the top it was flat and the ground sandy. The path ran briskly and pleasantly on in front of Tiburius and he followed it. It left the clearly-marked sand later and became black again, was wide and dry and pressed at every step against the foot, giving the sensation of walking on rubber. And so it wound on. Tiburius walked along it, resigned to his fate. Finally it became evening, the eerie calls of the blackbird sounded and Tiburius, buttoned into his inadequate coat, went on. – After a while it seemed as though something gushed somewhere below. – Tiburius went on, the gushing sounded nearer, but it was only water, which made the wood even eerier and from which no aid could be expected. Tiburius went on even faster, he went on and on – and unfortunately uphill again. At last, when he had gone around a very big rock which had appeared to darken everything before him, the path dropped down, and became sandy and gravelly. Also the tall firs were suddenly not near him any more, but instead all kinds of pleasant bushes with thick foliage, especially hazel bushes, always a sign that a wood is stopping and one is at its outskirts. But Mr Tiburius did not know these signs. He went on further amidst the bushes and on the sharp stones, it became lighter, the bushes stopped, the wood had finished and he stood high up on a meadow in the open air.

He was in a condition in which he had never been in his whole life. His knees were trembling and his body could only droop in his clothes with weariness. He felt his nerves trembling involuntarily through his whole body and his pulse throbbing. But here there was no prospect of help either. The sun had already gone down. All around in the cool blue breath of the evening stood mountains of all shapes, partly covered with forest, partly with rocks reaching upward. Far away behind the edge of a green wood, a very high mountain towered up. It had several protruding rocky crags. Between these crags were three very big snowfields which were now lit up rose-red and on which the peaks threw shadows. However, for Tiburius this exalting spectacle was terrifying. All around, no one and no living creature was to be seen. The gushing that he had already been hearing for some time in the wood was now comprehensible. At the bottom of the valley towards which the meadow where he stood fell away, a green burbling stream ran out over stones and ledges and hurried along. Apart from this, however, nothing moving or stirring was to be seen.

Tiburius saw that the path went over the meadow slope towards the water and he thought that, as the same green water, though in a much larger quantity, flowed into the resort, this brook might easily rush out into that green stream and possibly the path would follow it.

He decided therefore to follow the course of the path downhill. He mastered the raging desire of his body for rest – since the wet dew lay already all around on the grass – and went down the steep path with painful, forward-moving jerks of his knees. The mountain with the pink snowfields drew gradually back behind the wood until nothing was to be seen, except cold blue or green heights, interwoven with streaks of mist.

Tiburius reached the stream. It hastened along with the blue-green of its waters and its fleeting white froth – and what he had just thought did occur: the path went along beside the stream. He took it, therefore, and exerted all his powers, which seemed as though drunken and ebbing away, for a renewed and last effort.

When he had walked along like this for a while and darkness was already setting in, he suddenly heard footsteps behind him, above the sound of the rushing water of the brook fairly far below him. He looked round and saw a man walking behind him, having just caught up with him. The man was carrying an axe on his back, had several iron wedges over his shoulders and wore heavy clogs. Tiburius stopped, let him come up to him and then asked: 'My friend, where am I and how do I get out to the resort?'

'You're on the way to the resort,' answered the man, 'but in the Keis out there the paths divide again and the better one goes down into the Zuder Wood, you could get lost there. As I have to go that way anyway, you could go with me and I'll guide you out. – But how have you come here then, if you don't know where you are?'

'I am an invalid,' said Mr Tiburius, 'having treatment at the baths. I drove a good way along the road, then went for a walk and got lost in the wood, and I couldn't find my waiting carriage any more.'

The man with the iron wedges looked Mr Tiburius up and down from the side and, with a sensitivity which is often common in these people and is unjustly never credited to them, he walked, now that he had looked at him, much more slowly than was his wont.

'Then you went through the Black Wood, if you came over Bell Meadow down to the stream,' he said.

'Yes, I did come down to this stream over a steep curving meadow like a bell,' answered Mr Tiburius.

'Well, well,' replied the man, 'not many people like to go up there because it's so wild, and that was why you didn't know where you were.'

'Yes, indeed', answered Mr Tiburius, 'and who are you then, coming out into the gorge at nightfall?'

'I am a woodcutter,' said the man, 'and it's only by chance that I came out here today, because I had to bring a message to the foreman in the Zuder. So I brought my axe with me to sharpen it because my house is only half an hour away there to the left. We are felling in the clearings about six hours above the place where I met you. At present we always go up on Monday and down on Saturday. At other times we sometimes stay up there for some weeks. I helped today till afternoon and then I came down.'

'And when are you going up again?', asked Tiburius.

'I'll stay with my wife today,' said the woodman, 'then tomorrow at three o'clock in the morning I'll go to the Zuder to the foreman and from there back again to the clearing so that I'll still have an afternoon to work.'

'You do all that in a day?' said Tiburius. 'Does it go on like that the whole year round?'

'It is easier in the winter,' answered the woodman, 'then we are in the valley and often our time is just spent on the carts.'

'Well, well,' replied Mr Tiburius, as he walked painfully along beside the man.

The latter told him many other things about his trade, how they did it, how they lived in the pursuit of it in the high mountains and what dangers and adventures came to pass in doing so. While they were talking, they continued walking until the valley, as far as could be seen in the already advanced night, widened out and they were again descending a rather steep path. The woodman stayed close to Tiburius, supported him and led him down by the arm. When they were on the flat again and had put another stretch behind them, little houses with lights were visible.

'So,' said the woodman, 'here we are. I have gone out of my way with you, since you are so ill and couldn't go further. But it is very easy from here on. Just go down this street and then straight on, you will then recognise the houses. I must turn round because I have now almost two hours to go to get home and because the night is short and I must set out again at three.'

'Dear, good man,' said Tiburius, 'I cannot repay you because I have no money, for my servant always has that and he is not here. Only come with me to where I am staying so that I can reward your good deed, or take my stick and lend me yours, I shall stay here until late autumn, my name is Theodore Kneigt and if you or someone else brings the stick and exchanges it for yours, then I'll pay my debt conscientiously.'

'Don't forget,' said the woodman, 'that I still have to sharpen my axe. I can't afford to lose any more time. However, I'll take the stick very gladly and will indeed bring it back sometime; for I have two children and if you want to give them something, then that would suit me very well and their mother too.'

With these words they exchanged sticks and said goodbye. Tiburius walked slowly, supporting himself on the woodman's

short axe-handle, towards the fences of the little gardens belonging to the houses here and he heard the now much quicker
footsteps of the woodman who, laden with his iron wedges,
wooden clogs on his feet and without a stick – since Tiburius's
cane with the elegant gold knob was not to be counted – was
beginning his journey back to the hut two hours' journey away.

In the inn in which Mr Tiburius lived, they were all astonished
when they saw him arrive at night on foot with an axe-handle.
The innkeeper made timid inquiry, the others repeated it one to
another until it ran like wildfire into the other houses of the
town. However, Tiburius told the landlady quickly what had
happened, went up to his rooms, still with the axe-handle, sat
himself down in his comfortable winged bath-chair and demanded food. A little table was placed before the bath-chair and laid,
and various foods were placed on it. When he had begun to eat,
he asked if his carriage had come back. They told him it hadn't,
and he now realised that his coachman and valet were still
waiting at the glade. He therefore described the place and
ordered someone to be sent out to them immediately. After he
had eaten, his second servant, who had stayed at home,
undressed him and put him to bed. When Mr Tiburius was in
bed, he ordered that no one was to come into his little bedroom
until he rang, and when the servant had gone the invalid pulled
the two blankets in which he had wrapped himself up to his face;
for, after all this excitement, he wanted to induce a sweat since
this could perhaps prevent any consequences. After a short time
Mr Tiburius was drawing the deep breaths of the sleeper.

We do not know what happened in the night and can only tell
how things were the next day.

When Mr Tiburius awoke it was bright day. The sun shone in
and the red Chinamen on the silk screen appeared almost
flame-red because the sun was shining through them; however,
in spite of that they looked very friendly. Mr Tiburius looked at
them for a long time before he stirred. The warmth of the bed
was extremely comfortable. Finally he had to gather his wits to
find out what hurt him. His head did not hurt, he did not know
if a sweat had come or not, for he had been asleep, his chest did
not hurt either, his stomach was well, except that he felt very
hungry, and his arms were not stiff and felt no twitching or
strain. He took his watch which lay near the bed and looked at

her white stockings and rough hobnailed clogs stuck out. What Tiburius had taken to be a bundle was another white cloth which was wound around a flat basket so that it could be carried. But the cloth did not cover the basket completely but let it peep out in many places, disclosing its contents. These contents were strawberries. They were that type of small pungent woodland strawberry which is to be found in the mountains throughout the summer, by anyone who knows the proper places to look.

When Mr Tiburius saw the strawberries, a desire arose in him to have some of them, due particularly to the hunger he always felt on these walks in the wood. He recognized from the girl's dress that she was a strawberry-seller like the ones who often came to the resort, offering their wares for sale, partly at the street-corners and doors of houses and partly inside houses themselves. He had not looked at all at the girl's face. He stood for a while in his grey coat in front of her, then he said at last: 'If you're bringing these strawberries to market anyway, you would do me a kindness if you sold me a very small portion of them now on the spot; I'll pay you well, that is, if you come a little way with me to the road as I have no money here.'

At these words the girl looked up and gazed at him with a clear, unfrightened glance.

'I can't sell you any strawberries,' she said, 'but if you only want a very small portion of them, as you say, then I can make you a present of them.'

'I cannot accept them as a present,' answered Tiburius.

'Tell me, would you really like them?' asked the girl.

'Yes, I would really like them,' replied Tiburius.

'Then wait a little,' said the girl.

At these words she bent forward, untied the big knot in the cloth over the little basket, pulled back the corners and revealed on the flat basket a profusion of picked strawberries which must have been chosen with great care and consideration, because they were all very red, very ripe and almost equally big. Then she stood up, took a flat stone she had chosen, used it as a little dish, laid on it several big green leaves which she picked, and poured out onto it a heap of strawberries as big as it could take.

'There!'

'But I can't take them, if you are only giving them away,' said Tiburius.

'Since you said that you would really like them, you must take them,' she answered. 'I give them to you very gladly.'

'If you give them gladly, then I'll accept them,' said Tiburius, taking the flat stone carefully from her hand into his own. But he did not eat any of them at first.

She bent down again and wrapped the white cloth round the basket as it had been. When she had stood up again, she said: 'Now sit down on this stone and eat your strawberries.'

'But the stone is your seat, since you took it first,' answered Tiburius.

'No, you must sit on it because you are eating and I shall stand in front of you,' said the girl.

So Tiburius sat down to please her and held the little stone dish with the strawberries in front of him. He took first one in his fingers and ate it, then the second, then the third, and so on. The girl stood in front of him and looked at him with a smile. When he had only a few left, she said: 'Well, aren't they good?'

'Yes, they are excellent,' he answered, 'you have picked the best and most evenly-sized ones. But tell me, why aren't you selling your strawberries?'

'Because I don't sell strawberries at all,' she answered. 'I pick very fine ones and then Father and I eat them. You see, Father is old and was ill last spring. The resort doctor looked at him and then gave him something. He must be a foolish man because he said after a time that Father should eat lots of strawberries and then he would recover. What good are strawberries, I thought, they are only a food and not a medicine. But because one cannot be sure, I went into the wood and looked for strawberries. Father liked to eat them and I always took some extra from the wood so that there would be some left for me because I like them too. Father was cured long ago, I don't know whether the strawberries did it or whether it would have come about without them. But because they are so good, I still go to get us some.'

'There have been none to be had in the resort for a long time because it is now autumn,' said Tiburius.

'If you want lots of strawberries,' answered the girl – 'what's your name then, Sir?'

'My name is Theodore,' answered Tiburius.

'If you want a lot of strawberries at this time of year, Mr

Theodore', continued the girl, 'then you must go over to St Ursula's Clearings: because there they only ripen in the late summer. At the moment they are still nice enough. Go over sometime and pick some for yourself. At other times they are good in different places.'

Tiburius had meanwhile finished all his strawberries and he laid the little dish with the green leaves near him on the stone.

'I was only resting a little at this place and have to go on now,' said the girl.

'I'll go with you,' said Tiburius.

'If you want to, do,' answered the girl.

She bent down to the white cloth in which the basket was wrapped and which lay at her feet on the path, took the four corners neatly in her hand, lifted it and set off, carrying the basket at her side. Tiburius got up from his seat, brushed the pine needles that had fallen onto the stone from his grey coat and went with her.

She took him out onto the path which led to the rock-face and to his carriage. But when she came to the fork that had led Tiburius astray the first time, she turned along the well-defined path, leaving the one that led to the rock-face and to Mr Tiburius's carriage on her right. He walked at her side. The path led into a beautiful thick wood and continued through it. The girl, now spattered, now missed by the dancing lights of the wood, walked steadily on, so that Tiburius could accompany her without difficulty. When they had walked for a stretch, Tiburius thought he could recognise the big stone to which he had run that time and on which he had stood to call for his carriage and his servants.

'But I must ask you something which I don't understand,' said the girl as they walked along together.

'Ask me,' answered Tiburius.

'You said that you wanted to buy strawberries from me, that you had no money on the spot but that if I went out to the road, you would pay me well there. What does that mean? Is your money lying by the road?'

'No,' answered Tiburius, 'it is only that – but tell me, what is your name, if I may ask?'

'My name is Maria,' replied the girl.

'Well then, Maria, it is like this: I often go alone into the wood for a walk and my servant waits at the road. Because he buys everything we need and because he also pays for what I buy, I never carry any money with me. He has my money and gives me an account of it at set times.'

'But that is very unpleasant and a great inconvenience,' replied the girl. 'A person should have his own money with him and buy things and pay for them himself; then you need no one else and no accounts.'

'That's probably true,' said Tiburius, 'and you are right, but it has become a habit by now.'

'I wouldn't go on following a habit that was silly,' answered the girl.

So they went on amid different questions and answers. They walked for a long time in the wood. At last it thinned out, the trees were more scattered, meadows were visible here and there and the path went through them deeper into the mountains. At a lovely spot with deciduous trees and several stones lit up by the sun, Maria turned off the path and, pointing to a narrow little track which went up over an alpine meadow, she said: 'This is where you go up to our house. If you would like to come with me, you are welcome.'

'I'll come,' answered Tiburius.

She went in front, therefore, and he followed. They had not gone very far around the bends in the path, for the meadow was quite steep, when the house became visible. It stood in a wide comfortable hollow in the slope that formed a semi-circular rock-face at a distance from the house, protecting it on all sides, except to the south where the windows were. Therefore it was possible for many fruit trees to stand around the house and for their fruit to ripen, when in the whole region and especially at the altitude of this meadow conditions were not favourable for fruit. Nearer the rock face there were also bee-hives. The house belonged to the smaller type often found in that part of the mountains. Maria went ahead over the threshold of the open door and Tiburius followed her. She led him past the kitchen in which a maid was scrubbing to the living-room, brightly lit by the sunlight falling through the windows. At the white beechwood table sat Maria's father, the only inhabitant of the room and of the house, since the girl's mother was long since dead. She placed the little basket of strawberries first in an angle of the bench, pulling a chair for Tiburius up to the table and inviting him to sit down, while she told her father how she had found the gentleman in the Black Wood and that he had come up with her. Then she spread a little white cloth on the table, placed three plates on it, for her father, for Tiburius and for herself, and brought the strawberries, emptied into a painted wooden bowl. The maid also set milk on the table, with which the father ate the fruit brought for him. Tiburius ate very little and Maria said she would keep her share for the evening.

After Tiburius had spoken about various things for a while with the man, who was not old at all but rather on the threshold of old age, he got up from his chair to go. Maria said she would accompany him to the road along which he had then only to keep going in order to reach his servant.

The girl then led him on another equally narrow path down over the meadow. Just below the house they turned around the rock-face of the hollow and went diagonally down along its gentler outer side in exactly the opposite direction from which they had come. After a short time they came to the bottom of the valley and by going along it for a while among bushes and trees, they reached the road.

'If you continue now in this direction,' she said, 'then you'll come to the spot where your servant is, that is, if you went into the Black Wood along the little path past St Andrew's Wall and if you've left him standing there at the road.'

'Yes, that's where I went in,' answered Tiburius.

'Goodbye now, I'm going back home. Since perhaps you'd never find your way over to St Ursula's Clearing, I'll show it to you, if you'll wait for me the day after tomorrow on the stroke of twelve at the stone where you met me today. You can then pick enough strawberries for yourself; I'll show you the places where they are most plentiful at the moment.'

'Thank you very much, Maria,' answered Tiburius, 'for giving me a present and now for guiding me here. I'll definitely be there.'

'Do,' answered the girl as she turned round, already going off among the bushes.

Tiburius went along the road in the direction indicated. He walked for a fairly long time before he at last saw his carriage and his servants. When he reached them, they showed their amazement at seeing him not coming along his footpath today but along the road. He, however, gave no reason for this but got into the carriage and drove back to the resort. He told no one in the spa, either, about the meeting and that he had visited the house in the hollow in the mountains.

On the second day after that, however, he drove before noon to his usual spot. He got out, left the carriage and took the path towards his familiar rock-face. He went past it towards the beeches and took the forest path, going along it until he came to the stone they had agreed on. He sat down on it and waited. At this distance and in this wilderness no noonday bells could be heard, but Tiburius knew well the time at which they must all be ringing in the towers and spires of the land, for he had his watch in his hand; – and when this time had come, he saw Maria already coming towards him in the twilight of the wood, dressed just as before.

'But how do you know that it is now exactly midday, since there are no bells to be heard and since I don't see you have a watch?' asked Tiburius, when the girl had come up to him and stopped.

'Didn't you see the clock with the long chains hanging in our living-room the day before yesterday?' she answered. 'That clock goes very well and when it points to eleven, we go to our midday meal, then I get ready to go strawberry-picking and if I look at the hands before I leave, I know just when I will arrive here.'

'You came at exactly the agreed time,' he said.

'You too,' she answered. 'That is good; but come now, I'll guide you.'

Tiburius got up from the stone. He had his fine grey coat on again and so they went, the girl in the costume described above, he in his grey coat, through the wood. She had the little flat basket again with the white cloth around it but as it was empty, it hung loosely on her arm. She led Mr Tiburius a good way along the familiar woodland path which had once upon a time so terrified him, but was now so beautiful. When they came to the high fir-grove where the stakes lay across the path, Maria turned off it, going in amongst the stones and ferns. Tiburius followed. She led him without a path but in such a way that they walked on dry stones, avoiding the dampness in the moss and on the path. Later they came to dry ground. At times they walked on a barely recognisable path, at others only through rustling undergrowth, over the stones and scree of a thin wood. After more than an hour's walk they came to a slope cleared of trees all around and showing by its innumerable, still visible stumps that the trees had been cut down only a few years before. The south-facing slope was lit up by the warm autumn sun and so surrounded by mountains and rocks that no rough breezes could blow there. All kinds of shrubs and flowers grew here and in many places strawberry plants could be seen crowding round the tree-stumps.

'Let's pick here now from St Ursula's Clearing down,' said Maria, as she pointed to this strange tree-battlefield, 'and after a time we'll see who has more.'

With these words she went quickly away from Tiburius's side into the clearing among the sunny undergrowth and soon he could see her bending down here and there and picking. She must have put the little basket down somewhere because he didn't see it on her arm any more.

He wanted to be picking strawberries too, but he saw none. Where he stood everything was green or brown or some other colour – but he could not see a single red spot that would have meant a strawberry. So he went farther into the clearing. But here again he saw only green strawberry plants, all kinds of brown and yellow leaves, pieces of fallen tree-bark and suchlike: but no strawberries. So he decided to go even farther and look even more carefully. He must have succeeded too, because after a while he might have been seen stopping again and again. It was a strange sight to see the two people in the mixed under-growth of the clearing. The neat nimble girl moving dexterously between the branches and the man in his grey coat, from which it could be seen immediately that he had come out here to the wood from the town.

After some time Maria saw her companion standing, holding some strawberries he had picked on the flat of his hand. Having observed this, she went up to him and said: 'Look, you've brought no basket or other container to collect the berries – wait, I'll help you.'

With these words she took a knife out of the pocket of her skirt, went up a little hill on which stood a young birch-tree with a white bark, and with deft cuts separated a square of bark from the trunk as white, as strong and as supple as parchment. She took the square back to Tiburius, cut some slender twigs from the shrubs that were near him, stripped them clean, made some cuts in the delicate bark and in this way fashioned a little bag out of the bark and twigs, which could not only take the strawberries very nicely but also had the advantage that it stood on the inserted twigs as though on legs.

'So,' said Maria, 'now you have a little basket, pick busily into it, I'll keep filling mine up in the meanwhile and when you are finished and maybe need a second one, you have only to call.'

She went off again to her place and pressed on with her task – Tiburius also.

When she had as much as she usually gathered she went back to Tiburius and saw that he had his tiny little basket also almost full. She turned round in several directions to find more, so that his container should be full too. Then she brought him those she had found on green leaves and poured them into his bark bag.

'Now,' she said, 'We've both filled our containers and we'll be off.'

They went back again in the same almost ridiculous way they had come: through the undergrowth, ferns and stones, without a path, the girl in front and Tiburius in his grey coat behind. She guided him back to his path with the same certainty with which she had led him down to St Ursula's Clearing. When she came to the place where the path divided, she said: 'Now you can go out that way to St Andrew's Wall, you are nearer to the resort. I'll go left again home through the wood. I hope your strawberries taste good. You can put sugar on them too, wine if you like. If you come again, take a knife with you and make yourself a much bigger basket than the one you had today. If you want to come collecting with me, come again the day after tomorrow, I go every other day as long as the present fine weather lasts; once it rains, all the strawberries are ruined at this time of year and I don't go out any more. Now goodbye.'

'Goodbye, Maria,' replied Tiburius.

She went along her path to the left carrying her basket with the white cloth through the twilight of the wood as before; Tiburius went to the right and then drove back to the spa holding his strawberry basket in the carriage in front of him. When he was seen arriving back like this, and when the story of how he had gone strawberry-picking with a birch-bark bag and had driven back with it had spread to the neighbouring houses too, there was again much merriment. Tiburius, however, knew nothing about it; in the evening he ordered his servant to bring him some beautiful plates and he ate the strawberries he had gathered. He took no wine with them.

After this, he met her twice more. The first time he did indeed make a fairly big bag for himself with the knife he had brought with him, and he half-filled it with strawberries; the second time, however, he decided this occupation was too childish and he sat on a tree-stump with a book and read while Maria picked her strawberries. He went again this last time with her to her father's and, wearing the eternal grey coat to which he had become attached, he sat for a good while on a bench in front of the house, talking to the man, for the weather was very fine and the autumn sun laid its beams so warmly on the south side of the house that even the flies made merry around the two men as though it were the middle of summer. Then, knowing the narrow path down over the hill by now, he went off alone to the road and to his horses.

This warm pleasant day was indeed the last fine one, for very often, indeed almost always, it happens in the mountains that a very warm mild spell in late autumn is the harbinger of storms and rain. The lovely blue air no longer came from the beautiful fragrant rock-face which Tiburius had always seen from his window and which had surprised him at the beginning just after his arrival because the stones stood out on it so very high up; it was not even visible any longer, only grey billowing mists whirled unceasingly out from that region as though they were being emptied out of an immeasurable sack which could never become empty. A ceaseless wind blew out of the mists towards the houses of the spa and the wind brought a fine prickling rain which was horribly cold. Tiburius waited a day, he waited two, he waited several – but since the resort doctor himself said that there was now little hope that milder and more healthful days would come, and even that this weather was harmful rather than useful to the visitors, he had his travelling carriage packed and drove home. A few days previously, just as he was engaged in packing, the woodcutter had called, the same one who had shown him the way home from the Black Wood that time at night, bringing the stick that had been entrusted to him. He said he would have come earlier had he known that the knob was of gold, but he had only found this out yesterday. Tiburius answered that that did not matter and he was going to give him more for his services than the value of stick and knob together. He had given him the reward and the man had gone off amid many protestations of gratitude.

In the region in which Tiburius's country villa stood there were still quite fine, though slightly cloudy, days. Mr Tiburius drove out to the little doctor with the clapping device in his garden who was still extending his plantations. The doctor received Mr Tiburius as usual and spoke to him but did not tell him whether he thought he looked better or worse. Mr Tiburius told him he had been to the resort and that it had done him considerable good. He told him nothing of the life and doings of the resort nor of anything else that had happened in it. He stood near the plant containers and the doctor still worked without a coat in spite of the advanced season. Before the snow came, Tiburius had been repeatedly to the doctor's.

In the winter he put on high boots and a rough warm coat one day and tried a walk in the snow. It was successful and he did it again many times.

In the spring, however, when the sun was again letting its rays drop down warmly and pleasantly and when Tiburius had convinced himself from his books about the resort that there too the warmer season had set in, he got his travelling carriage ready again and drove off to the resort. Because he belonged to those who always like to stick to what is old and accustomed, he had already, the previous autumn before he left, rerented from his old landlord for the whole of the next summer the little apartment he had occupied.

When he had arrived there, when everything had been unpacked, when the silk Chinamen were resplendent around his well-ordered bed, he set about arranging things for the coming summer. He laid out the beautiful sketch-books he had brought with him this time on the table, onto which the blue rock face looked very pleasantly, he laid the packets of pencils he had prepared near them and also the little boxes in which he kept the fine files to sharpen the drawing pencils. Finally, when all that was done, he had the doctor called in order to discuss his future actions with him.

When everything was in order, he drove out to St Andrew's Wall. It was resplendent in full spring dress. The undergrowth, the leaves and plants of all kinds now had that marvellous laughing green instead of the brown and yellow of the previous autumn and many a fiery blue, red or white of blossoming flowers gleamed up out of it. The wood had that youthful light-green appearance and from many a fallen trunk that had appeared to be dead wood the previous year freshly-burgeoning leafy shoots stood out. Only, he thought, there would probably not be any strawberries yet at this time of the year.

He stood out for a while, and walked and looked about. When he had come out of the wood for the second time, he drew, and then went deep into his woodland path. Everything was quite different here too; the path seemed narrower because the grass grew right up to it everywhere and the trees and bushes had shot out long shoots and branches in all directions. Even the stones which he knew well had many a light green patch and in various places where only a meagre space could be found a little flower stood up.

When some time had passed in this way, when many very beautiful days had passed over the valley and the mountains, when he had once even walked out through the whole Black Wood to where the snowfields could be seen and from there back again, it happened one day as he strolled along the path in his grey coat with his sketch-books that Maria came towards him in person. Whether she was dressed the same or differently from the previous year he did not know, because he had never noticed – that he himself was exactly the same he didn't know either because he never thought of it.

When she had come quite near, he stopped and looked at her. She also stopped in front of him, turned her eyes to him and said: 'Well, are you here again already?'

'Yes,' he said, 'I've been in the resort for quite a time, I have often come out here too, but I've never seen you, naturally, as there are no strawberries yet.'

'That makes no difference, I often come here anyway,' answered Maria, 'because various medicinal and tasty herbs grow here which are very good in spring.'

After she had said this, she turned her bright eyes very clearly up to his and said: 'Why were you false that time?'

'I haven't been false at all, Maria,' he replied.

'Yes, you have been false,' she said. 'Whatever name one has from birth, it has come from God and one must cherish it as one's parents, be they rich or poor. Your name is not Theodore, it is Tiburius.'

'No, no, Maria,' answered he, 'my name is Theodore, my name really is Theodore Kneigt. People have called me Tiburius, it has come to my ears a few times and a friend at home always calls me that – if you don't believe what I say, I can prove it to you – wait, I have some letters which are addressed in my name – and if you are still in doubt, then I can show you my baptismal certificate tomorrow on which my name is written indisputably.'

At these words he searched in the breast-pocket of his coat in which he had several papers. But Maria caught him by the arm, restrained him and said: 'Don't, you don't need to. Because you've said it, I believe it.'

With some hesitation he let go of the papers in his pocket, withdrew his empty hand and Maria then took her hand from his arm.

After a while, Mr Tiburius asked: 'Then you inquired after me in the resort?'

Maria was silent a little at this question, then she said: 'Indeed I did ask after you. People also say other things – they say that you are a strange and foolish man – but that doesn't matter.'

With these words she prepared to go. Mr Tiburius went with her. They spoke about the spring, about the fine weather; and where the path forked, they separated – her path went left into the depths of the wood, his to the right towards the rock-face.

Mr Tiburius once also went up the hill to the hollow where her father's house stood, and after this first visit he came often, leaving the horses and servants waiting for him at the usual place on the road. He sat with her father, speaking to him about different things as they occurred to the old man – and he spoke too to Maria as she worked around the house or, if they were in the living-room, came to them at the table and listened – or, when they sat on the bench outside, stood near them holding her hand before her face looking out at the distant mountains or the clouds. Her father was indulgent towards the girl, let her do what work she wanted or let her wander off if it pleased her and walk about the wood at her leisure. Sometimes she accompanied Mr Tiburius a little way down the hill and did not hesitate to tell him when she would be coming into the wood again so that they could meet there.

Mr Tiburius did not miss these opportunities, they walked about together, she picked herbs into her little basket, showed him many of them growing and told him the names by which they were known in her country speech.

At last, Tiburius showed her his sketch-books. He was only able to do this after a long time. He turned over the leaves and showed her how he reproduced many objects of the wood and rock-face with fine-pointed pencils. She took the liveliest interest in the matter and was greatly delighted that with nothing except plain black strokes one could imitate the objects of the wood as faithfully and lovingly and truly as if they were standing there. From now on she sat near him when he drew, looked on intently and let her gaze go from the original objects to the lines in the book and back again.

After a time she even made suggestios and often said suddenly: 'That's too short – it's not like that out there.'

He recognised each time that what she said was correct, took a rubber, erased the lines and made them as they should be.

Sometimes after such sessions he accompanied her to her father's, sometimes she went with him to the rock-face. He never said anything to her about his carriage or that his servants were waiting for him outside the wood.

In this way a large part of the summer passed.

One afternoon when there had been strawberries again for a long time, as he sat at the rock-face drawing and as she, having set the full basket of strawberries near her, sat behind him on the stones and looked on while a tall, long-stemmed tiger lily blazed near them, he said: 'How is it, then, Maria, that you are not afraid in the wood and that from the moment when we met for the first time, you were not afraid of me either?'

'I haven't been afraid of the wood,' she answered, 'because I don't know what I should fear – I have been in it since childhood and know all the paths and areas of it, and don't know what to be afraid of. And I didn't fear you because you are good and because you are different from the others.'

'Well, how are the others?' asked Mr Tiburius.

'They're different,' replied Maria. 'sometimes I used to go down into the resort as almost everybody does here to sell various things – but then I didn't go any more except after all the visitors had gone, because they – and some were men in whom it was not at all fitting – always pinched my cheeks and said: "Pretty girl".'

At these words, Mr Tiburius put his pencil into his sketch-book, closed the book, turned round on his stone and looked at her. He was extremely startled, for she was indeed extraordinarily beautiful, as he noticed at that moment. Under the scarf that she always wore on her head the dark brown hair, softly parted, curved out, making the beautiful fine forehead appear even finer and more beautiful between its two sections; in spite of its fresh healthy hue the whole face was indescribably refined and pure, an effect increased rather than diminished by the rough clothes she usually wore. Her eyes were very large and shining, they looked at people very frankly when they were opened and were covered submissively by the lovely long lashes when they were closed. Her lips were red and her teeth white. Even now when seated her figure showed the corresponding height for her face and was slim and softly formed.

Having looked at her thus, Mr Tiburius turned round again, opened his book and went on sketching. However, he did not sketch much longer but said, half-turned towards Maria, 'I'd prefer to stop for today.'

He put the pencil back into the holder attached to the sketch-book, closed the book and strapped it up, picked up the things lying around and got up. Maria also got up from the stones where she had been sitting and arranged her basket. Then they went off together, he and his sketch-book under his arm, she carrying her full basket with one hand. From the rock-face they did not go towards the road but towards the forest, because Tiburius wanted to accompany her to that spot where her path branched off into the thicket before going towards the hill on which her father's house stood.

When they reached this spot they stopped and Maria said: 'Goodbye and don't forget to come early the day after tomorrow; for now the strawberries are ripe down in the Thur Clearings which are a much longer way away. You could come with me to

Father again, I'll prepare the strawberries for you both to eat. And now good night.'

'Good night, Maria. I shall be there,' answered Tiburius and turned back towards his rock-face.

But she vanished among the branches and trunks of the pine-trees.

Mr Tiburius appeared on the day as he had promised but she was already there waiting for him. When she saw him she laughed and said: 'There you see, you did come too late after all. I left home today exactly according to our clock and got here before you. Now you have to come down to the clearings with me and then you must come to Father's and then you have to eat some strawberries.'

Tiburius went to the clearings with her, he stayed there while she picked strawberries, then he went with her to her father's and ate the strawberries which she prepared for the two men in the usual way, while she ate hers on a separate little green dish.

But from now on Mr Tiburius was much shyer and more timid than before.

He appeared each time they arranged to meet in the wood, they walked about together as before, but he was more reserved than previously, he anxiously avoided the little word 'thou' so that he did not have to say it too often and sometimes when she was not looking he took a secret sideways look and admired some aspect of her beauty.

So the last part of the summer passed and autumn came, so that it was exactly a year since he had first met her.

Then it happened one evening that among the many thoughts that now strangely and without his knowing their origin often went around in his head, this thought came also: 'How would it be if you sought to make Maria your wife?'

When he had got this idea he almost went out of his wits with impatience, because it seemed to him as though all the unmarried men of the spa must have the most passionate and yearning desire to marry Maria. He had not been with her and her father that day: how easily someone could have driven out in that time and asked for her hand. He couldn't understand the carelessness with which he had been at her side all summer without having had his eye on this goal and initiated means for its approaching realisation.

He had the horses put to the next day early in the morning and drove out as far on the road as was possible without exciting notice, then walked up the footpath through the undergrowth over the hill to the little house. He had set aside his spa regime, which he had already been neglecting anyway.

When father and daughter wondered why he had come so early that day, he could give them no real reason. Because he was there Maria stayed all the time in the living-room. When she did go out once to see to some domestic task, he put his request to her father. When she came in again, the latter said to her: 'Maria, our friend here, who has visited us so often and in such a neighbourly way this summer, asks for your hand in marriage – if, as he says, you yourself agree to it gladly, otherwise not.'

But at these words Maria stood there like a blushing rose. She was red all over and could not bring out a single word.

'Well, well, it will be all right,' said her father. 'You need not give an answer now, it will be all right.'

After she had left the room at these words, after Mr Tiburius, to whom it had not occurred when he drove out that he should bring his personal papers with him, had told her father that he would bring him everything that related to himself and his circumstances, in so far as he had it with him, and that he would write immediately for what was missing, after he had gone away shortly afterwards and her father had gone out to Maria who was sitting on the garden seat at the back of the house, she said to him: 'Dear father, I accept him very, very, very gladly; for he is good as no other single person is good, he is so decent and upright and one can go about with him far and wide in the woods and in the wilderness, and he doesn't wear stupid clothes either like the others in the resort but is so simply dressed, almost as we are ourselves: but the only thing I am afraid of is whether it will be possible, I don't know who he is, whether he has a little house or anything to support a wife on, for when I was in the resort and asked after him I forgot to ask about these things.'

'Be easy on that score,' answered her father. 'The whole time he has been with us he has been so modest and trustworthy, his words so sensible and clear, and always very polite. Therefore he would not woo a wife if he did not possess what was fitting. One can be just as satisfied with little as with much.'

Maria was convinced and reassured by these words.

When Tiburius came on the following day her father told him at once that Maria had given her consent. Tiburius was so full of joy at this, he didn't know what to do or where to turn. Not until the next week when Maria herself said to him, as they sat on the bench in front of the house, that she would be his wife very, very gladly, did he, secretly before he went away, leave a present on the table which he had been carrying around in his pocket for several days.

It was a necklace with six rows of the choicest pearls which had been worn by the women in his family for many generations. When he came in the spring he had taken the jewel-case with him to the spa and many other things were in it which he had first to have altered and reset before he could give them to his bride as ornaments.

Maria did not know the great value of these pearls but she had a feminine instinct that they must be worth a lot — the only thing she did know with certainty, however, was that they lay indescribably beautifully and softly around her throat when she put them on.

All the documents and papers about his circumstances arrived and he showed them to her father. In the meantime he had also sent beautiful fabrics to the little house. Maria had had clothes made from them but of the type and cut that she had always worn hitherto. He had not stipulated anything and was delighted, and, when she was dressed, drove with her in his carriage before which the beautiful greys pranced through the busiest street of the resort.

Everyone was utterly astonished, because the meaning of various things now became clear, above all why Tiburius had recently rented a larger, beautifully furnished apartment. Not one person had had the slightest suspicion, even his servants had always thought he drove out only to sketch in the wood; meanwhile he had found this beautiful girl somewhere and was presenting her now as his bride. Into all the houses, rooms and chambers the rumours spread. Not once but more than a hundred times the old German proverb was repeated: 'Still waters run deep', and many a lascivious ageing connoisseur said significantly: 'The cunning old fox knew very well where to find himself a beautiful dove.'

Meanwhile, when the legal conditions had been fulfilled and the legal interval had passed, Tiburius brought Maria home as his wife and in the late autumn all the visitors who were still there saw him lift her into a beautiful well-equipped travelling carriage which stood before the house and drive off with her to Italy.

He intended to spend the winter there but instead he spent three years travelling through various countries before returning to the house that had meanwhile been built for him in Maria's beautiful native region. He had sold the house he had inherited from his father.

But how Mr Tiburius has changed!

All the silk Chinamen are gone, the elk skins on his beds and couches are gone – now he sleeps on plain clean straw with linen sheets over it – all his windows are open, a current of air flows in and out, he goes about at home in clothes as loose as those of his friend, the little doctor, who gave him the advice about the spa, and he manages his property just like the little doctor.

This doctor, who had written himself a prescription for his life, has been living near Tiburius now for several years; he has moved all his plants and glass-houses there on account of the better air and other more favourable conditions. When the matter of Tiburius's marriage came to his ears, he is said to have laughed very merrily. He respects and loves his neighbour extremely and although previously he called him Tiburius on short acquaintance, he does not do so any more but always says: 'My friend Theodore'.

His wife too, who disliked Mr Tiburius very much at the time of his folly, now esteems and respects him considerably; and she loves Maria heartily and tenderly, and is loved by her in return.

With that true, pure understanding that was characteristic of the strawberry girl, she found her feet quickly in her new life so that she seemed born to it and with her clear, innocent strength, the legacy of the forest, her household has become bright, laughing and gay, a creation which is unique, beautiful, faultless and all of a piece.

Tiburius is not the first to take a wife from the peasant classes but not all have fared as well as he. I myself knew a man whose wife squandered everything on her beloved, beautiful peasant body.

Because it became too lonely for him in the empty house in the hollow, Maria's father lives with his children where, in his little room, he has the clock that once hung in the living-room of his house.

With this the story of the forest path is finished.

– But finally a request: may Mr Theodore Kneigt forgive me for having called him Tiburius throughout; Theodore does not come as easily and quickly to me as good old Tiburius, who once growled at me so terribly when I said: 'But Tiburius, you are the most thoroughgoing fool and crank who has ever existed on this earth.'

Wasn't I right?

Epilogue

As I write this, news reaches me that the only sorrow, the only trouble, the only sadness that had clouded the marriage of Maria and Tiburius has been removed – his first child, a lusty crying boy, has been born.

Limestone

I am going to narrate a story that a friend once told us, in which nothing unusual happens, but which I have been unable to forget. Nine out of ten people who hear this story will blame the man who appears in it, the tenth will think of him often. What gave rise to the story was an argument that took place at a gathering of us friends as to how spiritual gifts are distributed in a human being. Some maintained that a person could be possessed of a certain gift to an extraordinary extent, yet possess the others to only a small degree. The so-called virtuosi were cited as examples here. Others said that the gifts of the soul were always present to a like extent, either all were equally great or equally mediocre or equally insignificant, and it only depended on fate which gift was especially developed, and this gave the appearance of inequality. Given other youthful experiences and contemporary circumstances Raphael could have been a great general instead of a great painter. Others again thought that where reason, as the supersensual capacity and as the very highest capacity of man, was present in great abundance, then the other subordinate abilities would be present also. The opposite, however, was not true, they said, a lower ability could stand out particularly, while the higher ones did not. But whatever talent is significant, be it high or low in itself, those which are subordinate to it must be significant also. As a reason for this they said that the lower ability was always the servant of the higher one, and that it would be a nonsense to possess the higher dominant gift and not the lower subservient one. Finally there were yet others who said that God made people as He made them, one could not know how He had distributed the gifts and therefore could not grumble at it because it was uncertain what might come to light in this connection in the future. Then my friend told his story.

You all know, he said, that I have been active for many years as a surveyor, that I am in the employ of the state, and that I am

sent off here and there on government surveying projects. Thus
I have become acquainted with various regions and various
people. I was once in the little town of Wengen with the prospect
of having to stay there for a considerable length of time because
my work dragged on and also became more extensive. I often
went to the nearby village of Schauendorf and got to know the
parish priest, an excellent man, who had introduced fruit farm-
ing there and whose achievement it was that the village, previously surrounded by hedges, thickets and undergrowth, now
resembled an orchard, lying in the midst of a wealth of pleasant
fruit trees. Once he invited me to a church festival and I said
that I should come later on, for I had some necessary tasks to
perform. When I had executed my tasks I set off for Schauendorf.
I went across the high-lying fields, I went through the fruit trees,
and as I approached the presbytery I saw that luncheon must
already have begun. There was not a single person in the garden, which, as is the case with many Catholic presbyteries, lay in
front of the house; the windows opening onto the garden were
open, I could see into the kitchen where the maids were fully
occupied round the fire, and from the dining-room came the
occasional rattle of plates and the chink of cutlery. As I entered
I saw the guests sitting round the table and an untouched place-
setting kept for me. The parish priest led me to it and begged
me to be seated. He said that he would not introduce those
present to me nor mention their names; I already knew some, I
would get to know others during the meal and, when we had
finished, he would introduce me to the rest. So I sat down and it
was just as the priest had foretold. I made the acquaintance of
many of those present, I was told the names and circumstances
of many others and, as dish followed dish and tongues were
loosened by wine, many a recent acquaintance became an old
one. There was only one guest whom I could not identify. He sat
there smiling and friendly, he listened attentively to everything,
he always turned his face towards the part of the room where the
most animated conversation was taking place, as though he were
driven by duty to do so, his facial expressions agreed with all the
speakers and if the conversation became livelier somewhere
else, he turned in that direction and listened to it. But he
himself spoke not a word. He sat fairly near the bottom of the
table and his black-clad figure loomed over the white linen

table-cloth; although he was not tall, he never stretched himself to his full height, as though he thought that would be unseemly. His dress was that of a poor country priest. His coat was very worn and threadbare, it was shiny in several places, in others it had lost its black colour and was rusty or faded. The buttons were of strong bone. His black waistcoat was very long and also had bone buttons. His two tiny little bands of white – the only white thing about him – hung down over his black neck-cloth and bore witness to his calling. As he sat there, sometimes a very small portion of a sort of ruffle peeped out of his sleeves, which he was constantly trying to push back surreptitiously. Perhaps the ruffles were in such a state as to make him rather ashamed of them. I saw that he did not take much of any dish and always politely thanked the servant who offered it. When the dessert came, he scarcely sipped some of the better wine, took only small pieces of sweetmeats and kept nothing back on his plate, as the others were doing, in order to take the customary little souvenir back for their loved ones.

Because of these peculiarities the man caught my attention.

When the meal was over and the guests stood up, I was able to see the rest of his body. His breeches were of the same material and in the same condition as his coat; they went below the knee and were fastened there with buckles. Then came black stockings, which were almost grey. On his feet he wore wide shoes with large buckles. They were made of strong leather and had thick soles. In this costume the man stood there almost alone, as groups formed to converse, his back almost touching the wall between the windows. His physical appearance matched his dress. He had an elongated, gentle, almost timorous face with very beautiful clear blue eyes. His brown hair was drawn together simply at the back and already had some grey in it, which showed that he was nearing fifty or that he must have suffered anxiety and distress.

After a short time he fetched out of a corner a cane with a knob of black bone, like his buttons, approached the master of the house and began to take his leave. His host asked him if he was going already, to which he replied that it was high time, for he had a four-hour walk to his presbytery and his legs were no longer as good as in his younger days. His host did not keep him. He took his leave generally, went out through the door and we saw him immediately walking through the cornfields and climbing the hill that bordered the village towards the west, to vanish there, as it seemed, into the shining afternoon air.

I asked who the man was and discovered that he was a priest in a poor area, that he had already been there for a long time, that he did not want to be moved and that he scarcely ever left his house except on very pressing occasions. –

Many years had passed since that luncheon and I had completely forgotten the man when my work took me once again into that fearful region. Not that it consisted of wildernesses, ravines, abysses, rocks and waterfalls – all that rather attracts me – rather, there was nothing there but lots of small hills, every hill consisting of bare grey limestone, not broken up into jagged pieces as is often the case with this sort of stone, but divided up into wide rounded shapes, with a long extended sand-bank all around them. A small river called the Zirder went through these hills in great loops. The waters of this river, which often reflected the sky and appeared dark-blue amidst the grey and yellow of the limestone and the sand, and the narrow strips of green which often ran along the water's edge and the other separate patches of grass which lay here and there among the stones, formed all the variation and refreshment there was in this landscape.

I lived in an inn, situated in a somewhat better and therefore very distant part of the region. A road went over a rise at that point and bore the name 'the high road', as is the case in many areas, and the inn had the same name. So as not to waste time going to and fro, I always took cold food and wine with me to where I was working and often ate my midday meal in the evening. Some of my men also lodged at the inn, others made do the best they could and built themselves small wooden huts out in the stony country.

Although this region, called the Steinkar, is not in fact so very isolated, few people will know it, because there is no reason to go there.

One evening, as I was coming home alone from my labours, for I had sent my men on ahead, I saw my poor priest sitting on a heap of sand. He had almost buried his great shoes in the sand and there was sand on his coat-tails. I recognised him instantly. He was dressed more or less as on the occasion when I had seen him for the first time. His hair was now much greyer, as though it had made haste to assume this colour, his long face had acquired visible furrows, and only his eyes were clear and blue as before. The cane with the black bone head was leaning at his side.

I stopped walking, went closer to him and shouted to him.

He had not expected a greeting, so he stood up hastily and thanked me. There was no sign on his face that he recognised me; indeed it was not possible he should do so, for at that luncheon he had certainly looked at me much less than I at him. He just stood there in front of me and looked at me. So, in order to initiate a conversation, I said: 'You will not remember me, Father.'

'I do not have that honour,' he answered.

'But I have had the honour,' I said, taking up his polite tone, 'of having sat and eaten at the same table as you, Father.'

'I do not remember that,' he replied.

'Are not you the same man, Father,' I said, 'who was once at a church festival in the presbytery in Schauendorf several years ago and who was the first to leave after the meal, because he had, so he said, a four-hour walk to his own presbytery?'

'Yes, I am the same man,' he answered. 'Eight years ago I went to the centenary of the consecration of Schauendorf church because it was the right thing to do, I stayed for the luncheon because the parish priest had invited me, and I was the first to leave after the meal because I had to walk four hours to get home. I have not been in Schauendorf since.'

'Well, I sat at the same table,' said I, 'and recognised you straight away.'

'That is amazing – after so many years,' said he.

'My profession entails dealing with many different people,' I replied, 'and taking note of them, and I have got so skilled at this that I can recognise people I have seen only once, and many years ago. And we meet again in this frightful place.'

'It is as God has made it,' he answered, 'there are not as many trees growing here as in Schauendorf, but it is often beautiful too, and at times it is more beautiful than any region in the world.'

I asked if he was living in the area and he answered that he had been parish priest in this karst region for twenty-seven years. I told him that I had been sent here to survey it, that I was measuring hills and valleys in order to depict them in a reduced form on paper and that I was living out at the inn on the high road. When I asked him if he often came this way, he replied: 'I like to go out to exercise my legs and then I sit on a stone to contemplate things.'

During this conversation we had started walking; he walked along beside me and we spoke of many indifferent things, of the weather, of the time of year, how these stones were particularly good at soaking up the rays of the sun, and so on.

If his clothes had been shabby at the luncheon, they were even shabbier now, if that were possible. I could not remember ever having seen his hat on that occasion, but now I was forced to glance at it repeatedly, for there was no nap on it at all.

When he reached the place where his path and mine diverged, and his led down to his presbytery in the Kar, we took our leave, saying we hoped we should now meet each other more often.

I went my way to my inn and kept thinking of the priest. His uncommon degree of poverty, such as I had never seen before in someone who was not a beggar, especially not among those who are supposed to shine forth as models of cleanliness and order, was constantly present in my mind. The priest was indeed almost pitifully clean, but it was precisely this cleanliness that emphasised his poverty all the more painfully, highlighting the looseness of the threads, the impermanent and insubstantial nature of his clothing. I looked again at the hills covered only with stones, I looked again at the valleys, where nothing but long sandbanks stretched out to the distance, and then I went into my inn to consume the roast kid that they often served me there.

I did not ask about the priest, in order not to receive a gruff answer.

From now on I often met him. Since I spent the whole day out on the karst and was often still wandering about there at evening, acquainting myself with different directions and sections within it, and since he was often out there too, we could not but meet. We got into conversation several times too. It seemed that he was not sorry to encounter me and I was glad too when I came across him. Later, we often walked about together among the stones or we sat down upon one and looked at the others. He showed me many little creatures and many plants that were peculiar to the area, and he showed me the

characteristics of the region and made me aware of the differ-
ences between many of the stone hillocks, which the most careful observer would have regarded as being of exactly the same
formation. I told him of my journeys, showed him our equipment and sometimes when we were working explained its use to
him.

As time went on, I went down a few times to his presbytery
with him. Where the worst of the stone opens up a little, we went
down over a gentler slope towards the Kar. A meadow lay at the
edge of the stones; several trees grew there, among them a beautiful big lime-tree, and behind the lime-tree stood the presbytery.
At that time it was a white two-storey building, which stood out
pleasantly against the kindly green of the meadow, the trees and
the grey of the stones. The roof was tiled. The attic windows
were covered with little shutters like doors and the windows of
the house itself could be closed with green folding shutters.
Farther back, where the landscape formed a nook, stood the
church with its red painted spire, as though hidden in the rocks.
In another part of the Kar, in a wretched garden, stood the
school. These three buildings constituted the entire place. Any
other dwellings were scattered round the area. Many of the
rocks had a hut near them, as though glued to them, with a
small garden for potatoes or fodder for the goats. Far away, out
towards the open countryside, was a much more fertile region
which also belonged to the parish and which contained arable
land, meadowland and pasture.

Within sight of the presbytery windows the Zirder flowed past
at the edge of the meadow and was crossed by a high foot-bridge
which stretched down towards the meadow. The surface of the
meadow was not much higher than the river-bed. This scene
with the high foot-bridge over the lonely river was all that was
visible from the presbytery, apart from the stones.

When I went into the priest's house with him, he never took me
into the upper storey, but always led me through a roomy porch
into a small sitting-room. The porch was quite empty, apart from a
long wooden bench which lay in a wide, shallow alcove in the wall.
Whenever I visited the house, a Bible, a great leather-bound book,
lay on this bench. In the sitting-room there was only an unpainted
softwood table, a few chairs of the same type round it, then a
wooden bench at the wall and two yellow-painted cupboards.

Otherwise there was nothing there, not counting a small very beautiful carved medieval crucifix of pearwood, which hung over the equally small holy water font at the doorway.

In the course of these visits I made a strange discovery. I had already noticed in Schauendorf that the poor priest was always surreptitiously pushing his shirt-ruffles back into his coat-sleeves at the wrist, as though he must be ashamed of them. He was always doing the same thing now too. So I observed this more closely and realised that he had no need to be ashamed of his ruffles, on the contrary, that he wore the finest and most beautiful linen that I have ever seen anywhere, as other glimpses of his clothing confirmed. This linen was of the most immaculate whiteness and purity, such as could never have been suspected from the state of his top-clothes. He must, therefore, take the greatest care in looking after this part of his attire. Since he never spoke of it, I held my peace too, as might be imagined.

Such was our intercourse as a part of the summer passed.

One day there was particularly hot weather out on the stones. Though the sun had not shone the whole day, it had penetrated the opaque veil that covered the whole sky to such an extent that its pale shape would always be seen and an insubstantial light lay around all the objects in this stony country, casting no shadow, and causing the leaves of whatever sparse vegetation could be seen to droop; for, although only a semi-sunlight penetrated the vaporous layers in the dome of the sky, there was still a heat as though three tropical suns were blazing down from a bright sky. We had suffered greatly, so that I sent my men home after two o'clock. I myself sat down under an overhanging rock which made a sort of cave, where it was considerably cooler than outside in the open air. Here I consumed my midday-meal, drank my chilled wine and read. Towards evening the cloud layer did not break up, as happens very often on such days, nor did it thicken, but lay over the sky in the same uniform manner as it had done all day. Therefore I left the cave very late, for, since the cloud blanket in the sky had not changed, so the heat had scarcely lessened and no dew could be expected that night. I wandered very slowly through the hills and then I saw the priest coming towards me through the sandhills, looking at the sky. We drew nearer and saluted each other. He asked where we had been working that day and I told him. I told him that I had been reading in the cave and showed him the book. Then we walked on together over the sand.

After a time he said: 'It's no longer possible for you to reach the inn.'

'Why not?' I asked.

'Because a thunderstorm is going to break,' he replied.

I looked up at the sky. The cloud blanket had grown thicker if anything and a very strange leaden light lay on all the bare stony surfaces we could see.

'It was to be expected all day,' said I, 'that a thunderstorm would come, but I do not think one can calculate how soon the cloud layer will thicken, cool and create wind and electricity and then pour with rain.'

'Indeed, it is probably not possible to say exactly when,' he answered, 'but I have spent twenty-seven years in this region and have much experience which tells me that the thunderstorm will break sooner than one thinks and will be very heavy. I think therefore that it would be best if you were to come with me to my house and spend the night there. The house is so near that we can still reach it easily, even if we begin to see lightning in the sky, there you are safe and can go about your business tomorrow as early as you like.'

I replied that it was not impossible, nonetheless, that the cloud layer would produce only a steady rain. In that case, I was protected; I had a light oilskin coat with me, I only needed to pull that out of my bag and put it round me and the rain could do nothing to me. Indeed, even if I did not have this protection, I had so often been wet to the skin in the course of my work that I did not want to be a burden to someone and put him out in his domestic arrangements just to avoid such an eventuality. But if a thunderstorm were really in the offing with very heavy rain or hail or even a cloudburst, then I would gladly accept his offer and ask him for shelter for the night, but I made it a condition that it should really be nothing more than shelter, that he would not put himself out and would go to no further trouble than giving me a small place in a safe haven, for I needed nothing more than such a place. Furthermore, I added, our paths coincided for a good while yet, so that we could put off the question, observe the sky in the meantime and decide finally according to its appearance.

He agreed and said that, if I did stay with him, I need not fear to be a burden to him, for I knew that he lived simply and no provisions would be made other than those which were necessary for me to spend the night with him.

After we had agreed upon this, we continued on our way. We walked slowly, partly on account of the heat, partly because this had always been our custom.

Suddenly a weak flash of light flew round us, reddening the rocks.

This was the first flash of lightning, but it was silent and no thunder followed.

We walked on. After a while further flashes followed and, as the evening had darkened considerably and as the cloud layer was also producing a twilight effect, the limestone was lit up rose-red in front of us by every flash of lightning.

When we reached the place where our paths diverged, the priest stopped and looked at me. I admitted that a thunderstorm was in the offing and agreed to go with him to his house.

So we took the path to the Kar and walked down the gentle stony slope to the meadow.

When we reached the presbytery, we sat for a while on the wooden bench in front of the house. The storm had now developed fully and stood in the sky like a dark wall. After a while, against the uniform, dark-coloured wall of thundercloud white, rushing clouds appeared, rimming the bottom of the wall of dark cloud in long swollen bands. Perhaps in that spot therefore the storm had already come, while no blade of grass nor leaf stirred where we were. Such racing, puffed-up clouds are often a very bad sign in thunderstorms, they always herald gusts of wind, often hail and cloudbursts. The flashes of lightning were now being followed by audible claps of thunder.

We went into the house.

The priest said that when there was a thunderstorm at night, it was his habit to put a lighted candle on the table, and to sit up quietly in the candlelight as long as the storm lasted. In the daytime he sat at the table without a light. He asked me if he should observe this custom today. I reminded him of his promise not to put himself out in the least on my account. So he led me through the porch into the familiar sitting-room and asked if I should like to take off my things.

I usually carried a box on a leather strap over my shoulder, in which were drawing materials, drawings and also some surveying instruments. Next to the box was attached a bag in which were my cold food, my wine, my drinking glass and my arrangements for cooling the wine. I took off these things and hung them over the back of a chair standing in a corner. I leant my long measuring rod against one of the yellow cupboards.

In the meantime the priest had left the room and came in now with a light in his hand. It was a tallow candle in a brass candlestick. He put the candlestick on the table and put a brass snuffer near it. Then we both sat down at the table and stayed there to wait for the storm.

It seemed to be on its way. Once the priest had brought the candle, the little light that had still been coming through the windows vanished, they became black panels and dense night had fallen. The lightning became more piercing and in spite of the candlelight lit up the corners of the little room with every flash. The thunder grew heavier and more penetrating. So things continued for a long while. At last the first gust of the storm-wind came. The tree that stood in front of the house trembled quietly for a second, as though touched by a brief puff of air, and then became still again. After a little while it trembled again, this time for longer and more strongly. After a short interval there came a strong gust, all the leaves rustled and the branches must have been shaking, to judge by the sound we heard inside, and now the noise became continuous. The tree by the house, the hedges round it and all the bushes and trees in the neighbourhood were caught up in one single roar, which only intermittently slackened before increasing again. Through it the thunder boomed. The claps became more and more frequent and more and more distinct. But the storm was not yet overhead. There was still an interval between the lightning and the thunder, and the lightning, bright though it was, was still not coming in jagged flashes but as a general momentary illumination.

At last the first drops of rain struck the window panes. They beat hard and individually against the glass, but others soon followed and in a short while the rain was pouring down in streams. It increased quickly as though rushing and chasing itself, and was finally so heavy as to make it seem as if whole connected masses of water were falling down onto the house, which was groaning under the weight so that the groaning and creaking could be heard inside. The thunder could scarcely be heard over the streaming of the water, the streaming of the water became a second thunder. At last the storm was overhead. The flashes of lightning shot down like threads of fire and the thunderclaps followed quick and hoarse upon them, triumphing over any other uproar, and causing the window-panes to tremble and clatter as the claps ended and petered out.

I was glad now that I had followed the priest's advice. I had rarely experienced such a storm. The priest sat calmly and simply at the table in his sitting-room, with the light of the tallow candle shining on him.

Finally there came a clap of thunder as though it would lift the whole house from its moorings and fling it down, and a second followed. Then there was a pause for a little while, as often happens with such phenomena, the rain came to a sudden halt for a second, as though startled, even the wind paused. Things soon continued as before, but the main force was broken, and everything went on more smoothly. Gradually the storm slackened, it was now only a steady wind, the rain was weaker, the flashes of lightning were paler and the thunder rolled more feebly as though fading away out towards the open country.

When the rain was only a steady drizzle and the lightning only a flicker, the priest got up and said: 'It is over.'

He lit the stump of a candle and went out. After a while he came in again, carrying a tray with several things for supper. From the tray he put a little jug of milk on the table and poured out two glasses. Then he placed strawberries on a little green-glazed dish and put several pieces of black bread on a plate. By way of cutlery he put a knife at each place and a small spoon, then he carried the tray out again.

When he came in again, he said: 'This is our supper, I hope it will suffice for you.'

He went to the table, folded his hands and said a silent blessing; I did the same and then we sat down to our supper. We drank the milk from the glasses, we cut ourselves pieces of black bread with the knives and ate the strawberries with the spoons. When we were finished, he said grace again with folded hands, fetched the tray and carried out what remained.

In my bag I still had a portion of my midday-meal and there was still wine in my bottle. Therefore I said: 'If you will allow me, Father, I will take the remains of today's midday-meal out of my bag, as it will go bad otherwise.'

'Do just as you please,' he answered.

So I took my bag and said: 'Then you will see how I dine on my wandering life, Father, and what sort of vessels I use for eating and drinking.'

'You must know,' I went on, 'that, however much one praises water and especially mountain water, and however useful and wonderful this liquid is in the great economy of nature, if one is working all day long in the open in the sunshine or walking about among the hot stones and on the hot sand or scrambling among the rock-faces, then a drink of wine mixed with water is incomparably more refreshing and strengthening than the purest and most exquisite water in the world. I soon learned this in my work and therefore I always provide myself on all my journeys with wine. But only a good wine is of service. So I had some good pure wine sent to me to the inn and every day I take some of it with me out into my stony hills.'

The poor priest watched me as I unpacked my equipment. He examined the small tin plates, of which several could be packed into a small flat disc. I placed the little plates on the table. I added knives and forks from my box. Then I cut slices of fine white wheaten bread, which I had sent to me twice a week, then slices of ham, of cold roast meat and of cheese. I spread this out on the plates. Then I asked him for a bottleful of water, for I explained that that was the only thing I did not carry with me, for I was bound to find it anywhere in the countryside. When he had brought a jug of water, I spread out my drinking utensils. I took out the bottle, still half full of wine, I placed two glasses – I always carry a spare one – on the table, then I showed him how I cooled the wine. The glass is put into a container of very loose fabric, the fabric is moistened with a very thin liquid called ether, which I always have with me in a little bottle. This liquid evaporates very quickly and very intensely and in doing so creates a chill which makes the wine cooler than if it had just come from the cellar, even as though it had been on ice. When I had cooled two glasses of wine in this way, mixed them with water, and put one at his place, I invited him to eat with me.

As though to honour my invitation, he took a tiny little bite of the foods, sipped from the glass and could not be brought to take anything else.

I also ate only very little of the food I had put out and then packed everything away again, ashamed of the impoliteness I was guilty of in my hastiness.

I cast a quick glance at the priest's face, but there was not the slightest trace of displeasure in it.

When the table was empty, we sat for a while in the light of the tallow candle and talked. Then the priest went about preparing my bed. He carried a big woollen blanket in, folded it in four and put it on the bench by the wall. He made a pillow out of a similar blanket. Then he opened one of the yellow cupboards, took an extraordinarily beautiful fine white linen sheet out of it, unfolded it and spread it over my couch. When I saw the uncommon quality of the linen in the light of the candle, I involuntarily turned my eyes towards him and he blushed.

As a coverlet, he placed a third woollen blanket on the bed.

'That is your bed, as good as I can make it,' he said. 'Only tell me when you are ready to sleep.'

'I'll leave that to you, Father,' I answered, 'you go by whatever is your usual time for going to sleep. I am not tied to any particular time, my way of life means that sometimes I have a long sleep, sometimes only a short one and that sometimes I go to bed early and sometimes late.'

'I am not tied to any particular time either,' he replied, 'and can organise my sleep according to my duties. But since it is later today than usual on account of the storm and since you will most probably get up very early tomorrow and go to the inn to fetch things, I think sleep would be best and we should go to bed.'

'I entirely agree with you, Father,' said I.

After this conversation he left the room and I thought he had gone to his bedroom. I therefore got undressed, to the extent that I usually do, and lay down on my bed. I was just going to put out the light, which I had placed on a chair near my bed, when the priest came in again. He had undressed and was now wearing grey woollen stockings and a grey woollen jacket. He had no shoes on, but walked on his stockinged feet. In this costume he entered the room.

'You are already in bed,' he said, 'I came to wish you good

night before going to bed myself. So, sleep as well as you can on that bed.'

'I shall sleep well,' I replied, 'and wish you the same.'

After this exchange he went to the holy water font which hung under the small beautifully carved crucifix, sprinkled himself with holy water and left the room.

By the light of my candle I saw him lie down in the roomy porch on the wooden bench in the shallow alcove and put the Bible under his head as a pillow.

When I saw this I jumped up from my bed, went into the porch in my night clothes and said: 'This will not do, Father, this was not what I intended, you should not be sleeping on this bare bench and giving me the better bed. I am accustomed to sleeping on all kinds of beds, even in the open air under a tree, let me take this bench and you take the bed you wanted to give me.'

'No, my dear Sir,' he answered, 'I have not given you my bed. Normally there is never a bed where yours is now. I sleep every night where I am sleeping now.'

'On this hard bench and with this book as a pillow, this is how you sleep every night?' I asked.

'Just as you are accustomed from your work to sleeping on all kinds of bed, even in the open air,' he replied, 'so I am accustomed in my profession too to sleep on this bench with this book as a pillow.'

'Is it really possible?' I asked.

'Yes, it is so,' he answered. 'I am telling you the truth. I could make myself up a bed on this bench just like the one I made for you; but a very long time ago I began to sleep in these clothes on this bench here, just as you see me, and I am still doing it today.' As I was still hesitating, unconvinced, he said: 'You can be quite happy about it in your mind, quite happy.'

I no longer objected, for his argument that he could have made himself a bed too was especially convincing.

After a while, during which I continued to stand there, I said: 'If it is an old custom of yours, reverend Sir, then indeed I have no more objections, but you will understand that I argued against it in the beginning, for people usually sleep on a soft bed.'

'Yes, they do,' he said, 'and become accustomed to it and think it has to be like that. But it can be otherwise too. A person can get used to anything and the habit then gets very easy, very easy.'

With these words I went back into the room and lay down again on my bed, after I had wished him good night for the second time. I now remembered that indeed I had never seen a bed, no matter how often I had been in the priest's dwelling on previous occasions. I mulled the matter over for a while, and could not avoid feeling how pleasant the priest's extremely fine linen was against my body. After a short time the priest indeed proved that he was used to his couch, for I could hear from his soft, regular breathing that he had already fallen into a deep sleep.

I too was quiet now and there was a dead silence in the presbytery, the wind had stopped, the rain was only barely audible and stray flashes of lightning only touched the window now with a dull glow, so my eyelids grew heavy too and after I had extinguished the candle, I heard a few drops fall on the window-pane and then it seemed to me as though there was the merest flicker of lightning and then there was nothing more. –

I slept very well, woke late and it was already broad daylight when I opened my eyes. It seemed to me as though it was a gentle noise that had caused me to wake up fully. When I opened my eyes completely and looked around, I saw the priest in the porch in his grey night-clothes, busy brushing the dust from my clothes. I rose quickly from my bed, went out and interrupted him in his task by saying he should not do this, I could not accept this service from him, it was not fitting to his position, the dust did not matter and if I wanted to get rid of it, then I could remove it quickly myself with a brush.

'It does not befit my position as a priest, but it does befit my position as your host,' he said, 'I have only one old maid-servant who does not live in: she comes at certain times to do my few tasks and is not here today.'

'No, no, that's neither here nor there,' I answered, 'may I remind you of your promise not to put yourself out.'

'I am not putting myself out,' he replied, 'and I have almost finished already.'

With these words he gave the coat a few more strokes with the brush and then let me take both brush and clothes from him. He went out of the porch into another room, whose existence was unknown to me till then. Meanwhile I got dressed. After a time he came out fully dressed. He was wearing the old black clothes he wore all day and every day. We went to the window. The scene had changed completely. It was a really lovely day and the sun rose beaming in an infinite blue. What an extraordinary thing a thunderstorm like that is! This great commotion is caused by the most delicate, the gentlest thing in Nature. The sky's fine invisible vapours, suspended harmlessly in infinite space during the heat of the day or during the heat of several days, increase all the time, until the air at ground level becomes so heated and so rarefied that the heavier air higher up subsides; the lower vapours are cooled by it or they are touched by another breath of cold air, whereby they form into cloud masses immediately, create electrical combustion and spark off a storm, thus causing new cold, creating new vapours which are set in motion by the storm and which spring together and precipitate themselves in a mass upon the earth in the form either of ice or raindrops. And when these have poured down and the air is a mixture of hot and cold again, then it is often pure and clear the next day, capable of again absorbing the vapours created by the heat and so gradually beginning the same interplay again, causing the alternation of rain and sunshine which gives joy to people, animals and plants and makes them flourish.

The infinite quantity of rain the night before had washed the limestone hills smooth and they lay white and gleaming beneath the blue of the sky and the rays of the sun. As they stretched away one behind the other, they exhibited their broken shining colours in soft gradations of grey, yellowish, reddish and pink, and between them lay the long sky-blue shadows, more and more beautiful the further away they were. The meadow in front of the presbytery was fresh and green, the lime-tree had lost its older and weaker leaves in the storm and stood there as though new-born, and the other leaves and bushes round the house raised their wet, shining branches and twigs towards the sun. Only in the vicinity of the foot-bridges was there another, less pleasant spectacle caused by the storm. The Zirder had broken its banks and had flooded a part of the meadow, which as I said above is only slightly higher than the river-bed. The lower part of the high foot-bridge led directly into the floodwater. If one disregarded the damage to the meadow that the flood probably caused by depositing sand on it, then this sight was beautiful too. The great sheet of water shone beneath the rays of the sun, it added a third harmonious shimmering note to the green of the meadow and the grey of the stones, and the bridge made a strange dark line above the silver surface.

The priest showed me several places very far away which could not usually be seen, but which were visible and distinct today in the purified air like clear pictures.

After we had spent a short time contemplating the morning scene, which had drawn our eyes involuntarily to it, the priest brought in some cold milk and black bread for breakfast. We consumed them both and then I got ready to go. I hung my box and my bag over my shoulder on the leather strap, took my rod from the corner near the yellow cupboard, took my white broad-brimmed hat and thanked the priest heartily for giving me shelter during the heavy storm.

'I hope the accommodation was not too plain and bare for you,' he said.

'No, no, Father,' I answered, 'it was so very kind and good of you, I only regret that I disturbed and inconvenienced you: in future I shall pay close attention to the weather and the sky, so that no-one else will have to suffer for my carelessness.'

'I gave you what I had,' he said.

'And I should like very much to be able to do the same for you,' I replied.

'People live side by side, and can often do each other a favour,' said he.

With these words we had reached the porch.

'I must show you my third room too,' he said. 'Here I have a room in which I can dress and undress without anyone seeing me and where I store all sorts of things.'

With these words he led me out of the porch into a side-chamber or rather into a storeroom, the door to which I had not noticed. In the storeroom there were again only very simple objects. Its entire furnishings consisted of a large free-standing softwood cupboard in which clothes and other similar things were kept, probably including the woollen blankets for my bed, a few chairs and a shelf on which lay loaves of black bread and a jar of milk. When we had stepped out of the room again, he locked it, we said good-bye and promised to see each other again soon.

I stepped out into the cool, pure air onto the wet meadow. I was probably still thinking it was strange that we had only ever been on the ground floor and that I had clearly heard footsteps overhead at night and in the morning, but I did not let the thought trouble me again and walked on.

I did not take my proper path but turned towards the Zirder. If you survey a region, if you spend many years mapping regions and their configurations on paper, you take an interest in how they are constituted and become fond of them. I went towards the Zirder because I wanted to see what effects its flooding had produced and what changes this would have introduced in its immediate vicinity. When I had been standing for a while near the water contemplating its ripples, without being able to observe any other effect than the flood itself, I suddenly witnessed a spectacle that was new to me and acquired companions such as I had not had hitherto in this stony country. Apart from my workmen, with whom I was so well acquainted and they so well with me that we must have appeared to each other at times like our tools, I had seen only a few people in my inn, some wanderers on their way and the poor priest among the stones. Now things were to change. As I was looking I saw a lusty, cheerful boy run across the foot-bridge from the far bank, which was higher and so not flooded. When he came to the end of the bridge that led down into the floodwater of the Zirder, he crouched down and as far as I could see through my pocket telescope, he untied his shoelaces and took off shoes and socks. But when both were off, he did not go down into the water, as I had assumed he would, but stayed where he was. Straight away a second boy came and did the same. Then a barefoot boy came and stopped too, then several others. At last a whole swarm of children came running across the bridge and as they came to the end of it, they ducked down, just like a flock of birds that comes flying through the air and then swoops down on a small spot, and I could easily see that they were all busily taking off shoes and socks.

When they were ready, one boy went down off the bridge and carefully entered the water. He was followed by the others. They paid no heed to their trousers but went deep into the water in them, and the little skirts of the girls floated round their legs. To my astonishment I now also saw out in the middle of the water a larger, black-clad figure, which was none other than the poor priest from the Kar. He was standing almost up to his hips in the water. I had not seen him before nor been aware of him entering the water, because I had kept my eyes turned towards the bridge, only looking straight ahead when the children were walking towards where I was standing. All the children went towards the priest and after they had spent a while speaking to him, they turned towards the bank on which I was standing. Since they walked with different degrees of care, they spread out on their way through the water, appearing like black dots on the shining surface and arriving individually at the spot where I stood. When I saw that there was no danger in the generally shallow floodwater, I stayed where I was and let them come. The children arrived and stopped in front of me. At first they looked at me with shy, defiant faces; but as I have been fond of children from my youth, loving them especially for their future promise as human beings, and since I have been blessed with a number of them myself in my marriage, and since finally there are no creatures that recognise as quickly as children do who likes them, trusting people accordingly, I was soon surrounded by a circle of chatty, active children, who were anxious both to put and to answer questions. It was easy to guess where they were going, as they all had their school-bags hanging on their shoulders on leather or linen straps. Because I too had my bag and my box on a leather strap over my shoulder, I must have presented a comical sight standing like an overgrown schoolboy among the little ones. Some were bending down trying to put their shoes and socks on again, others were still holding theirs as they looked up at me and talked to me.

I asked them where they came from and was told that they came from the outlying houses of the parish and were going to school in the Kar.

When I asked them why they had all waited on the foot-bridge rather than entering the water individually as they arrived, they said their parents had told them to be very careful and if the Zirder meadow on the far side of the bridge was flooded, not to go into the water alone but only in a group.

'But what if the water on the meadow were deep enough to reach over the head of an adult?' I asked.

'Then we would turn back,' they answered.

'But if the water only built up when you were off the bridge and out on the meadow, what would you do then?'

'We don't know that.'

I asked them how long they took to get from their houses to where we were and was told an hour. Their houses could indeed be as far away as that. They were situated on the far side of the Zirder in just as infertile a region as the Kar, but their inhabitants were engaged in many business activities, in particular they burned lime and sold it far and wide.

I asked them if their parents had also told them to take care of their shoes and socks, and was told they had, and this inconsistency amazed me, for they were holding their dry shoes and socks in their hands while standing in front of me in trousers and skirts that were wringing wet.

I asked what they did in winter.

'We wade across then, too,' they said.

'But if there is snow water on the meadow?'

'Then we don't take off our shoes but walk through it with them on.'

'And if the bridge is icy?'

'Then we have to take care.'

'And when there is a very bad snowstorm?'

'That doesn't matter.'

'And if there is a great deal of snow on the ground and no path visible?'

'Then we stay at home.'

At that moment the priest came up to me with the last of the children. It was high time too, for the children had already become so friendly that a tiny little boy, who carried the alpha and omega of all knowledge on a little card, wanted to say his alphabet for me.

When the priest caught sight of me in the midst of the children, he greeted me in a very friendly way and said how nice it was of me to hurry up to render assistance too.

I was startled at this assumption, but said immediately that I had not hurried up to render assistance, for I had not known that children would be crossing the bridge, but if assistance had been necessary, I should certainly have rendered it.

During this conversation, as I saw him standing there among the children, I noticed that he must have been much deeper in the water than they, for he was wet almost to his waist and this would have been up to the neck for many of the children. I could not understand this contradiction and asked him about it. It was easy to explain, he said. The farmer from the Wenn, who owned the part of the flooded meadow on which he had just been standing, had had some stones dug out of it two days before and taken away. The hole was still there. When the priest saw the meadow by the Zirder covered in water that day, he had thought the children would probably pass quite close to this hole and one of them might come to grief. For this reason, he said, he had intended to stand near the hole to avert the danger. But because its sides were steep, he had slipped in himself and once he was standing in it, he stayed there. One of the smaller children could even have drowned in the hole, it had been dug so deep. Someone must see to it that the hole was filled in again, for the water was muddy during a flood, making it impossible to judge the depth and unevenness of the ground beneath.

The wet children pressed round the wet priest, they kissed his hand, they spoke to him, he spoke to them or they just stood there, gazing trustfully up at him.

But at last he told them to wring out their wet skirts, squeeze the water out of all their clothes or brush it off and put on shoes and socks if they had them, then they should start to walk so as not to get a chill, placing themselves in the sun so as to dry off more quickly, and then they should go into school and behave themselves there.

'Yes, we'll do that,' they said.

They followed his instructions immediately, they bent or crouched down, they wrung out their skirts, they pressed the water from the legs of their trousers, or they squeezed it from pleats and flaps, and I saw that they were very practised at this. Nor did their soaking matter so much, for they were all wearing either unbleached or red or blue-striped linen clothes, which would soon be dry, scarcely showing that they had been wet; and as for their health, I thought, these young bodies would easily cope with a wetting. When they had finished squeezing out the water, they began to put on their shoes and socks. When they had finished with this too, the priest said good-bye to me again, thanked me again for coming and went with the children along the path towards the Kar.

I called after the children to work very hard in school and they called back: 'Yes, yes', and went off with the priest.

I watched the figure of the priest going across the wet meadow towards the Kar school in the midst of the crowd of children, then I too turned and took the path towards my stones. I no longer intended to return to the inn, but to find my people and the place where we were working at once, partly because I had no time to lose, partly because I was anyhow still provided with the remains of the food that the priest had refused the evening before. I also wanted to reassure my men, who were bound to have heard that I had not been to the inn the night before and might therefore be worried about me.

As I climbed up into the limestone hills, I thought of the children. How great inexperience and innocence is. On the authority of their parents they go to a place where they could meet their death; for the Zirder in flood is very dangerous and, given the ignorance of the children, can be incalculably dangerous. But they know nothing of death. Even if they speak its name, they do not know its essence and their aspiring life has no feeling for annihilation. If they were on the brink of death themselves, they would not know it and they would die before they found it out.

As I was thinking this, I heard the bell from the church tower in the Kar, still audible out among the stones, calling people to the morning Mass which the priest would say and the children would attend.

I went further in among the stones and found my men, who were glad to see me and who had brought me food. –

Since I stayed for a long time in the area, I could not avoid hearing a lot about the priest from other people. I discovered that it was really true that he had been sleeping for many years in his porch on the wooden bench with the Bible under his head, something I had anyway not doubted from his own statement; that it was true too that he wore only the grey woollen clothes in summer and used only one blanket in winter. He wore his clothes for such a long time and kept them going so long that no one could remember him ever getting new ones. He had rented out the upper storey of his presbytery. A man had come, a former civil servant, now retired, who wanted to spend his pension in the place where he had been born. He had taken advantage of the circumstance that the priest was letting his rooms to move in there with his daughter and so always have before his eyes the scene in which he had spent his childhood. The fact that a man was coming back to this area to soothe and cheer his old age, an area from which anyone else would have been striving to escape, was another proof to me of how sweet the place of our birth is, in the words of the poet, and that it never lets one forget it. People said that the priest ate only a piece of black bread for breakfast and supper and that his servant Sabine prepared his midday-meal in her house and brought it over to him at the presbytery. This usually consisted of hot milk or soup or in the summer only cold food. If he was ill, he never sent for a doctor or for medicine, but stayed in bed and fasted until he was better. He used the income from his tenant and from his living to do good to people, whom he chose very carefully. He had no relatives and no friends, it was said. In all the years he had been in the parish no one had ever visited him. All his predecessors had been parish priest in the Kar for only a short time and then left; but he had been there for a very long time and it looked as though he would stay until the end of his days. He never went on visits in the neighbourhood, indeed he did not have much to do with people at all and if he was not going about his priestly business or in the school, then he was reading in his sitting-room or walking across the meadow into the karst or wandering about there in the sand or sitting solitary with his thoughts.

The rumour had spread in the neighbourhood that he must have money on account of his way of life and he had therefore already been burgled three times.

I had no way of knowing what was true or untrue among these details. Whenever I visited him I saw his calm, clear blue eyes, his simple manner and his bitter, unfeigned poverty. Whatever his past had been I did not probe it and did not want to.

I had also heard him preach several sermons. These were filled with simple Christianity and if there were many criticisms to be made of his eloquence, the sermons were nonetheless clear and calm and there was such goodness in them that they sank into the heart.

My period of working in the region grew longer and longer. The clumps of stones in this inhospitable landscape put such difficulties in our path that it looked as though we should need double the amount of time necessary for a similar area of tamed and fertile land. Added to this was the fact the authorities had given us a deadline by which we had to be finished, by setting a date by which we had to start work on another part of the country. I did not want to have it be said that we were dilatory. I therefore exerted myself to the utmost to get the work moving swiftly. I left the inn, I had a wooden hut built for me in the part of the karst where we were working, I lived there and had my and my men's food prepared together over one fire. I gathered everybody together and had them live at the work-site or nearby in specially erected huts, and I took on several new men as unskilled assistants, in order to progress with real diligence and speed.

So we now began hammering, measuring, driving in pegs, drawing out chains, erecting plane-tables, gazing through theodo-lites, drawing lines, measuring angles, calculating and so on. We moved on through the stone hills, and the signs of our passing spread over the limestone. Since it was an honour to be allowed to survey this difficult corner of the globe, I was proud to do it handsomely and elaborately and so I often worked long into the night in my hut. I drew many of the sheets a second time and rejected the less successful ones. The material was ordered appropriately.

It is understandable that the priest should slip to the back of my mind with all this work. But when I had not seen him for some time out on the karst, I became uneasy. I was accustomed to seeing his black figure among the stones, visible from afar because he was the only dark point in the grey limestone plain at dawn or against the reddish limestone under the rays of the sinking sun. I therefore asked after him and discovered that he was ill. I immediately decided to visit him. I used my first free time for this, or rather, I kept the first evening free, and went to him.

I did not find him on his usual bed in the porch but in the living-room on the wooden bench on which he had made me a bed on the night of the storm. The woollen blankets I had had that time had been put under him, and he had allowed this because he was ill. A coverlet had been spread over him too to cover his body and the pine table had been pulled up to his bed, so that he could put books and other things on it.

This was how I found him.

He lay there quietly and could not be persuaded even now to accept a doctor or medicine, not even the simplest remedies which were brought to him in his room. His reason was the strange one that it was a divine temptation to want to interfere, for God had sent the illness and God would remove it or let preordained death follow. Neither did he have very much faith in the efficacy of medicaments and in the skill of doctors.

When he saw me his face looked very cheerful and it was clear that he was glad I had come. I asked him to forgive me for not coming till now, I had not known that he was ill, for I had not left my hut on the karst because of the quantity of work I had to do, but I had missed him, had enquired after him and now I was here.

'That is kind, that is really kind,' he said.

I promised that I would now come more often.

On questioning him more closely about his condition I realised that his illness was not so much serious as protracted and so I went away assured. Nonetheless, one day I ordered post-horses and travelled up to town to take advice from a doctor I knew, and explained to him all the symptoms I had elicited from the priest in the course of several visits. He assured me that I had judged correctly and that the illness was not dangerous, that Nature could do more than man and that the priest would recover though after a somewhat lengthy period.

I now went frequently to the priest's house and I grew so used to spending a little while sitting on the chair near his bed in the evening and chatting to him that gradually I came to do it every day. After my day's work I walked out of the karst over the meadow into the presbytery and completed my evening's work later in my hut by candlelight. I was able to do this all the more easily as I now lived fairly close to the presbytery, which had certainly not been the case when I lived in the inn. But I was not the only one to take an interest in the priest. Old Sabine, his help, not only came across to the priest's dwelling more often than she was really obliged to, she spent most of the time she could spare from her own household, which consisted only of herself, in the presbytery, doing the little services that a sick person requires. Apart from this old woman, a young girl, the daughter of the man who rented the upper storey of the presbytery, also called. The girl, who was extremely beautiful, brought the priest soup or other things or enquired after his health or brought a message from her father to know whether he could be of assistance to the priest in some way. The priest always lay very still when the girl was in the room, he did not move under his coverlet and pulled the blanket up to his chin.

The schoolmaster often came over and a couple of the priest's colleagues from the neighbourhood arrived too, to ask after his health.

Whether it was the illness that put the man into a gentler mood or whether it was the daily intercourse that brought us closer, we had become much better acquainted with one another since the priest's illness. He spoke more and gave more information about himself. I sat at the pine table which stood near his bed and arrived there punctually every day. Since he could not go out and could not go into the karst, I had to report the changes that were taking place there. He asked me where the blackberries were already beginning to ripen at Kulter Hollow, whether the grass up towards Zirder Heights, which always turned such a beautiful green in spring, had already started to get dry and yellow, whether the hips were ripe already, whether the limestone was getting more weathered, whether more pieces of it had fallen into the Zirder and whether the sand was increasing, and such things. I told him all this and described other things too, I told him where we were working, how far we had got and where we would begin the next day. I explained many things about our work which were unclear to him as I did so. I sometimes read aloud for him too, particularly from the newspapers that I had sent to me twice a week by messenger.

One day, when he had taken a considerable turn for the better, he said that he had a favour to ask me.

When I replied that I should be glad to do him any service that was at all in my power, that he only had to say what he wanted and I would certainly do it, he answered: 'Before I tell you my request, I must first tell you a story. Understand, I am not telling it because it is important, but so that you can see how things turned out like this, and so that you will be more inclined to fulfil my wish. You have always been very kind to me and recently, as I discovered, you even went up to town to ask a doctor about my condition. This gives me the courage to turn to you.

'I am the son of a well-to-do tanner from our capital city. My great-grandfather was a foundling from Swabia, who walked into town with his staff in his hand. He learned the tanner's trade thanks to the kindness of some benefactors, he went round various tanneries and worked in them, he travelled to different countries to earn his bread by plying his trade and then to learn the way this trade was carried on elsewhere. Having been instructed, he returned to our town and worked in an eminent leather business. There he distinguished himself by his knowledge, and finally became the foreman; the owner of the business entrusted many business matters to him and put him in charge of various experiments with new processes. Meanwhile, my great-grandfather attempted some small business ventures, buying raw materials cheaply and selling them again. So he amassed a small fortune. When he was already getting on in years, he bought a large garden in a distant suburb, which bordered on derelict land. On this land he built a tannery and a little house, married a poor girl and now ran his own business and his own commercial ventures as his own master. He built it up and died a respected man, well-thought-of by business people. He had only one son, my grandfather.

'My grandfather carried on his father's business. He expanded it even further. He built a large house at one side of the garden, so that the windows opened onto where subsequently there would be a street. At the back of the house he built workshops and warehouses. Grandfather loved building in general. Apart from the house he built other workshops and various commercial buildings round a great courtyard. He sold the unused land next to our garden, and because the city was in the middle of a great expansion, these lots of land fetched a very high price. He surrounded our garden with a wall which had regular spaces in it filled with iron railings. He developed the business considerably and built the great storehouses in which the merchandise we produced ourselves and that in which we dealt could be stored. Grandfather again had only one son to carry on the business, the father of myself and my brother.

'Father only built the drying-rooms on top of the workshops, and he built a small wing onto the house on the garden side and a glass-house. In his day, a road had already been built in front of the windows of the main building, lined with houses, paved with stones and filled with people walking and driving. From my childhood I can still remember that our house was very big and spacious, that it had many courtyards and different areas which were used for our business. I like most of all to remember the beautiful garden in which trees, flowers, herbs and vegetables grew. The workmen, stained almost a yellowish brown from their work, went around in their linen clothes in the rooms of the building and in the courtyards, bales of leather lay piled up in the great storeroom at ground level and in the two smaller ones leading off it, skins hung on poles in the drying-loft and in the great sorting-rooms they were separated out and graded. In the warehouse they lay neatly in compartments. There were cows in the byre, in the stable there were six horses and in the coach-house there were coaches and carriages, and I can even remember our big black dog, Hassan, who lived in the great courtyard and let everyone in at the gate there, but no one out.

'Our father was a big, strong man, who moved around the spacious rooms of the house, inspected everything and directed everything. He hardly ever left the house, except on business, or when he went to church; and when he was at home and was not supervising the business, he sat at his desk, writing. He could often be seen in the garden also, walking about with his hands behind his back, or just standing there, looking up at a tree or contemplating the clouds. He enjoyed fruit-growing, employed a gardener for this alone and sent for grafts from all over Europe. He was very good to his men, he payed them sufficient, saw that each got his due, but also that each fulfilled his obligations. When one of them was ill, he went to visit him himself, asked him how he was and often gave him medicine himself. In the house he was generally just called "Father". He was against display, he dressed rather too plainly and insignificantly than too imposingly, his house was simply furnished and when he drove out in a carriage, then it had to look very ordinary and middle-class.

'We brothers were twins, and our mother had died at our birth. Father had held her in great esteem and did not therefore take a second wife, for he was never able to forget her. Because there was too much noise on the street, we were put in the back wing giving onto the garden, the one father had built. The room in which we lived was large, with windows looking onto the garden; this room was separated from the rest of the house by a long corridor, and so that we did not have to go through the rest of the house every time we went out, Father had steps built up to the garden-wing, by means of which one could go directly into the garden and from there out into the open.

'After mother's death, Father had entrusted the running of the household to a servant who had already been in mother's service before her marriage, and had more or less been her governess. Mother had commended her to Father on her death-bed. She was called Luise. She was in charge of everything to do with food and drink, with laundry, crockery, furniture, cleaning stairs and rooms, heating, airing, in short, of everything to do with the inner workings of the household. She was set over all the maids. She also looked after the needs of us two boys.

'When we grew older we were given a tutor who lived with us. Two handsome rooms near ours were furnished for him, and the three rooms together constituted the whole part of what was called the garden-wing. From him we learned all that children have to learn at the beginning of their schooling; our letters, reading, writing, arithmetic. My brother was much cleverer than I was. He could remember his letters, he could combine them into syllables, he could read clearly and connectedly, his sums always came out right and his letters were always written evenly and on the same line. Things were different with me. I could not remember the names of the letters, then I was unable to say the syllable they made up, and when I was reading, the long words were very difficult and I was in torment when there was no comma for a long stretch. I followed all the rules in arithmetic but ended up usually with quite different figures from those I was supposed to get. When I was writing I held my pen very carefully, looked fixedly at the line, moved evenly up and down, and yet the letters were not even, they dipped below the line, they leaned in different directions and I could not make a fine line with the pen. Our tutor was very keen, my brother showed me many things too until I could do them. In our room we had a big oak table at which we studied. There were several drawers along each of the long sides of this table; one side was used by my brother to keep his school things in, the other by me. In each of the corners at the back of the room was a bed and next to the bed was a bedside-table. At night the door between our room and our tutor's bedroom stood open.

'We went into the garden very often, and amused ourselves there. We often drove through the town behind our greys, we drove into the country too or somewhere else, and our tutor always sat in the carriage with us. We went out with him, we took walks either along the top of the city walls or along a tree-lined street, and if something worth seeing came to town and Father allowed it, we went with our tutor to see it.

'When we were instructed in the primary school subjects, we went on to those of the grammar school and our teacher told us that we would have to pass an examination in them given by the headmaster and the professors at the grammar school. We studied Latin and Greek, we studied natural history and geography, arithmetic, essay-writing and other things. We were given religious instruction by the worthy curate from our parish church and Father set us a good example in religious and moral questions. But it was just the same now as it had been in our earlier lessons. My brother learned everything very well, he did his exercises well, he could translate Latin and Greek into German, he could do algebra, and his letters and essays were as if written by a grown-up. I could not do that. I was certainly very industrious, and at the beginning of every subject things did not go so badly, I could understand the material and could say it and do it; but when we progressed, I became confused, things got muddled, I could not find my place and had no understanding of the concepts. When I was translating from German I understood all the rules perfectly, but there were always several contradictory rules to apply to any given word and when I had done my task, it was always full of mistakes. It was just the same when translating into German. There were always such strange words in the Latin or Greek text which could not be fitted together and when I looked them up in the dictionary, they were not there and the rules that we had learned in our grammar were not followed by the Greek and Latin authors. Things were best in two subsidiary subjects that Father had ordered us to learn, because we should need them in the future, that is, in French and Italian, for which a special teacher came to the house twice a week. My brother

and our tutor took a lot of trouble over me and tried to help me.
But when the examinations came, I was not up to standard and
my results were not good.

'Several years went by like this. When the time had passed that
Father had allotted for us to learn these things, he said that we
must now learn the business, which he would hand over to us at
his death and which we should carry on together as honourably
and as respectably as our and his forefathers had done. He said
we must be taught it in the same way as our forefathers, so that
we should know how to act in the same way as they. We must
learn all the knacks and knowledge of our trade from the bottom up, we must first be able to work at our trade as well as any
good or outstanding workman, so that we could judge the workers and their work, so that we should know how to deal with the
workers and be respected by them. Only then should we proceed to learn the further aspects necessary to the business.

'Father wanted us also to live as our workpeople lived, so that
we should understand their position and not be strangers to
them. Therefore he wanted us to eat, live and sleep with them.
Our previous tutor left us, giving us each a book as a keepsake,
we moved out of our schoolroom and went across to the
workers' quarters.

'Father had picked out the best craftsman in our employ, who
was also the foreman, to be our teacher and to keep an eye on us
generally. Each of us was given a place in his workshop, was
provided with tools and had to begin like any apprentice. We
came together to eat at the same table as our workers, but we sat
at the very bottom with the apprentices. We slept in the apprentices' dormitory, and next-door slept the foreman who was the
only one to have his own room. For that reason the foreman
always had to be not only a very skilful worker but distinguished
too by his justice, morals and way of life. No one who was not was
ever given this position in our firm. He was in charge of the
apprentices in particular because they still needed to be trained.
We were given the same bed as the apprentices to sleep on and
for clothing we wore the same costume as all our workers.

'So we began. But it was just the same here too as in all previous things. My brother worked quickly and the pieces he made
were beautiful. I did things just as the foreman told us, but my
pieces did not turn out as they should and were not as beautiful

as my brother's. However, I was extremely hard-working. In the evening we often sat in the great workers' rest-room and listened to their talk. There were workers too who set a bad example, but we were not supposed to be led astray by them, rather to be strengthened and put off by them. Father used to say that he who wants to live must get to know life, the good and the bad, and must not be weakened by the latter but strengthened. On such evenings I liked to fetch things the workmen sent me for – wine, cheese and other things. For that reason they were very fond of me.

'When we had been trained in one workshop, and could do those things, we went to another one, until we were given our articles and could enter the commercial site as apprentices. When we had finished there too, we entered the office to learn the paper side of the business.

'At last, after a lengthy period, our years of apprenticeship were over and we entered the room of the sons of the house and were given the same simple clothes to wear as our father wore.

'Not long after the completion of our apprenticeship and when my brother was already involved in all parts of the business, our father fell ill. He was not so ill that any danger was feared and he did not have to stay in bed either, but his strong figure wasted, it grew thinner, he walked around the house and the garden a lot and did not take such an interest in the business, as it had previously been his custom and his joy to do.

'My brother took over the direction of the firm, I did not need to interfere, and finally Father spent the greater part of the day, when he was not in the garden, in his sitting-room.

'Around this time I asked to be allowed to move back into our old schoolroom and to live there. This request was granted and I moved my possessions down the long corridor into it. Because Father was not issuing any instructions or orders to do with the business and because my brother did not entrust any work to me, I had leisure to do what I wanted. Because no one had reproached me for not getting sufficiently good results in my school-subjects, I decided to do them all again and to learn everything properly. I took a book out of the drawer, sat down with it and read the beginning. I understood it all, learned it and remembered it. Next day I repeated what I had learned the previous day, tested myself to see if I still knew it and learned a new portion as well. I only set myself a small amount but I tried to understand that and to store it thoroughly in my memory. I gave myself exercises to do and they came out right. I took out the exercises that our tutor had given us before, did them again and did not make any mistakes this time. I did the same with the other books as I had done with the first. I studied very hard and gradually I was busy in the study the whole day long. If I had some free time, I liked to sit with the book our tutor had given us as a keepsake in my hand and think about the man who had been with us then.

'In the schoolroom everything was the same as it had once been. The great oak table still stood in the middle of the room, it still had the scars we had cut in the wood either on purpose with a knife or by accident with our tools, it still exhibited the dried-up rivers of ink that were the result of an accident with the ink-well which no amount of washing and scouring could remedy. I pulled out the drawers. In mine my textbooks still lay, with the red ink or pencil marks showing how far we had to learn; my exercise books were still there, in which our exercises were worked out and the red ink with which the teacher had marked our mistakes stood out strongly; old dusty pens and pencils still lay there. It was the same with my brother's drawers. His old school things lay there in excellent order. I now studied at the same table at which I had studied a number of years before. I slept in the same bed and had the bedside-table with the light next to it. But my brother's bed remained empty and was always covered over. In the two rooms in which our tutor had lived then, I kept some chests with clothes and other things, but apart from this they were unoccupied and contained only the old furniture. I was the sole occupant of the back garden-wing and this state of affairs lasted several years.

'Suddenly our father died. It was a frightful shock to me. No-one had believed that his death was so near or that he could be in any danger at all. He had indeed kept himself to himself more and more recently, his figure had become rather wasted and he often spent several days in bed, but we had got so used to this condition that it appeared normal to us in the end; every inhabitant of the house had looked on him as a father, he was such a necessary part of the household that his departure was unthinkable and I had really never thought that he could die or that he could be so ill. In the first moments everything was in confusion, but then the arrangements for the funeral were made. All the poor people of the suburb, men from his line of business, his friends, many strangers, his workmen and his two sons followed his coffin. Many tears were shed and people said that an excellent man, an exceptional citizen and an honourable businessman had been buried. After a few days the will was read and it said that we two brothers were the heirs and that the business should pass to us both jointly.

'After some time my brother told me that the whole burden of the business now lay on our shoulders, and I revealed to him then that I had caught up on Latin, Greek, natural history, geography and arithmetic, in which I had made scant progress at the time we were being taught them, and that I was now almost perfect in these things. But he answered that Latin, Greek and the other subjects were not necessary in our profession and that I had taken this trouble too late. I replied that, just as I had caught up on all these school subjects, so too I would now learn gradually the things directly necessary to our business. To this he said that if the business had to wait for me, it would have perished by the time I was ready. But he promised that he would see to things as well as was in his power and that he would leave it to me to do what I liked, that I could keep an eye on things, that I could assist him, that I could carry on learning the business, and that my portion should be kept for me in any case undiminished.

'I went back into the schoolroom, did not interfere in business matters because I did not seem to understand them, and my brother left me there. Indeed, he even sent me better equipment and provided me with several comforts, so that my time in that room should not be unpleasant for me. After some time he appeared with our lawyer, with officials of the law and with witnesses, friends of Father's, and gave me a legal document on which was set out what claims I had on the inheritance, what was my share and what was my due in the future. My brother, the witnesses and I signed the document.

'I carried on studying and my brother directed the whole of the business. At the end of a quarter, he brought me a sum of money, saying this was the interest due to me from my portion of the inheritance which was invested in the company. He said he

would give me this sum once a quarter. He asked if I was satisfied
and I answered that I was very satisfied.

'After another period had passed, he once made the point to
me that my studies should lead to something and asked me if I
were not inclined to work towards one of the learned professions, for which the things I was now occupied on could be the
preparation. When I answered that I had never thought about it
and that I did not know which profession would be right for me,
he said that that was not necessary yet, I should just gradually
take the examinations in the knowledge I had now acquired, so
that I should have certificates in my hands to prove my preparation, that I should try to acquire the knowledge I lacked, so
that when the time came to decide on a particular profession, I
should have gathered more experience and should then be in a
better position to decide in what direction to turn.

'I liked this suggestion very much and agreed. After some
time I took the first examinations in the lower subjects and
passed them extremely well. This gave me courage and I pro-
ceeded with zeal to learn the other subjects. My heart trembled
inwardly with joy to think that I might belong to one of those
professions that I had always looked on with such respect and
that served the world with their scholarship and their skill. I
worked very hard, I was miserly with my own time, I scarcely
went into other rooms in the house and when another period of
time had passed, I was able to take another examination with
great success.

'So I lived entirely in the back garden-wing, was allowed to go
on doing so and was able to devote myself with a good conscience to my efforts.

'The back of our garden bordered on a second garden, which
was not really a garden but rather an untended green with a tree
here and there. On the other side of the railing of our garden
ran a path which was part of this other garden. In that garden I
always saw really beautiful white sheets and other linen hung up
to dry on long lines. I often looked at it, sometimes from my
windows, sometimes through the railing if I happened to be in
the garden. When the washing was dry, it was put into a basket;
a woman stood by and organised this. Then wet washing was
hung up in its place, after the woman had wiped the lines
stretched between posts. This woman was a widow. Her husband

had had employment which had paid well. Shortly after his death his kind old master had died and his son had such a hard heart that he gave the widow only just enough to keep her from starving. She therefore rented the little garden next to ours, and rented the little house too which stood in the garden. With the money her husband had left her she arranged the little house and the garden so as to be able to take in washing for people who trusted her, fine laundry and any other kind. She had coppers built into the little house and other equipment to boil the washing and to soak it. She had washrooms installed, she prepared places where the washing could be washed and ironed and folded, and she had a drying-room erected for periods of bad weather and for the winter. In the garden she had posts hammered into the ground at equally-spaced intervals, rings fastened to the posts and lines, which were often changed, pulled through the rings. Behind the little house flowed a brook which was what had led the widow to set her laundry up here. Water was pumped from the brook into the coppers by means of conduits and a washhouse had been erected over the brook. The woman employed many girls to work and do things properly; she stood over them, directing and showing them how to do everything correctly and, because she did not let the washing be handled with brushes and rough tools and took care that it was very white and that worn patches were mended, she acquired so many customers that she had to extend the laundry and employ more washerwomen. High-born ladies often came and sat with her under the big pear-tree in the garden.

'This woman had a little daughter, a child, no, she was no longer a child – I did not in fact know at that time whether she was still a child or not. This little daughter had very delicate red cheeks, and she had delicate red lips and innocent brown eyes, which gazed pleasantly about her. She had big gentle eyelids with long eyelashes, which looked delicate and modest. Her dark, smooth hair was parted neatly by her mother, and it lay beautifully round her head. Sometimes the girl carried a long basket of fine cane; over the basket there was a white, very fine cloth, and in the basket there must have been very special linen which the child was taking to some lady or other.

'I just loved to watch this. Sometimes I would stand at the window and look across at the garden in which there was always washing hanging, except when it was night or bad weather, and I was very fond of the white things. Sometimes the girl would come out, sometimes she went onto the green and performed various tasks, or I saw her standing at the window studying, although the little house was very much hidden behind branches. Soon too I got to know at what time she would deliver the washing and then I sometimes went down into the garden and stood at the iron railing. Since the path went past the railing, the girl had to pass me. She knew very well that I was there, for she was always embarrassed and drew herself up as she walked.

'One day when I had seen the girl with her washing coming from afar, I quickly put a very beautiful peach which I had already picked for this purpose through the railings onto her path and went into the bushes. I went so deep into them that I could not see her. When a sufficient period had passed for her to have gone by long ago, I came out again; but the peach still lay on the path. Then I waited for when she would come back again. But when she had already returned and I looked, the peach still lay on the path. I took it back again. The same thing happened again some time later. The third time I stayed where I was as the peach lay with its soft red cheek on the sand and, when she came near, I said: "Take it." She looked at me, hesitated a while, then bent down and took the fruit. I no longer remember where she put it, but I do know for certain that she took it. After some time had passed, I did the same again and she took the fruit again. This happened several times and finally I held the peach out to her with my hand through the railings.

'At last we got to speak to each other. I cannot remember what we said. It must have been something ordinary. We also took each other by the hand.

'In time I could no longer wait for her to come with her little basket. I was already standing every time at the railings. She stopped when she came up to me and we talked. Once I asked her to show me the things in the little basket. She parted the linen covering with its little strings and showed me the things. There lay ruffles, fine sleeves and other things that had been ironed. She told me what they were called and when I said how beautiful they were, she replied: "This linen belongs to an old countess, a noble lady, I always have to carry it to her myself, so that nothing will happen to it, for it is so fine." When I said again: "Yes, it is beautiful, it is extraordinarily beautiful," she answered: "Indeed it is beautiful, my mother says that after silver linen is the first possession in a household, it is fine white silver too and if it is dirty, it can be cleaned until it is again fine white silver. It is our noblest clothing and nearest our skin. That is why mother collected so much linen that we had enough after father's death, and that is why she has undertaken the laundering of other people's linen, and does not allow it to be touched with rough and unsuitable things. Gold is precious too, but it is not a household object, it is only a decoration." At these words I remembered that I had always seen the finest white linen on the speaker's body, just visible at her neckline or at her cuffs, and that her mother wore a snow-white cap with a fine ruffle framing her face.

'From this moment on I began to collect very fine linen, like the countess's, and to buy all kinds of silver household objects with the money my brother gave me every quarter.

'Once, when we were standing together as usual, her mother came past close by and called: "Johanna, you should be ashamed of yourself." We were indeed ashamed and ran away from one another. My cheeks were burning with shame and I should have been very startled to have come across someone in the garden.

'From that time on we no longer saw each other at the railings. I went into the garden every time she passed by but I stayed in the bushes so that she could not see me. She passed with reddened cheeks and downcast eyes.

'In the two rooms next to my living-room I had chests placed, constructed with shallow upper drawers, into which I placed my silver, but deep lower ones, into which I put the linen. I placed together what belonged together and tied it up with red silk ribbons.

'After a long time, I no longer saw the girl pass by the iron railing, I did not dare to ask after her, but when I finally did so I found out that she had been sent to another town and that she had married a distant relative.

'I thought then that I would weep my soul out of my body.

'But after a while something frightful happened. My brother dealt with a big money-changer, who always gave him money for running expenses up to an agreed credit limit, and collected his money again according to the circumstances. I do not know if other people undermined my brother's credit, or whether our banker became mistrustful himself, because two firms that owed us a great deal of money failed and cost us our fortune, but he refused from now on to honour bills of our house. My brother had to cover several of them and he had not enough ready money to do so. The friends he turned to became mistrustful themselves and so it happened that our creditors brought an action against us, that our house, our other possessions and our goods were valued to see if they were sufficient, without having recourse to the sums owed to us. When this became known, all those who had a claim on us and wanted it paid came forward but those who owed us money did not. My brother did not want to tell me anything, so that I should not be hurt, he thought he could brush through it. But since we were ordered to sell our house immediately to cover our banking debts, he could no longer hide it from me. He came to my room and told me everything. I gave him the money I had; for my needs were very small and I had been able to save a great part of my income. I opened the narrow upper drawers of my chests and put all my silver onto our oak study table and offered it to him. He said it was not enough to save the house and the business and he refused to accept it. The court did not make any claim on me but I could not bear my brother to let a claim go unfilled and burden his conscience, so I added everything I had to the other assets. It was enough to pay all the creditors what they were owed and to satisfy them down to the smallest detail. But our beautiful house with its rear-wing and our beautiful garden were gone.

'I do not know what other blows fell, but the prospect of beginning a small business with the rest of the money and gradually pulling ourselves up again came to nothing in a short time.

'My brother, who was unmarried, grieved so much that he took a fever and died. I alone and several people to whom he had done good followed the coffin. Since there had been a single son as the only child and heir since my grandfather's day down to us two brothers and since our house-keeper Luise had died a long time before, I had no relatives and no friends.

'I had got the idea of becoming a proclaimer of the Lord's word, that is, a priest. Even if I were unworthy, I thought, yet

God might give me enough of His grace for me to become a not quite contemptible servant and representative of His word and His works.

'I collected my certificates and documents, went to the seminary and asked for admission with bated breath. It was granted to me. I moved into the seminary at the appointed time and began my novitiate. It passed well and when I was finished, I was ordained a servant of God. I had my first ministries as a curate to older priests in the parishes entrusted to them. There I came into various situations and got to know the human race. I learned spiritual and secular things from the parish priests. When such a number of years had passed that people could not think badly of me if I applied for a parish, I asked for the present parish and got it. I have been here for twenty-seven years and will not leave it now. People say the living is bad, but it brings in enough for a preacher of the gospel to live on. They say the region is ugly, but that is not true either, one must just look at it in the right way. My predecessors were moved from here to other parishes. But because my fellow priests of my own age or somewhat younger who are still alive distinguished themselves greatly during their novitiate and are superior to me in every characteristic, I shall never ask to be promoted from here to somewhere else. My parishioners are good people, they have not closed their minds to some of my words of instruction and will not do so in the future either.

'But I have another more worldly and more particular reason for staying in this place. You will find out what it is some day if you grant the request I am going to make of you. I come now to this request, but I must say something else before I mention it. I began to save in this presbytery for a purpose, the purpose is not a bad one, it concerns not just a temporal good but another good too. I will not tell you what it is now, it will be revealed one day, but it is for this that I began to save. I brought no fortune with me from my father's house. Whatever money came in was used for various things and there has been no income at all for years. From my father's inheritance I have only the crucifix that hangs there by the door over the water-font. My grandfather bought it once in Nuremberg and Father gave it to me as a present, because I always liked it. So I began to save from the income of my living. I wore simple clothes and tried to keep them a long time, I got rid of my bed and slept on the bench in the porch and put my Bible as a witness and a help under my head. I kept no more servants and pay old Sabine for those services which are sufficient for me. I eat what is good and beneficial for the human body. I have rented out the upper storey of my presbytery. I have already been reprimanded for this twice by the episcopal consistory, but now they let it go. Because people thought I had ready money, which indeed was true, I have been burgled three times, but I began again from the beginning. Because the thieves took only money, I tried to remove it from their clutches. I have invested it against security, and when there are small amounts of interest, I always add them to the capital. So I have not been molested for many years. In this long period my condition has become a habit and I love it. I have only one sin on my conscience with regard to this saving. I still have the beautiful linen I acquired and kept in the school-room in our garden-wing. It is a serious fault but I have tried to remedy it by even greater savings in my bodily needs and other things. I am so weak that I cannot rid myself of this fault. It would be too sad if I had to give the linen away. After my death it too will bring something in and I do not use the greater part of it, after all.'

Now I knew why he was ashamed of such magnificent linen.

'I do not like it,' he continued, 'that I cannot help the people here as I would like; but I cannot take the money away from my purpose and not everyone can be a benefactor to the extent he would like, the greatest fortune would not be big enough for that.

'See, now I have told you everything about how things were for me in the past and how things are with me now. Now comes my request. Perhaps, when you remember all that I have told you, you will accede to it. But it is troublesome to carry it out and only your kindness and goodness allows me to utter it. I have deposited my will at the court-house in Karsberg Castle. I assume that it is safe there and I have the receipt here in my house. But all human things are changeable, and fire, devastation, enemy attack or some other misfortune can happen and endanger my will. Therefore I have made two exactly similar copies, to be deposited as safely as possible, so that they will appear after my death and their purpose will be fulfilled. My request therefore is that you should take one copy into your hands and keep it safe. I shall either keep the other one here or give it to someone also, to be kept until it can fulfil its purpose equally. And you must allow me to write you a short letter from time to time, after you have left this region, to let you know that I am still alive. When the letters stop, then you will know that I am dead. Then you must have the will sent by a reliable messenger and against a receipt to Karsberg, or to wherever the officials are who can put it into effect. This is all just a precaution, in case the legally deposited will should get lost. The will is sealed and you will discover its contents after my death, if you are not disinclined to grant me my request.'

I told the priest that I granted his request with pleasure, that I should preserve the document as carefully as my own best things which would be irreplaceable if they were destroyed and that I should gladly fulfil all his instructions. Nonetheless, I hoped that the moment was still very distant in which the seals on the will and its two companions would be broken.

'We are all in God's hands,' said he, 'it can happen today, it can happen tomorrow, it can take many years. For the sake of the goal towards which I am working, along with my pastoral duties, I hope that it does not come so soon; but God knows what is best and indeed He does not need me for the accomplishment of this task.'

'But since I could die before you,' I replied, 'I will put a written instruction with the will for safety's sake, which will transfer my obligations to someone else.'

'You are very good,' he answered, 'I knew that you would act like a friend, I knew it for sure. Here is the document.'

With these words he pulled his document from under his pillow. It was folded and sealed with three seals. He placed it into my hand. I examined the seals, they were perfect and undamaged and bore a simple cross. On the top page of the document were the words: 'Last Will and Testament of the Parish Priest in the Kar'. I went to the table, took a sheet of paper out of my pocket-book, wrote on it that I had received a document from the parish priest in the Kar on the day named, sealed with three seals bearing a cross, and carrying the legend: 'Last Will and Testament of the Parish Priest in the Kar'. I gave him this receipt and he pushed it under his pillow. I put the will meanwhile into the bag in which I kept my drawings and other work.

After this conversation I stayed for a considerable time with the priest, and our conversation turned to other indifferent subjects. Sabine came in to bring him some food, the girl from the first floor came down to ask after his health. When the stars were standing in the sky, I went back to my hut through the pale stones and the soft sand and thought about the priest. I put the will into my trunk, where I kept my best things, in order to put it into safe-keeping later at home.

The period after the priest's narration passed for me in my wilderness of stones as it had passed previously. We measured and worked and drew. I collected material during the day, visited the priest towards evening, sat for a few hours at his bedside and then worked by night in my hut, while one of my men roasted me a small piece of meat on our improvised cooking-place.

Gradually the priest recovered, at last he got up, as the doctor in the town had predicted, then he was able to go out in front of his house, then he went into the church again, and finally he came out into the karst, wandered around in the hills or stood near us and watched us working.

But everything comes to an end and so did our long stay in the karst. We had moved forward all the time, getting closer and closer to the boundary of our designated area. Finally the pegs were set up along it, we had measured up to it and after a small amount of paperwork, a complete image of the Steinkar region was mapped out on many sheets of paper in our portfolio. The rods, pegs and tools were taken away immediately, the huts were torn down, my men separated according to their destinations and the karst was again empty and free of these inhabitants.

I packed my trunk, said goodbye to the priest, to the school-teacher, to Sabine, to the priest's tenant and his daughter and to other people, had my trunk brought to the inn on the high road, walked there myself, ordered posthorses and when these arrived, drove away from the scene of my former activity.

I must mention a very strange feeling that overcame me as I did so. A deep sorrow took hold of me as I left the region, which had seemed so frightful to me the first time I entered it. As I drove further and further into more populous places, I felt compelled to turn round in my carriage and look back at the stones whose reflections shimmered so gently and softly, and in whose hollows lay the beautiful blue shadows where I had spent such a long time, while I was now driving out to green meadows, to patchwork fields and under high, soaring trees.

Five years later I was in the neighbourhood and seized the opportunity to visit the karst again. I found that the priest walked about in it from time to time as before, or sometimes sat on one of the stones looking around. His clear blue eyes had remained the same.

I showed him the letters I had received from him, which I had kept. He thanked me very warmly for having answered each of them, he was glad of my letters and often reread them. He showed them to me, as we sat as of old again at the pine table in his living-room.

The sky-blue ribbon of the Zirder flowed through the stones; these were still grey and the sand lay at their feet. The strips of green and the few bushes were the same as always. In the inn the landlord, the landlady and nearly all their children were the same too, even the same guests seemed to be sitting at the tables, so unchanging are the people who travel over the hills on business in those areas.

After this visit to the region, I neither went there again on business nor did I find the time to make a special journey. Many years passed and the priest's wish that God would allow him to live on for a long time to accomplish his purpose seemed to be coming true. Every year I received several letters from him which I answered regularly, and regularly they arrived again the next year. There was one thing I thought I noticed, that is, that the letters looked rather as though the writer's hand were trembling.

Many, many years later a letter from the schoolteacher arrived. In it he wrote that the priest was ill, that he was talking of me and that he had said: 'If only he knew that I was ill.' He was therefore taking the liberty of letting me know this, uncertain as to whether he was doing the right thing, and he therefore asked me to forgive him for being so importunate.

I answered that I could not regard his letter as being importunate but that he had done me a service in writing it, for I was very concerned about the priest in the Kar. I asked him to write to me more often about the priest's health and if it grew

worse, to tell me this immediately. And if God should send him
the fate of all mortals unexpectedly soon, then he should let me
know this without delay too.

To reassure the priest I also wrote to him that I had heard of
his illness and that I had asked the schoolteacher to send me
frequent reports of his health; I begged him not to exert himself
to write to me, that he should have his bed made up in the living-
room and that his indisposition might vanish again in a short
time as in earlier years. I told him that my work would not allow
me to pay him a visit just at present.

Nonetheless, he wrote me a few lines in answer that he was very,
very old, that he was waiting patiently and that he was not afraid.

After the schoolteacher had sent two letters in which he said
that there was no change in the priest's condition, a third came
which announced that the priest had died after receiving the
Last Sacraments.

I reproached myself, put everything aside and got ready for
the journey. I took the sealed document out of my cupboard, I
took the priest's letters as well to confirm if necessary that the
handwriting was the same and set off for Karsberg.

When I arrived there I received the information that the priest's
will had been legally deposited in the castle, that a second one
had been found among his effects, and that I should appear in
two days' time at the castle to present my will, whereupon all
three could be opened and examined.

During these two days I went to the Kar. The schoolteacher
told me about the priest's last days. He had lain there quietly
during his illness, as he had done during that other illness when
I had visited him so often. He had again taken no medicine,
until the parish priest from the Wenn, his neighbour, who had
given him the Last Sacraments, made clear to him that he
should use secular remedies too and leave it to God as to
whether they worked or not. From that moment he took
everything he was given and let people do anything they wanted
with him. Again he lay in his living-room, where a bed had been
made up for him with the woollen blankets. Sabine was with him
all the time. When he got to the point of death, he made no
special preparations, he just lay there as he did every day. It was
not possible to find out whether or not he knew that he was now
dying. His manner was just as usual and he spoke of ordinary

things. Finally, he fell quietly asleep and all was over.

They undressed him in order to prepare him for the laying-out. His finest linen was put on him. Then he was dressed in his threadbare clothes and over them a surplice. In this costume he was laid out. People came in great numbers to see him, for they had never seen anything like it; he was the first parish priest to die in the Kar. He lay there with his white hair, his face was gentle, only much paler than usual, and his blue eyes were closed. Several of his priestly colleagues came to bury him. As he was lowered into the earth, many of those present wept.

I asked then after the tenant on the first floor. He came down to the porch of the presbytery, where I was, to talk to me himself. He was almost completely bald and was therefore wearing a black skullcap on his head. I asked after his beautiful daughter who had been a lithe young girl at the time when she used to visit the sick priest in my presence. She was now married in the capital and the mother of almost grown-up children. She had not been with the priest either in his last days. The tenant told me that he would probably have to move to his daughter's now, for he would certainly lose the apartment when the living was filled again, and he would not find another one in the Kar.

Old Sabine was the only one who had not changed. She looked just as when she had nursed the priest in his illness during my first visit to the Kar. No one knew how old she was and she did not know it either.

I had to remain in the porch of the presbytery because the living-room and the storeroom next to it were sealed up. Only the wooden bench, the priest's bed, stood in its place, for no one had noticed it. But the Bible no longer lay on the bench, I was told that it had been taken into the living-room.

When the two days that had to elapse before the reading of the will were up, I went to Karsberg and presented myself at the appointed hour in the courtroom. There was quite a number of people there, including the leaders of the parish council and the witnesses who had been called. The two wills and the list of the priest's effects lay on the table. My receipt for the priest's will, which had been found among his effects, was shown to me and I was asked to produce the will. I handed it over. The handwriting and the seals were examined and the will was recognised as valid.

In the usual manner the legally deposited will was opened first and read. Then followed the one brought by me. It was word for word the same as the first one. Finally, the will that had been found in the priest's house was opened and it too was word for word the same as the first two. The date and the signature were the same in all three documents. All three wills were declared immediately to be three copies of the same will.

But the contents of the will surprised everyone.

The priest's words, omitting the introduction in which he called on God's help, placed the dispositions of the will under His protection and declared himself to be in full possession of his faculties, ran like this: 'Each person finds or should seek something to accomplish apart from his employment and his profession, so that he can do all that he is called upon to do in his life and I too have found something to accomplish apart from my pastoral duties: I must remove the danger the children from the houses in the Steinkar neighbourhood are in. The Zirder often rises and can then become a raging torrent, which appears quickly, as happened twice in the first years of my ministry because of cloud-bursts, which then washed all foot-bridges and other bridges away. The banks are low and the bank on the Kar side is even lower than that on the other side. Three dangers are possible: either the bank on the Kar side is flooded, or the other bank is flooded as well or the foot-bridge is washed away. But the children from the houses round about must cross the foot-bridge to go to school. When the bank on the Kar side is flooded and they enter the water from the bridge, any one of them can slip into a pit or hollow and come to grief there, for the muddy water hides the bottom during a flood; or the waters can rise so quickly, while the children are wading through them, that they cannot reach dry land in time and all are drowned; or they can get onto the foot-bridge from the far side, can find the water on the Kar side too deep, can delay too long hesitating and discussing what to do until the far bank is also under water which is too deep – then the bridge has become an island, the children are standing on it and can be washed away with it. And if none of these things happens, in the winter their little feet wade through meltwater which has lumps of ice in it, which is very injurious to their health.

'To remove this danger for the future I began to save, and my instructions are as follows: from the sum of money that shall be found in my possession after my death, augmented by the money which shall result from the sale of my effects, a schoolhouse shall be erected in the midst of where the schoolchildren live, then such a portion of the money shall be invested as to provide for the teachers in the school; further, a portion of it shall be invested so that a yearly compensation shall be paid from the interest to the schoolteacher in the Kar because of the loss of his pupils, and finally, if there is anything over, it shall be the property of my servant Sabine.

'I have made three identical wills for greater security and if any disposition or statement is found in my papers that does not have the same contents and date as these wills, then it is invalid.

'But to lessen the danger in the meantime, I go out onto the meadow every day by the river bank and see where there are any ditches, holes and hollows and put a post in them. I ask the owner of the meadow to level out all holes and hollows as soon as possible and he has always acceded to my requests. I go out when the meadow is flooded and try to help the children. I have got to know the weather, in order to foresee a flood and to warn the children. I never go far from the parish, so as not to be negligent. And I shall do this in future always.'

The accounts of the priest's savings up to the date of the wills were included with them. The accounts from that date until the day of the priest's death were found among his papers. These accounts had been kept with great exactitude. One could see from them how careful the priest had been in his saving. The tiniest amounts, even pfennigs, were included and new sources of finance, the most unlikely ones, were tapped, so that a small trickle of money should flow from them.

The fifth day after the opening of the priest's will was set aside for the auction of his effects.

As we left the court-room the priest's tenant said to me through his tears: 'Oh, how I misjudged that man, I almost took him for a miser. But my daughter knew him much better than I did, she always loved the priest. I must write to her immediately about this.'

The schoolteacher from the Kar blessed the priest, who had always been so good to him and so glad to spend time in the school.

The other people about the neighbourhood found out the contents of the will too.

Only those people whom it most nearly concerned, the children, knew nothing of it, or if they did hear of it they did not understand it and did not know what had been planned for them.

Because I wanted to be present at the auction too, I went back to the Kar and decided to spend the four days visiting many of the places in the karst and in other areas where I had once worked. Everything was unchanged, as though this region had added the characteristic of immutability to that of simplicity.

When the fifth day had come, the seals on the priest's house were broken and his effects were auctioned. Many people had gathered, for the will had made the auction remarkable. Striking incidents occurred during it. A priest bought for a tidy sum a coat found amongst the dead man's clothes, the shabbiest garment that could be found among clothes that were not actually ragged. The Kar parish council bought the Bible in order to donate it to their church. Even the wooden bench which had not even been locked away found a buyer.

I bought something too at the auction, the little carved wooden crucifix from Nuremberg and all the rest of the beautiful fine sheets and tablecloths. My wife and I still have these things today and use the linen very rarely. We keep it as a reminder of the deep, lasting and tender emotion that made the poor priest keep these things and never use them. From time to time my wife has the linen washed and ironed, then she admires the indescribable beauty and purity of it, and then the folded items are tied up with the old, faded red-silk ribbons, which are still there, and put back into the cupboard. –

Now comes the question as to the outcome of all these things.

The sum of money which the priest had saved and that which resulted from the auction of his effects were together much too small to pay for the establishment of a new school. They were too small even to build a medium-sized house of the type usual in the area, let alone a schoolhouse with classrooms and accommodation for the teachers, to endow a salary for them and compensation for the previous teacher.

This was in the priest's nature, that he did not understand worldly things and had to be burgled three times before he invested his money.

But since evil is always essentially pointless and has no effect in the universal plan, while the good bears fruit, even if it is embarked upon with insufficient means, so it happened here too: God did not need the priest for the final accomplishment of His plan. When the affair of the will and its insufficiency became known, the rich and well-off people all around came together and in a short time had subscribed a sum that seemed adequate to achieve all the priest's intentions. And if any more should be necessary, then each declared that he would make an additional payment as well. I added my mite also.

If I had parted from the region with sadness the first time, now tears flowed from my eyes as I left the lonely stones. –

Now, as I speak, the school has long been standing among the houses in the outlying Steinkar region, it is standing near where the schoolchildren live in a healthy, airy spot. The teacher lives in a building with his family and his assistants, the teacher in the Kar receives his yearly compensation and even Sabine has been given her portion. She refused to take it and made it over straight away to the schoolteacher's daughter, of whom she had always been very fond.

The only cross in the churchyard that marks the grave of a priest stands on the mound of the originator of all these things. Sometimes a prayer may be said there and many a person will stand in front of it with an emotion of which the priest was not the object while he was alive.

Fiction published by Angel Books

ALFRED DÖBLIN

A People Betrayed *and* Karl and Rosa
(The trilogy November 1918: A German Revolution *complete in 2 volumes)*
Translated by John E. Woods
0 88064 008 1 and 0 88064 011 1 *(paperback)*
Published in the USA by Fromm International Publishing Corporation, New York

FYODOR DOSTOYEVSKY
The Village of Stepanchikovo
Translated by Ignat Avsey
0 946162 06 9 *(cased)* 0 946162 07 7 *(paperback)*

VSEVOLOD GARSHIN
From the Reminiscences of Private Ivanov *and other stories*
Translated by Peter Henry and others
0 946162 08 5 *(cased)* 0 946162 09 3 *(paperback)*

GERHART HAUPTMANN
Lineman Thiel *and other tales*
Translated by Stanley Radcliffe
0 946162 27 1 *(cased)* 0 946162 28 X *(paperback)*

HEINRICH VON KLEIST/LUDWIG TIECK/E. T. A. HOFFMANN
Six German Romantic Tales
Translated by Ronald Taylor
0 946162 17 4 *(paperback)*

ALEXANDER PUSHKIN
The Tales of Belkin
with The History of the Village of Goryukhino
Translated by Gillon Aitken and David Budgen
0 946162 04 2 *(cased)* 0 946162 05 0 *(paperback)*

HENRYK SIENKIEWICZ
Charcoal Sketches *and other tales*
Translated by Adam Zamoyski
0 946162 31 X *(cased)* 0 946162 32 8 *(paperback)*